THE NAKED GHOST

A novel

by Jay Gross

AmiGadget Press

Lexington, South Carolina

2011

THE NAKED GHOST
A novel
by Jay Gross

ISBN 978-1-879211-01-8

For information regarding rights or licensing, contact the copyright holder
in care of AmiGadget Press, PO Box 1696, Lexington, SC 29071, or visit
blog.jaygross.com online.

First printing: May 2011

Published by:
  AmiGadget Press
  P.O. Box 1696
  Lexington, SC 29071

  www.amigadget.com

for lost friends

Acknowledgements

Special thanks to the Twisted Scribes Writing Group, Fran Rizer, Ray Wade, John Koelsch and the late Leonard Jolley. Their able assistance, kind words and encouragement brought me back to this work again and again.

CHAPTER ONE

Phil 'Em Up

"Tacky of Real Estate Dude not to show up," Casey grumped for the eleventeenth time after a sweaty hour in an open convertible parked in front of Phil's Texaco Groc & Ser Sta in the heart of Bryson, Georgia. "I'm hot, in the Fahrenheit sense of the word, and mad in the road rage sense of the word, plus some things in the four-letter sense of some other choice words. And I'm thirsty in the H-Two-Oh sense of the word."

"Thirst I can fix." Whit shifted in the driver's seat, fished a tenspot from his pocket. "As for mad, I'm steamed, too. Maybe the guy doesn't need a fat commission. I'd call Dad's lawyers to take over if our cellphones hadn't fizzled out ten miles south of here. And since you're going in there again for sodas, how about trying the agent again. Give him one more chance."

Casey blew upward to cool his forehead. "I'd rather desiccate to dust and blow totally away than go in there again. You go. Call Whoziname, or your old man's lawyers. Call Dial-a-Shrink, whatever. I've already warmed up the spectators for your performance."

True. Half an hour and considerable perspiration earlier, Casey had sidled through the tattered Colonial Bread screen door of the Groc & Ser Sta and made with the down-home Cajun-bred super-polite. "May I please use your phone?"

"Shore, Son. Ya'll're th' city bucks a-wantin' the Vydah place, ain'tcha?" A handsome, iron-built man, Phil Trane didn't hold with ceremony. He spoke his mind, and forcefully—with such force, usually, that people rarely questioned what he said, or paid much attention, either. In tiny Bryson, Phil knew everything that went on, everything planned to go on, and everything that had gone on for all the years he'd lived in Bryson, which was most of the years he had lived, forty-eight of which he admitted to. In tiny

Bryson, though, everybody else knew everything that was going on, since rarely did anything go on.

Bryson's two gas stations–slash-tractor overhaul centers–slash–groc-ser-sta's glower at each other from opposite sides of Main Street at the far end of town, exactly two blocks of overarching shade trees from the near end of town. Although people get gruff truths from Phil Trane, they fare far worse across the street at Bob Roberts Shell. The families have bickered for most of a century. The brands of gasoline differ, but the ambiance is the same, parallel scenarios on opposite stages according to generations of spite filled tradition.

Like Phil and his Texaco cronies, Roberts and his Shell regulars mostly do nothing, but they do it with a *panache* that defines the small town of Bryson in the red clay hills north of Atlanta. Theirs is the social circle, the political system, the debate squad, the rumor mill, and the entertainment committee, all in one. Or rather, all in *two* diametrically opposed factions, each sustained by disdain for the other.

Under the sagging wooden canopy of Phil's aging station, Phil's aging camp teeters in ramshackle slat-bottomed chairs propped against weathered clapboard. Come sundown, they can claim little else but having sat, spat, and chewed the fat for another whole day. They eat pork rinds and drink Yoo-hoos, preach, grumble and pass the time as generations of their kin have done since the station's peeling green paint was crisp and new. Since the bleached and broken asphalt still steamed with fresh oil. Since the old people in the chairs were themselves young boys, shushed and shooed by their fathers and grandfathers. This generation, this century, Phil's place is a gas station instead of a general store. A mite newfangled, but it'll do.

Across Main Street, barely three hundred feet away, Roberts' crowd sits, spits, and chews fat, too. Although the two sides haven't come to blows recently, Main Street's oft-patched macadam, like the Rubicon, cannot be lightly crossed.

A perpetual storm cloud shades the Shell side with ill winds and bad luck, like Al Capp's immortal Joe Btfsplk. Fresh from a Midnight Madness sale at Grant's Town & Country in neighboring Antioch Springs, a simple grass trimmer inexplicably developed high torque and exploded, injuring Roberts' helper. Dropping off freight at the antique store, a driverless van truck ran amok and took out the Shell's hand cranked kerosene dispenser and a rack of tires. The station's plate glass bears so many cracks it looks like a mosaic made with duct tape. On both sides of the street, these events and many others remain the stuff of conjecture as to their causes, real or imagined, spirit or human, earthbound or divine. Scientific theories and other rumors abound.

"City bucks, that's us." Casey edged toward the grimy telephone atilt among the clutter on the high, linoleum covered counter. "Mr. Bundrick told us you wouldn't mind if we met him here, and he's late."

"Phone's yonder." Phil fondled a socket wrench. "Local Calls Only, like the sign says."

The phone had no buttons, no dial.

"Just pick it up, Son," Phil said. "We ain't ever got no dialin' phones over here. When th'operator answers, that'll be Ernestine. Tell her who you want."

Eavesdropping, Phil's porch regulars snickered.

Casey hefted the ancient phone. "Bryson Realty, please... You don't need the number?"

"Ernestine's got ever'body's number by heart, Son," Phil said while Casey waited, jittery, through three long rings... four... "No answer I bet," Phil said. "That's Bundrick. You boys'll bake well done b'fore he'll talk to ya. He cain't do it, any more'n he c'n come down an' show that prop'ty."

Casey propped the handset on his other shoulder.

Phil kept talking. "Son, ain't nobody in this town'll go out t'that Vidah Simple place with you, particularly not Bundrick. You'll see—won't he, Reb?"

"Yyyyyyep." Reb Creech spat at the deep shadow his chair cast.

Casey waited four more rings. "Thanks." He bolted for the Fiat. Hopping into the car, he told Whit his Bryson phone experience was hardly one to write home about, at least not civilly, and complained—some might say "bitched–" that even ET couldn't phone home on a backwoods system with no connection to the rest of the world, much less to reality, and not a cell tower for two counties and which way is home?

"Okay, this is my adventure. I'll go handle it." Whit took a deep breath and eyed Reb, Phil, and Bud leaned back against the clapboard comfy as you please, masticating their plugs. Bud Speaks, whose toothlessness didn't support "chawin'," sucked on a hand rolled cigarette pinched between first and third fingers stained a deep ochre from Prince Albert's vaporous embrace. Whit's gaze moved to the gloomy gathering on the opposite side of the street. Same scene there, but with heavy frowns and ominous wheezing, not a good vibe on the lot. "Motley bunch. Which ones do you think are the Hatfields?"

"They all look like real McCoys to me." Casey grimaced. "I inspected the ones at Phil's Curbside Sweat Lodge and Down Home Cruising Spot up close and thankfully impersonal. The geriatric unit tonguing the homemade ciggie looks like the poster boy for Iron Lung Huggers of Amurika. The tall one built like a truck with bushy eyebrows clued me in. Talk to him. He acts like he owns the planet."

Whit tapped the ignition keys against the steering column. "We are privileged to observe here a cherished local phenomenon."

"Loitering?"

"It's Bryson's version of Piedmont Park. Except they're just settin'–not 'sitting.' And chawin', instead of something more useful like cruisin'. I'm going to the phone. Sit tight."

Casey smirked. "I'm set-nnnghhh' right here. Where would I go? There isn't a porn shop for forty miles. And the nearest mall is–oh never mind."

Whit marched to the station. "One more time on the phone, there, Good Buddy?"

"Shore 'nuff." Phil winked at Reb. "Local Calls Only, like the sign says. Good Buddy. Just pick it up–"

"Operator? Bundrick, right. How did you know?" Whit pulled the phone cord to its limit so the porch regulars could overhear his half of the conversation.

"Is this Mr. Bundrick's office... May I please speak with him?"

The men laughed, wheezed, slapped their knees.

"He wore out the church key, did you say?" Whit frowned. "Do you mean he's drunk?"

The men broke into belly laughs, gasped for air.

"Excuse me? I don't see how that has anything to do with my speaking to him," Whit said, forceful.

After a torrent of coughing and laughing that echoed off the town's buildings, the men snickered while Whit held on for a long minute at the phone.

"Bundrick, this is Whit Garrett..." Whit raised his voice. "Garrett... We've been waiting for over an hour. Are you interested in making this sale? Are you singing?"

Long, pregnant pause.

"Bundrick!" Whit shouted more at Bryson, Georgia, than into the phone. "When you sober up, call the number I gave you and leave a voicemail. I might, just might, return your call." Whit clunked the receiver into its cradle.

Phil heaved himself up from his chair. "Son, jes' hol'on."

Whit turned to glare. Phil made eye contact and held it.

"Ol' Bundrick cain't show that place t'you n'r nobody else," Phil said. "I done tol' y'friend. Go on out an' look f'y'selves. It ain't Bundrick's fault, but 'e shouldn't a-tol' y'all t'wait fer 'im, 'cause he knowed he couldn't come meet ya."

"How do you know so much about it, Mister--?"

"Trane. Call me Phil. Ever body does. I own this place, such as it is, and I own that Vydah place yall're a-wantin'. Such as it is, I reckon."

"You? Own? Uh, just a sec." Whit beckoned to Casey.

Reb and Bud exchanged meaningful glances, creaked the worn wood of their chairs.

"Mr. Trane," Whit said, "this is Casey dePaul. Mr. Trane *owns* the property we looked at yesterday."

Casey's mouth dropped open.

"Call me Phil, ever body does." Phil plopped down in his wooden desk chair and, with a fluid motion that brought precipitous creaks, convinced it to lean into its familiar position against the wall.

"Anything y'all want t'know, jus' ask me. Bundrick's drunk as usual, an' I'm the one that knows, anyhow."

Resounding snickers from the porch chorus.

"You're not putting me on?" Whit asked.

"Naw, Buster," Reb said. "Ol' Phil don't never put nobody on." Reb's high-pitched voice squeaked out of a scrawny, leather covered frame on which a farmer's rags had been hung out to dry.

Unhurried, Phil cleared his throat, mopped his forehead with his sleeve and resettled his baseball cap. "I been the proud owner of that place f'twenty-odd years. Me an' m'Uncle Jeb, we owned it together before then, but when he died the whole thing passed to me. My daddy got it at a tax sale with m'Uncle Jebediah. To plant corn on, I reckon, but that never come to pass."

Whit cleared his throat.

"There's no tellin' how much money them two didn't spend a-takin' out legal papers. But they both died b'fore they re'lized s'much's a nickel out've it. The place's mine, now, good as can get without 'nother mess of money bein' spent." Phil reset his cap, a crisp new Atlanta Braves model. "So, I reckon if'n y'all want it, like ol' Bundrick was a-sayin' this mornin', I'll durn shore sell it. Bundrick, he ain't nothin' but a dark cloud. You want thunder, you got t'come t'ol' Phil."

"Tax sale," Whit said. "How clear is the title?"

"I ain't studied with it in a while." Phil raised his cap again, smoothed his close-cropped salt-pepper hair. "Y'all seen the place?"

"Yesterday." Whit said.

Casey shuddered. "Been that. Done there. Ran away from the scary T-shirt."

"From the way this little feller's spooked, I figgered ya'll'd've a'ready been out there. Hit's a doozer, ain't it?" Phil lurched up from the chair and stood at the door.

"A doozer." Casey stuffed his hands in his back pockets.

"Ya'll don't know, do ya? That no 'count Bundrick! Fellers, that Vidah place is a sore spot all the way to the county seat. I'll give you a piece of advice you'd do good to heed and hinder, and that is: don't go near there if you ain't got good life insurance."

Whit stepped back a pace. "Is that a threat?"

"Nawww, Son. I don't reckon anybody round here'd bother you unless'n you crossed 'em, even Ol' Bob Roberts yonder. He's a mean un. Some say he's into all kind of kinky stuff. I mean, sex-wise. He shore rules over 'is helper like he was lord and master. S'far as bein' dangerous, though, Roberts is a struttin' rooster. All chicken shit, scuse th'expresion, and no chicken salad. Y'got t'watch y'back, though. He's one to sneak around in the night a-settin' fires an' such. A womanizer, too, if he c'n find one that'll have 'im. His wife left 'im b'fore he got the chance t'be a wifebeater. Good thing he ain't ever had no kids."

Phil took a breath. "That Vydah place is pure-tee hainted, shore as c'n be." He lowered his voice. "Hainted."

Reb and Bud snickered. Reb spat at a junebug.

Whit said in a tone of dismissal, "I don't believe in ghosts."

"Nobody does," Reb said. "Not till they come face to face with 'em. Y'all'd do well t'mind Ol' Phil's words."

Bud spat, drowning the junebug in tobacco juice. "Them house cats out yonder'll convince ya. Folks've seen 'em jump into holes in space."

"I believe in ghosts," Casey said. "We have plenty of them in southern Louisiana where I come from–along with witches and vampires and voodoo queens. Personally I've never seen any ghosts, that I know of, but I'm convinced they exist."

"Smart boy." Bud wheezed, drawing deeply on the stub of his cigarette.

"Well," Phil said, "I got good reason to believe in them ghosts, and a whole passel of other things. 'Roun' here, the ghosts 'emselves've convinced people. Near 'bout ever body in this town's had contact with 'em, and ain't none of us denies b'levin'."

Casey looked around, nervous. "Cats? Glass ones? White?"

"Anyway," Phil went on, "no matter if you b'leve in ghosts or no, y'don't saunter around a graveyard at night."

Bud wheezed, coughed, spat. "Tha's truth."

Phil plopped down in his chair. "They's ghosts in town, includin' right across yonder, a-keepin' ol' Bob Roberts runnin' fer 'is Band-Aid box. Real ghosts, not made up ones. Believe it or don't, but likely you'll be drove teetotally nuts, just like the last hunnert people that's come roun' here a-tryin' to prove otherwise. Then you'll end up going off to Milledgeville or California or wherever it is they send crazy people nowadays."

CHAPTER TWO

The Roadless Travel

Abandoned mansion, must sell, has some problems...

The country lane tunneled through encroaching oaks, its surface having surrendered to weather, undergrowth, and time. In a flash of polished red, Whit Garrett threaded his vintage Fiat through the overhanging branches. He dodged some of the bigger holes, scattered garrulous birds, and screeched-braked-sideslided to a billowy stop at an ironwork gate where pure elegance puddled.

"Terminally fabulous," Whit said. "This place is abandoned?" He gestured past pristine metal flourishes, toward a verdant expanse of lawn peppered with pecan trees, dotted with pink camellias, and embellished with ornamental shrubs. "Are you sure we made the right turns?"

Casey brushed leaves from his lap. "What turns? Real Estate Man 'reckoned' you take the only road out of town. Also the only road *into* town, see? Go till it ends. And did it ever. Hang a left into the woodsy road. I give you: woodsy road, nigh onto roadsy woods. Go down, and I do mean *down*, through selfsame woods." He hefted a healthy grasshopper from the dash to the outside. "Till it stops at the gate. *Voilà, la* gate. So, turns? What turns?"

"*Wrong* turn, obviously. Even if this place is the only place, it's way too fancy to be *the* place, so this can't be the place."

Casey thumped an oak leaf from Whit's knee. "Oh, my elementary Sherlock? Are we in the wrong place at the wrong time doing the wrong thing in the wrong way? Do let's go back to Atlanta and do the wrong thing in the right place for a long time." He evicted another 'hopper.

"Something is not in, meaning *is out of*, whack."

Casey's hand described a grand flourish in the air. "Fifty miles from home sweet condo, here in this gorgeous garden of proverbial Big Eden, with the smell of freshly pollenated country air soothing our smogged sinuses, where-oh-where does your great power of deductive cynicism indicate out-of-whackness?"

Whit frowned at a neat mansion that crowned a gentle slope just visible in the distance. "'Has some problems,'" he quoted. "The first problem was the number-ten obstacle course to get here. I can deal with that. I have contractors who can deal with it. But buttcheek-deep in dense forest, this place isn't a bit overgrown. The road? *That's* overgrown, as in paved tree branch."

"Paved?" Casey peered over the door.

"So, why isn't the house dilapidated? And the grounds?"

"Hermits," Casey said. "Are we going in, or just sitting out here under the redbug trees?"

Whit hnmphed. He reached across the open-top two-seater to feel around in the confusion of the car's glove compartment.

"Was that a cat? Peeking through the great gay gate?"

Whit looked, shrugged, hnmphed. "I didn't see any cat. And the gate's gay? Ohhh, okay, I see your point."

"Creepy Real Estate Guy told us all I need to know in two words." Casey wheezed-mimicked, "'Place's hainted.'"

Whit hnmphed. "Haunted my ass."

"Probably." Casey flashed blue eyes and an imp's grin.

Whit seized a brass key ring and closed the glove box, leaving a crumpled blue envelope peeking out. "Here, Smarty. See if you can get that brand-new-looking, umpty-year-old lock on that brand-new-looking but supposedly dilapidated, Forties-fruity and incidentally magnificent gay-for-days gate to yield to your dreary humor."

Casey hopped out over the convertible's door. "Wrought iron, tons of it. Nice." The polished brass lock glinted in the sun, although the outsized *passe-partout* that fit it looked like an escapee from an *Antiques Road Show. Dirt* road. The lock fell open at Casey's touch, and the massive gates swung in. They caught with loud clinks in iron swirls at either side of the brick-paved entrance. The hinges didn't squeak.

Casey pointed at a granite block that defined the threshold. He read the inscription to Whit and the mockingbirds, *"Vita Sempre,"* while hooking the key ring through his belt loop. On the right.

"So! This is the right place," Whit said. "'*Sempre*' must be what Bendrick or whatever his name is couldn't pronounce. Get in, Butch." He revved the car's engine and eased it forward as Casey snapped to attention to play gatekeeper.

Casey's face lit up. He hopped into the car as it rolled past. "It's something like 'always life,'" he said. "Loosely translate 'live forever'? Even looser, 'happily ever after, maybe.'"

"Latin? That's way loose."

"Italian." Casey said. "And I am not."

"All I know is *eine kleine* German, a bit of Russian from Piotr downstairs, some French and a little Greek."

"Your German is barely passable," Casey said. "But your French is *magnifique*. And as for that Greek—"

Whit revved the engine. "Don't get too loose translating the Italian or Uncle Giorgio won't front us tickets to the opera."

"My lips are sealed and if his were, too, I might go with you to his dinners. But I'll have to admit he has great taste."

"Maybe that rock is a tombstone for Old Man Sempre's son Vita." Whit eased the car forward. "Buried in the driveway face down, so the fam can keep riding over his ass."

"Cute."

"Are you looking at those bricks?"

"Bricks. How many guesses? Old as the hills. I'd say, north side of the kiln? Or maybe they baked up a new batch, like Williamsburg. They look old on purpose so people will respect them." Casey grinned. "Like you."

"Thank you for the dissertation on roast brick. Check out the edging." Whit pointed.

"Were you thinking of taking the gardener to task, or hiring her to fix your balcony rock garden?"

"There's not a blade of grass in the bricks or touching the bricks, Brick," Whit said. "Somebody's keeping this place up better than the White House Rose Garden. We must be in the wrong place. Right?"

"Nahhh. They had a gaggle of slaves left over from before the wawwuh, and—"

"Be serious a minute—"

"Ick, do I have to?"

"If this really is the place from that classified ad, we're not waiting one nanosecond before snapping it up," Whit said.

"Really, Dahling, how you do go on. But, go on."

Whit put the car in gear. "It's damn tacky of them to make us drive fifty miles chasing wild goose. April Fool's was *last* week. Let's go in so I can give these Yankees a proper Southern cussing."

"Comb time!" Casey commandeered the rear-view mirror.

"Maybe they're brother-loving Philadelphians into fooling li'l ol' Southern folks," Whit said.

"For what?" Casey coaxed just the right swoop into the blond locks that kissed his forehead.

"Grits and grins? Awww, they're lonely. And this far out in the boonies who would there be on the social register to ever come calling? Yankees or otherwise."

"Ooo, maybe they're going to hold an orgy." Casey adjusted his clothes. "That classified ad was the invitation, see? Like in L.A. and wherever else the Eleanor Rigbys of the world hang out? That's why they sent us keys." He pocketed the comb. "Maybe it's Village weirdos. Or San Franweirdos. Heavy into anything weird?"

"Yeah and weird for anything heavy. Maybe they want to trap us." Whit frowned. "Or kidnap us. Closets, everyone! Quick, look straight, so they won't get any ideas."

"Me? You can't be serious."

"Think of it as performance art."

"Acting is such a strain." Casey crossed his arms. "Them Dawgs really whupped 'A' on them Ailerons last night at Dodgeball, eh Bo? Hol' m'beer."

"Point taken." Whit stopped the car where the driveway widened into a forecourt paved with brick in concentric swirls. A path of limestone set into polished rock meandered through exotic ornamental plants to the front of the house, and brick paths led through rose-trellised, arched portals built into high brick walls. Inches from ground level, the imposing entrance comprised heavy cased panels that flanked twin walnut doors polished to a warm glow.

"How Italian. How Renaissance. How Italian Renaissance!" Casey poised his knuckles. "Do we barge in with the key, or shall I do the knock-knock thing?"

"Nobody's home," Whit said, confident. "Ours is the only car, and our footprints are the only ones in the pine pollen. No way Martha services burbs this far out."

In Atlanta gayspeak, "Martha" has little to do with "Vineyard", or "Stewart," or even "Graham." "MARTA" is Atlanta's far reaching subway, bored through solid granite in the city, and elevated as necessary to connect distant bedrooms to urban boardrooms.

Casey kept his hand ready to knock. "So the recluses haven't left the house since the last rain. Whit, these hermits know our address–they mailed us the key. Obviously they're in Burb Buckhead right now breaking into our condo and stealing our cat."

"Duh?" Whit patted his pockets for the key. "Hermits don't invite people to drop by for tea, much less strangers they don't even know. And we don't have a cat."

"Okay, they're eccentric athletes training for the Olympic bi-marathon. They run to Decatur thrice a week to keep in shape." Casey winked. "And steal people's cats."

"Atlanta is finally over the Olympics, and I'm sure the Olympics will someday recover from Atlanta. *Meowww.*"

"Maybe there's an underground pneumatic tube. *Whisk!* Galleria Mall in thirty-two seconds. And if we did have a cat, the hermits could be in Atlanta right now making off with Neuteronomy and all his kittens."

"We live in a high-security, gated high-rise with bank-vault doors and twenty-four-seven Barneyfifes. But when we get home, do check for missing pussies." Whit felt for dust along the top edge of a panel. He showed an unsoiled fingertip to Casey. "Passed down through decades of tax sales and estate settlements. Unoccupied since before man set boot on moon? Hnmph! This place is better maintained than daddy's condominium."

"What was that you said about a little pussy?" Casey licked the back of his hand, catlike.

CHAPTER THREE

The House Dressing

Generous eaves shaded the house's stuccoed exterior. The one-story edifice stood quite tall, with expansive windows on one side of the front entrance, balanced on the other by wood panels, iron fretwork, and window boxes overstuffed with flowers redolent of a rainbow of spring blossoms. Neat and elegant, cozy and inviting, with solid construction of the finest materials.

"Committee designed, but *so* beautiful." Casey stood back to admire the layered window and cornice moldings, the terracotta tile work, and the copious iron flourishes.

"Definitely," Whit said. "Spanish influence roof. French doors. Fine Southern Greek Revival cornices. Freudian windows."

"Freud designed windows, in addition to guilt? How totally Italian. I think I hear a *duetto buffo*, even now."

"Windows this huge have got to be somebody's fetish." Whit knocked sharply. "And Freud wasn't Italian. He didn't even like lasagna."

"It all works together," Casey said. "My compliments to Old Man Vita. Cottage-like, but really huge." Casey grabbed himself by the waist and hip-swiveled a foxtrot. "Can't you just hear a swing orchestra, the swish of satin gowns dusting the floor to Billie Holiday? Jacques Brel, Edith Piaf? Backstreet Boys?" He adjusted his clothes for impending social interaction.

Whit pounded on the door again. "Our checkbook is burning a hole in my pocket, even as you speak. But for me to live here, it would need major changes."

"For me to live in it, it would have to be moved fifty miles south-by-south-southeast and reinstalled within mocha-smelling distance of Caribou Coffee and Out Write Books." Casey jumped back. "What was that?"

"Sounded like glass breaking. Someone *is* home. Shhh," Whit said. "Somebody's breaking in. Let's go around back."

"Around back to Atlanta!" Casey grabbed Whit's arm.

"Come on, there's adventure to be had."

"I can be had, too," Casey said. *Sotto voce.*

"After the adventure is over when we're sitting at home wishing we were out having an adventure." Whit pulled Casey by the arm to the corner of the house.

More sounds of breaking glass. Casey froze. "We were warned. Let's hit the road."

Whit dragged him like a sandbag to an arched opening in the high brick wall that joined the edge of the house. "Look, there's the cat from the gate, acting like he owns the place. For all the trouble of driving over here, I want to know what's going on."

"For all the trouble of finding out what's going on, I'd rather not know. Call them from our clock-infested home." Casey tightened his grip. "Wouldn't you know the cellphones won't work this far from reality."

"That's funny." Whit stopped short at a broken window.

"I'm laughing myself silly."

"I'd believe *shaking* yourself silly." Whit poked at the ground with his toe. "A place this devotedly perfect would not have broken windows."

"We *are* listening to someone breaking glass? Hellooo? Can we go now? Places to see, people to do. I think I left a Boston butt in the oven. And there's salad to toss, crackers to eat, philosophy to discuss. I've got a haircut appointment at the dry cleaners. Did we forget to feed the cockatoos?"

Whit pointed at the ground. "Not a shard in sight. And your mom's the one with the cockatoos. We're short on '-atoos.'"

"Okay, Mister Punster, the window was knocked in from the outside. No shards. That's how it works with breaking and entering, also with brats playing baseball or chess or whatever."

Whit cupped a hand to his face and leaned against the empty space. "Pitch black."

Casey shouted to the house. "Shucks, folks, don't mind us. We're just peeping Toms from the Big City, in town for the big orgy and parade."

"Admit it strikes you strange."

"Strange? You mean the part about driving fifty miles to see a haunted house, or the part about peering into strangers' windows? Try the back door?"

"Now you're talking. Come on."

Casey seized Whit's arm.

Whit pulled him across a stone-paved terrace peppered with deco planters. A fluffy white cat peered around the house behind them and dashed out of sight. "Those iron chairs–how French."

"Luvvv-ly verannnda," Casey intoned in his best O'Hara. "Perfect for quiche, *frommage*, Beaujolais, cranberry pear and apricot torte with gingerbread crust in sour cream custard with Cool Whip topping."

"It smells like fresh bread. Where could that come from?" Whit looked around. "That huge wall of French windows."

"Hugely haunted," Casey stage-whispered. "And it knows I'm getting hungry."

"Ghosts can't harm you if you don't believe in them. Do you believe in ghosts?"

"Yup. And I believe in hermits, robbers, highwaymen, ax murderers, bashers, slashers, thugs, thieves and can we go now?"

"Ax murderers my ass," Whit said.

"Tempt. Me!"

"Please fix your impudent gaze on that creature in the far reaches of the lot."

"The gardener? Ask him if nobody's here so we can go home."

Whit shaded his eyes from the sun. "What is he doing?"

"The technical term is 'staggering.' He's drunk. *Tsk,* those twenty-martini lunches up at the General Store."

"Maybe he's old. Okay drunk *and* old." Whit waved. "Maybe it's Bunnick. Hellooo."

The figure took no notice. Several hundred yards away, the gardener leaned on a hoe, sloshed from side to side, and approached the terrace in a random, circuitous route that in time would cover much of the acreage between.

"The help you get these days." Casey tsk'd. "Probably has hedges to trim, too."

"Weeds to weed, catheters to change. Maybe he's not the gardener," Whit said. "What around here would you use a hoe on?"

"Tourists! Can we go?"

"I'll go knock on the back door. Stay here."

"I'm with you, remember?" Casey made a dramatic gesture of covering his eyes and allowing himself to be pulled by the arm.

Whit led the way up the porch's three brick steps. An extra-wide affair of dark, shiny wood panels, the back door had tiny windowpanes in complex fretwork on its upper half.

Wide windows opened onto the porch at waist height. Sheer curtains, pure white, flapped in gentle breezes through spaces left by broken panes. Whit frammed the doorpost.

Guarding the rear, Casey leaned out over the balustrade. "The gardener's gone!"

"Probably fell in a hole." Whit knocked louder.

"Poor hole." Casey peered in cautiously. Classical piano music, a cat's contented *miaow*, and more sounds of breaking glass wafted through the broken window panes. He pulled Whit away. "Maybe their royal highnesses are having a fight and don't want to be bothered with guests right now. We should knock on the front door like people with manners."

Whit smoldered. "The hermits are the ones with no manners."

Whit and Casey hiked the rest of the way around the house. As they passed the car, Casey took advantage of its side mirror to adjust his hair. With a nod from Casey indicating coif readiness, Whit pounded the twin front doors in turn, the sound echoing off the distant serpentine wall that encircled the property. After a long silence and no answer at the door, the two exchanged exasperated glances. "Pass me the keys Bunnick sent us." Whit held out his hand.

"Are there other houses in this area we wanted to look at—a pond site on the other side of the Interstate?"

"Saw that, hated it. Keys?" Whit wriggled his fingers.

"The Keys are sooo nice this time of year. We'll send them a nastygram from Key Largo. Key West? Key Frame? Call them pre-verts and ax-murderers, and invite them to take their tea in Claxton with Georgia's other fruitcakes."

Whit wiggled outstretched fingers. "Claxton is fruitcakes as in baked. Milledgeville is half-baked as in cuckoos' nest. The keys?"

"I'm chicken."

"The keys, my aging friend who is no longer chicken for I don't dare mention how long."

"So I'm eighteen going on twenty-nine," Casey said. "My gosh, the time. If we leave now, we can *just* make happy hour at Pernicious Patsy's."

"Quit stalling."

Resigned, Casey held out the metal treasure.

While Whit fiddled with the gleaming brass lockset, Casey whispered, "The gardener's watching us."

"Let him!" Whit shouted. "Keys don't fit. Let's try the back."

"My thoughts exactly. The back way out of here."

At the back door, Casey gripped Whit's arm. "That gardener can sure move. He's way over there, now. Doesn't seem possible."

"Maybe there's a gaggle of gardeners on roller blades."

"Twins. But one's a hundred-year-old bum disguised as a drag queen, and the other's a hundred-year-old drag queen disguised as a bum."

"I smell hyacinths. Are they still watching us?"

Casey peered over his shoulder. "Yes, she is." He waved elaborately and hid in front of Whit. "I've got gardening to do at home. I think I left my zinnias in the oven. And can we please leave this burg, as in *now*?"

"On the way here you dubbed Bryson a charming little village. Now it's demoted to burg?"

"Any quaint little village that harbors a haunted house gets kicked downstairs," Casey said.

Unseen, the white cat peeked around the corner and darted off, fading to transparent as he ran.

"Poppycock!" Whit said with an exasperated *hnmph*. "I'm ready to break a window."
Crash.

"Somebody inside beat you to it." Casey seized Whit's arm with both hands.

"I didn't hear a thing. Let's go see what it was."

"'Didn't hear a thing,'" Casey mimicked. He stopped short. "Whit! Somebody's stealing our car!"

In the distance, a car's engine started, its tires spun in place, and a small dog yapped frantically. "Run!" Whit took off like an Olympic sprinter, but stopped after a few steps.

Casey jogged up beside him, tugged him forward."

"That's not our car." Whit yanked Casey to a stop. "The Fiat has a much lower pitch."

The dog yapped. The engine's roar continued. Tires screeched.

"How observant." Casey sighed relief. "Let's go catch them before they–"

"The driveway has no gravel. It's brick."

Bam! Yelp-yelp-yelp-yelp!

"Oh, Whit, the dog's been hit! Come on!"

The sound of the car's engine died away as Whit and Casey neared the driveway.

Casey stared in disbelief.

"How did they do that?" Whit puzzled, looked around. "At this distance? Outdoors? That would take speakers to make any audiophile jealous."

"Speakers." Casey said, shaky, his gaze zombielike. "Ghost speakers. Speaking loud and clear. Saying 'GO HOME!'"

The white cat trotted off.

Whit fidgeted, holding onto Casey's shoulder. "There's—"

"—no such thing as ghosts." Casey spoke in a soft monotone without conviction. "Whit, I'm scared." Same monotone, *with* conviction.

CHAPTER FOUR

Things That Don't Exist

Whit cleared his throat and spoke with the confidence of an engineer who has just solved a precedential math problem. "Somebody's trying to scare us."

"They're doing a fabulous job!" Casey blew upward, setting blond silk aflutter. "It's some ghost body, I just know it. That creepy Bundrick dropped hints when I had him on the phone. Casey wheezed-coughed-quoted, "Cain't sell a prop'ty that scares off m'prospects.' Well now we know. So?" He made let's-get-out-of-here motions with his eyebrows.

"Now, my shaking sweetie," Whit said loud enough to startle bluebirds far across the lawn, "one way or another we get into this fugitive-from-Ripley's Italian Re-renaissance home for wayward circus magicians. We find out what in the name of all divas that ever graced a silver screen is going on." Stalking the front door, Whit sorted through the keys on the Bryson Rlty & Prpty Mgmnt & Ins red, white, and blue tagged ring.

"I'd rather find out by long distance. Martinique?"

"Too meet-up-with-exes."

"Paris?"

"Too we-just-got-back. Casey, are you cold?"

"I'm frightened out of my tits."

"You mean wits?" Whit asked.

"No, tits. Wits was ten minutes ago."

"Aren't you curious?"

Casey snapped his fingers. "I gave my curious bone the day off. A non-existent car drag-races out of a gravel driveway that isn't here and smacks a non-existent dog that yelps into the next dimension. No car, dog or gravel. There's an awesome amount of doesn't-exist around here. Unless you count the ghosts." He put his arm around Whit's waist. "Hold me. Please, or I'll run."

"With pleasure. What an adventure."

"This terrifying episode defnitely qualifies as adventure," Casey said, blue eyes blazing. "Because I truly wish I was sitting at home pining for adventure."

"That I can fix," Whit said. "Let's go."

Exultant, Casey bounced into the car. Whit got in, but sat staring at the porch as Vita's front door swung open. Wide.

"I don't believe it," Whit said.

"I do. Let's ride."

The white cat peeked out through the open door, fluffed himself, and oozed back into the shadow inside the hall.

"We can't leave it open," Whit said. "I'll go lock it."

"Let the pussycat do it."

Whit trudged to the porch and pulled the door. It wouldn't budge. He backed up a step. "I'm tired of these parlor tricks!" He screamed into the house.

"Miss Manners! You didn't say please or thank you," Casey chided in his best Martha Stewart recipe recitative. "Let's just leave. Please! Thank you!"

"Screw manners. I aim to kick some Connecticut ass." Whit wrenched the door handles back and forth and yanked the door shut. He narrowed his gaze and rattled the handle. Locked.

As Whit shook the left door's handle, the right-hand door swung open and a cool breath of sweet smelling air wafted out. Whit claimed victory. "Comb your hair, we're going calling. I'll teach these creeps some proper Southern manners or dish out some shiners!"

"How butch," Casey said. He left his hair unchecked and joined Whit on the porch.

Whit stepped into the house. "Hell-lowww," he yelled, knocked on the doorjamb. "Company coming!" With a flick of his neck he flung his light brown mane back and yanked the reluctant Casey through the doorway.

Casey whistled. "Five stars for terminal elegance."

Whit shouted. "I think it SUCKS!" He pulled Casey farther into the room. "Doors that big would do the Pantheon proud. And is this rug a Kirman? Big enough for a polo match."

"That hall bench looks like it saw action in the Revolution," Casey said. "Hmmm, from the looks of everything else I bet that delightful little framed Man Ray on the wall is neither a print nor a copy. Probably worth ten times Tara's asking price."

Whit stared. "More like ten *dozen* times. My trembling friend, it appears you are in the presence of someone with exquisite taste."

Casey grinned. "Yeah, and you're cute, too."

"You, too. Let's look around."

Casey held fast to Whit's arm. The commodious, hexagonal room had massive pairs of paneled, walnut doors centered in each wall. Warm afternoon sunlight streamed through grand windows, a beveled glass transom, and side window panels that, along with waist high Doric pedestals of walnut burl, flanked the entrance. The columns supported white marble busts that Michelangelo might have admired.

"Eclectic eccentric," Casey said. "Like you, Whit. Okay, been here, seen this. Don't want it, too scary. Places to see, checkbooks to balance, karaoke to sing, banana boats to load. Can we go now?"

Whit stared. "I. Don't. Believe it."

Behind them, unseen, a translucent poodle padded across the floor and oozed through the still-closed doors to the next room.

"Wow." Casey shivered, followed Whit's gaze to an enormous chandelier whose multitudinous prisms, disturbed by cool zephyrs, suffused the hall with brilliance. "Brrr, sudden cold draft, and I don't mean Molson. Feels like a polar bear licked my cheeks, and I don't mean face. I'm a sucker for rainbows, but I get a creepy feeling this museum isn't open on Mondays. Can we go?"

Whit whistled. "Did that classified ad say this place costs eighty grand or eighty million? And today isn't Monday."

"I'm already scared into next week." Casey gripped Whit's arm. "Ooo. That chill again. Price is no object to saying no way, no sale, no thanks." Neither of them noticed a white cat, half transparent, lick itself visible in the corner behind Casey.

"Consider it sold. Should we look in the other rooms or just rush to the nearest bank for a money order?" Whit waved his free arm expansively. "Okay, Door Number One, Door Number Two, or? There are plenty to choose from."

Casey cast a longing glance over his shoulder.

"Forget it. Door Number Out is Rice-A-Roni. If you're still spooked, hang on to me. Tight. Then if anything happens neither one of us can run fast and we'll die together, ever so dramatic, like the movies."

"Cute. Let Mister DeMille know when you're ready for our closeup."

"Time's up. You get Door Number One." Whit nudged Casey leftward. With a flourish worthy of perforated celluloid, he flung the doors wide.

The room's wall space not given over to floor-to-sky-high-ceiling windows sported rich cherry library shelves filled with bound volumes. A huge oak desk and a cozy group of squarish leather chairs and Art Deco lamps held down the far end. The pegged cherry floor shined as though plucked from a magazine ad. Persian rugs asserted soft puddles of blue and pink against the polish. Cut crystal wine services, on gleaming silver serving trays, decorated the space with prismatic shimmers.

"No ghosts in here," Whit said.

Casey hnmphed, taking in the room's splendor.

Whit pointed across the hall. "Door Number Three?"

The poodle marched outside, returning from a passage through the wall near the doors Whit had dubbed "Three." Unseen.

"There's that chill again." Casey tightened his hold.

Whit opened the doors. Bedroom.

"Ooo," Casey said. "The room that makes a house a home."

"This doesn't look abandoned to me." Whit examined the top of a dresser.

The white cat peered in.

"Brrr." Casey shivered. "Ooo, that bed. Did you ever see anything like it?"

"In books," Whit said.

"Right, your old man's an architect."

"Those urns and intertwining nude figures? Definitive Adam style. Way French. Way fashionable a couple centuries ago."

"Cherubs. How quaint."

Whit laughed. "Industrial strength quaint. I doubt a forklift could move that bed. Think Krell metal, only heavier."

"Think Versailles, only more ornate." Casey looked around and whistled. "Think The Hermitage, only with more art. "The bed's made, pillows fluffed." Casey sniffed. "Smells like roses. This wardrobe—towed behind the Mayflower with a rope? Cedar lining. Mmm. It has clothes in it."

Whit tsk'd. "Yes, but the residents were punk rockers. All Forties hats, see?" He mimed cocking a hat to just the right angle. "Yet there are signs this crib is not being lived in."

Casey doffed the imaginary hat and readjusted his hair in a gilt-framed mirror that claimed most of the space between a pair of lacy windows. "Such as, Mister Smug?"

Whit tapped the books on a bookstand beside the bed. "Full Moroccan, custom bound by a true artisan, like the ones across the hall in the library." He picked up a book: *Wild Geese and How to Chase Them: An Informal Discussion of Living as an Art.* "It's by Charles Allen Smart." He opened to the verso. "This one's 1941." Another book. *The Brass Cannon.* Novel, published '33. First edition."

"Not your romance thriller of the Post Modern persuasion. So?"

Behind Whit's back, out of sight, the fluffy white cat jumped into space, disappeared, and materialized across the room among the pillows on the bed. He licked his fur a few strokes and curled up to nap.

"Ooo, here's a recent one." Whit hefted a book from a corner table. *Bel Ami International Art Competition.* "It's a portrait catalog. 'Eleven paintings by noted American and European artists submitted in competition for the selection of the one to be featured in the Loew-Lewin motion picture based on Guy de Maupassant's novel "*The private affairs of Bel Ami*". The exhibition,' blah-blah, 'until the end of, hmmm, 1947.'"

The mysterious cat emitted a loud purr.

"Hey, kitty," Casey cooed. "Are you sleeping off your guilt? Was that you breaking all that glass?"

The cat looked up, yawned, curled up again.

"Silver Persian," Whit said. "Just like Jan's terrorpuss."

Blond Jan, pronounced with a "Y" but spelled with a "J," and his partner live across the hall from Whit and Casey. Their imaginatively named cat "Snowball" escapes to the hallway as often as possible. He's the Swamp Fox of the condo complex, waging guerrilla war for independence on wayward socks, plants, and other residents.

Whit beckoned Casey to the dresser. "The perfume bottles?"

"Coco Chanel would coo Collette silly."

"Evaporated, empty." Whit said. "No hair in the hairbrushes. These vases? No flowers, even though this is spring and there's a huge rose garden and a full-time, so to speak, gardener."

"Disgusting gardener." Casey fondled a comb. "I don't even want to think about that... *person*. So okay they've got antique taste in literature and hay fever to boot. Wha– Do I hear music?"

"Someone's practicing scales on a piano in the other part of the house."

Casey pondered. "That's not scales, it's the beginning of Saint-Saëns *Carnival of the Animals*. Don't let go of me."

"Not a chance. Now the music that wasn't there isn't there any more."

Behind them, unseen on the bed, the white cat morphed himself into a porcelain figurine.

Casey drew a finger across the dresser top, puzzled at his unsoiled fingertip, and held it up for Whit's inspection. "The housekeeping staff is non-union. Did the butler do it? Are we in the Twilight Zone? And what did the butler saw?"

"Ellie Mental, my dear Casey. Vita Sempre is haunted." Whit punned on Ellie D. Mental, a somewhat famous female impersonator who plies Atlanta's bars when not occupied with day job duties as an appellate court justice.

"Leave her out of this. She only sent us the newspaper clipping about this place. The ad said nothing about ghosts, just 'has some problems.' Besides, you know Ellie and her thirty pages of caveats." Casey froze. "The cat!"

"Meow?"

"C-c-c-cat! Bed!" Casey shook, shivered, and hid his face in Whit's white shirt.

"A little pussy on the bed?" Whit didn't turn around.

"Look. At. The. Cat. On. The. Bed."

"Looks normal to me."

"Normal for glass! He's turned into something Moorcock would gladly claim."

"Very nice. But that's Moor-*croft*. Moor*cock* does books, and wasn't there a real cat a few minutes ago?"

"When we were standing beside the bed there was. As real as anything gets in this place. I heard him purring."

"I did too. So the cat wandered off to Limoges, which is more likely than Moorcroft, anyway." Whit dismissed the issue with a wave of his hand. "Big furry deal."

"Could we just big deal out of here?"

"Sure."

Casey perked up. "I didn't think you believe–"

"–ved in ghosts? I don't. We can get out of here into the rest of the house."

"Whit, look!"

In the hallway, the front door swung closed. The brass latch clamped shut and its metallic chink echoed through the hall.

"Whit?" Casey's eyes pleaded, urgent.

"Relax. I've already inspected that door. It unlocks from the inside. We're safer now than with the doors open. Slashers can't sneak in, and we can leave this Hotel Californication anytime we like."

"Ohhh." Casey moaned.

"Come on, Comic. You did notice that Ellie's mysterious ad from the *Weekly Intelligencer* touted this as a one-bedroom estate? The bedroom's decor is, well, you saw it. And the wardrobes contain zero women's clothes. Sooo?"

"Whit, you don't think those ghosts are...? Were? Family?"

"Probably." Whit led the way to the pair of doors in the entrance hall. "A place this perfect, this huge? Better decorated than Donna Jean's Chicago penthouse? But only one bedroom? Do the math." He wiggled the door handles. "Ready?"

"Do it."

"Curious bone working now." Whit shook the handles noisily.

"Open the door!"

Whit flung the doors wide, opening the tap on daylight. "More Persian rugs," he used his toe to tip the nearest corner of a huge one into place from where it had flopped over. "Ceiling's way high. Fabulous beveled inset paneling, obviously executed by supremely skilled craftspersons. More art. Way fine."

"What. A. Dump!" Casey quipped in his best Bette Davis, which considering his nervousness wasn't up to his usual high standard.

The cat peeked in, playful, as though sizing up a mouse.

"These guys have a major window fetish, along with any other fetishes they might have," Whit said. "They better have one enormous heating system to keep up with that huge French wall of Italian glass in the winter."

"Radiators," Casey said. "Bunch of them in the front hall. More in here. Forced air AC. See the returns?"

"Straight out of Sweets 1940. The boiler has to be the size of the QE-2. You did notice the clock?" Whit uncoiled his arm.

"How could I not, speaking of fetishes. It's taller than you, Mister Six-Foot-Two, though not as good looking. Older than the Republic. Unlike you, Mister Just-Over-Thirty."

Whit nudged Casey toward the back corner of the room where the grandfather timepiece presided. The clock's base bore a small brass plate: Wilcox & Perkins, 1818. Its brass pendulum bob, massive and gong shaped, glinted like new. Polished weights and chains, walnut case curved in more ways than not. Gothic numerals, lunar dial. *Tempus fugit.* The hands had stopped at 2:32 in the afternoon during a crescent moon.

"It's the kind of clock you only read about in auction catalogs." Whit strolled around the clock, nodding approval.

"Unbelievable." Casey indicated the whole room. "What is this? A clubhouse for the Terminally Strange?"

"Maybe for the terminally wealthy," Whit said.

"Okay, it's a retreat for deposed royalty? A gangster hideout? A day spa for rich weirdos... fallen movie stars? Atlanta's own Sunset Strip. Where's Max?"

"Playing with his organ." Whit flashed an imp's smile.

"Tired. Someone was playing that piano earlier? Where are they?"

Sounds of shattering glass came from beyond a pair of massive doors, slightly ajar, in the back wall.

"Stay here," Whit whispered, moved toward the sound. If anything happens, run for the car."

"You don't have to worry about me running," Casey said, hugging the clock. "I've suddenly developed quite an interest in the fifty-yard dash."

CHAPTER FIVE

Mean Cuisine

"Shh!" Whit looked over his shoulder at Casey. "Fifty yards would barely get you to the front hall."

"The half marathon's sooo strenuous."

Whit stalked the doors.

"I'll miss you," Casey mouthed as though starring in a silent movie, eyelashes aflutter.

Whit pushed one of the doors open and peered into the room beyond. After a few seconds, he broke into a broad smile, opened both doors and stepped backward through them, out of sight.

"Nothing," he said from around the corner. "Nothing but a *Pleasantville*-perfect kitchen big enough to make cozy dinners for two hundred of our closest friends."

"What broke?" Casey clung to the clock.

"Don't know."

"How did it break?" Casey hugged the clock tighter.

"Don't know," Whit parroted.

"Who broke it?"

"Don't know."

"You got my address in Atlanta?" Casey bolted. Whit caught up with him halfway across the Persian rug, asserted a reassuring arm around Casey's waist and wheeled him around.

"Come on. There's nothing here that can hurt you."

"'There's nothing here that can hurt you,'" Casey mocked. "Nothing except the slashers and the pre-verts. And Limoges the cat, peering around the corner even now. And Yankees that go bump in the night!"

Whit pulled the reluctant Casey, who feigned a swoon, to an Eames chair beside the clock. He dusted the broad seat with an imaginary handkerchief and, holding Casey by the shoulders, guided him into the chair. Patting Casey's head, he crossed the room to the window and gazed at the lawn that undulated down to a brick serpentine fence in the distance. "This is some place." He sat at the piano and opened the keyboard. The pastoral plaint of Rachmaninoff's "Vocalise" filled the room.

"I didn't know you played piano," Casey said. "And so beautifully!"

"My step-moms—two of them in turn—insisted that my brother and I take piano lessons, but I stubbornly refused to practice." Whit held up his hands for Casey to see. "It's a player."

"No way, a player Steinway? I'd believe it comes *with* a player, maybe a cute twenty-something Russian prodigy with no vowels in his name and designs on Carnegie Hall."

"You play, don't you?"

Casey put on a convincing Marilyn Monroe. "The radio." He mugged. "I had piano lessons, too. Daddy insisted on it. But I migrated into other forms of entertainment."

"I made it through the first page of 'Gypsy Rondo.' What is this piece? Not Chopin? It's..."

"Ummm, something to do with voices, vices, whatever. Rachmaninoff. Way famous."

Whit teased. "Not famous enough for you to remember its name. Hnmph! A place this elegant could have piano rolls cut by old Rocky himself."

"How do you turn it off?"

"It'll run down—no electricity here for decades." Whit got up and made a slow turn. "You think they didn't finish the wood panels?"

Casey twisted around to a solid white wall behind him. "Odd in the middle of all this opulence. Has to be a repair of some kind, probably associated with a stash of Amontillado."

Whit eyed the blank wall suspiciously. "Did you notice the dining room as you ran by?"

Casey strolled to the deep cased opening which let into the dining room. The cat hopped onto the piano, curled into nap position and morphed into a porcelain figurine worthy of the finest French tradition. "Frank Lloyd Wright would hardly lay claim," he said, "but it's nicely appointed by a fanatic eclectic. Nothing the crowned heads of Europe wouldn't treasure, mind you. Enough crystal to keep the butler nervous as a ca—way far very nervous. And a table—is that Hepplewhite?—huge enough to... to..."

"Park a limousine?"

"Warm."

"Land a 747?"

"Warmer."

"Cover most of Kansas and part of Nebraska?"

"Got it!" Casey leaned against the doorjamb. "Only two chairs. They don't do much entertaining."

"Oh, they're very entertaining, and they're not even here."

"I hope," Casey muttered. He reached over to pet the white cat on the piano but pulled his hand back and stuffed it into his pocket. He didn't notice that the cat stirred and settled into a different napping position before returning to its ceramic state.

"Let's check out the kitchen."

"Yummm," Casey said. "Can I hold onto your arm?"

"If you promise not to ask me about those crashes."

Sounds of breaking glass came from around the corner.

Casey swallowed. "What crashes?"

More shattering from the kitchen. Loud.

"Shall we?" Whit yelled at the doorway. He extended his elbow. Casey entwined both his arms into it and let himself be led-pulled-dragged through a butler's pantry lined with glass-front cupboards full of china and crystal, service for twenty in each of several patterns. Nothing broken.

With pink and white checkerboard tile and cream trim, the kitchen proved a spacious, utilitarian affair with two side-by-side commercial stoves—cooking space to handle a sizable army. A walk-in refrigerator built into the back wall sported heavy chrome handles on its pink, enameled steel doors. Hung on chains from the ceiling, chromed racks accommodated a dizzying array of gleaming chef's paraphernalia. Tiered mesh vegetable baskets hung to just above counter height. Empty. A wall of shelves displayed cookbooks, teapots, French *café* presses, shiny brioche tins, scalloped torte pans, copper molds, while a nearly symmetrical array of wood-handled knives adorned a square butcher block on casters near the door to the butler's pantry. Spacious work tables of enameled steel made the kitchen postcard-worthy picturesque, if not modern.

"I love it," Casey said. "I wouldn't change a thing!"

"I hate it," Whit said. "I'd re-build the whole area, redefine this wasted space, lose the retro tile and bring the place up to date. I couldn't cook in this kitchen."

"You? Cook? All you make for dinner is reservations—and I love you for it. Do you suppose that cooler still works?"

"Do I detect an afternoon cream soda craving? Forget it. That thing was worn out before your grandma DePaul."

"Let's not bring her into this." Casey peered into a cupboard. "Wow, this stuff looks perfect. Here." He tossed Whit a pound-size can of chocolate sauce.

"Publix-shelf condition." Whit put the can down gently. "If this isn't a museum, it ought to be."

"Ooo, I always wanted to be a museum piece," Casey cooed.

Whit led the way to the breakfast nook. "A little nooky in the nook?"

"Cute," Casey said, indicating the nook.

"There's something here from every wave of fashion since Lincoln was in diapers." Whit tugged Casey's shirt up, over his midriff.

Casey grabbed Whit's hand. "Ohhh, too spooky for nooky."

Whit hugged Casey and patted his back. "Not to worry. Whit is here to protect you from things that don't exist." He plunked himself down onto a bench seat under a large window. The lace-curtained window just touched the top of a trestle table of natural oak. "Decision time. To buy, or not to buy. That is the bare bodkin. Whether this what-a-dump is worth blowing the big bucks," Whit said. "Or suffer the zings and narrows—"

"Spare poor William further parody, please," Casey interrupted. "I doubt even Ripley would believe this place. And there *is* that ghost thing. Looks like people live here and don't live here, have always lived here and haven't ever, all at the same time. Like people slept here last night and no one's ever slept here. Ripley for days. There's probably a coffee table made out of matchsticks lurking in a secret passageway that leads to a dungeon full of I don't even want to think what full of."

"Clocks." Whit nudged Casey. "This isn't getting us anywhere. Look at simple facts, instead of conjecturing about non-existencies." He counted "points" as he listed them. "It's fifty miles, give or take." One finger. "It's gorgeous, you have to give it that." Two fingers. "It's private, and huge." Three, four. "So, chase scene to the cutting room floor. Do. We. Want. To. Make. An. Offer?" Five. "And it has a great clock." Ten fingers.

"Buy Vita Italiana Hauntississimo? Ask me when I'm sipping Chai far from scaring distance. Besides, eighty grand wouldn't buy the contents of one of those cupboards at a flea market ten minutes before closing time, much less this whole place. And surely not the matchstick coffee table."

Whit hnmphed. "Very astute, Mister Financial Planner. I figure eighty thousand is the down payment or some other stupid bait-switch ruse. Maybe the second mortgage, the fifteenth, the monthly payment, whatever."

"There's art here that the High could only wish for. The Man Ray in the front hall? You'd have to steal a thing like that. Mere money would not buy one."

"International art thieves strike Bryson, Georgia. Winslow Hits Homer in the Bottom in the Ninth. Whistler's Mother Bakes Ghost Flavored Cookies."

"Cute."

Casey adopted a high tenor worthy of W.C. Fields. "Getcher matchstick coffee table here. Free ghost with any purchase, half as cheap at twice the price. Also comes with a broken clock."

"It's secluded. You could tan all over your gorgeous body with nobody to bug you. Except me. And huge. Soirées like Atlanta-town hasn't seen since General Sherman came calling."

"Who would drive fifty miles from Lenox to a party? Or even an orgy? Ghost orgy, at that–" Casey tightened his grip on Whit's arm. "Anyway, you don't think the art goes with the deal? Forget the Man Ray."

"Rays, plural. Rayogram in the dining room. Didn't the real estate guy–Bedrick?–say 'partly furnished,' whatever that means." Whit blew into Casey's ear.

"He also wouldn't show the place. Sent keys. Those vague references he made to 'problems'? I've figured it out. Casey whispered, "It's haunted," and licked Whit's earlobe.

"I don't believe in–you know. But if it bothers you, we'll get Mother Patricia and Toni Ann over here for a proper MCC exorcism. Nine pounds of sage, a boatload of garlic, a couple gay priests with purple pope hats, whatever it takes to evict the non-existent ghost."

"Ghost-zzzzz. Plural. Multitudinous. Slashers, too, and bashers and perverts, Yankees and Ohioans, and–and I want to go ho-o-ome." Casey looked into Whit's eyes. "Uh-oh. You really want this haunted hacienda. It's the clock. You've got that little gleam in your eyeballs, and it's not about–"

Whit gazed into Casey's baby blues. "It's irresistible if the art comes with it. And the clock. Atlanta's expanding. Do I see a McDo in Bryson's future?"

"Oh Whit, I'll just die if they put Martha under our vegetable garden. That noise, and those awful construction men!"

"Construction men my ass." Whit hnmphed.

"Dream on, Sweetie." Casey thumped Whit's shoulder.

Slow, shuffling footsteps approached.

Casey gasped, buried his face in Whit's shoulder. "I just know it's a ghost."

"Have you ever met any ghosts?"

"Not that I know of." Casey's words muffled into Whit's white shirt.

"Sings like the gardener." Whit glared toward the door. The stumbling, shuffling sounds approached as someone slur-sang a drunken ditty in a voice that rivaled a driveway for gravely. Whit leaned around to peer through the door. "Ol' Grandad himpersonalself, in the key of A."

Casey inclined an ear. "And B-flat, C and C-flat. He's all over some twelve-tone."

The gardener oozed-swayed-stumbled through the doorway and leered. He cradled a liter jug of blackberry wine, which he brandished in sloshy circles.

"Afternoon." Whit smiled, nodded amicably.

"Likewise." Casey leaned away from Whit on the bench.

"Hummmnnnohhhggg." The gardener sang-mumbled-wailed the next line of the song. Dilapidation-on-the-hoof sported worn-out overalls, a worn-out red flannel shirt torn in more places than it was whole, and worn-out work shoes borrowed, no, hand-me-downed from a sewer rat. Sticking through or out in plentiful places, his worn-out long underwear looked more like discarded axle grease than any color Sears would admit the garment comes in. He sported a bristly white beard and a veritable shock of dirty grey hair at his ears, emphasizing the vacancy of his round, bald pate. A gnarled visage made all the grime look quite at home on his haggard frame. In a garbled, nasal tenor, he emitted another line of tunelessness.

"I don't think he speaks that language," Casey said.

The gardener glared back, his eyes clear.

"Howww dooo you doooooo," Casey mocked in E-minor, snaked a hand around Whit's waist. "We're lovers, see? We're here, we're queer, so it's okay if we neck. Get over it."

"Watch out." Whit freed his arms, prepared for confrontation. "We don't know if he's dangerous."

"He's too drunk to be dangerous, except to his liver."

The gardener lunged toward the table, waved his bottle wildly, gargled the song.

Whit jumped to his feet, ready to do battle. "Hold it, buster." He inhaled deeply, struck a defensive pose, and fixed an intent glare on the gardener, who lurched closer.

"I take it all back," Casey said, urgent. "I'm a dyke in drag. You wouldn't hit a lady?"

"He's not going to hit anybody," Whit warned, "unless he's suicidal."

The gardener sprawled onto the opposite window seat, took a long, thirsty pull on the bottle and belched.

"Maybe he's deaf."

"Possibly. He acts like he's so drunk he could blow chunks at any moment. Better get up, we might need to flee."

Casey extricated himself from the window seat. "It's the Mad Puker of Bryson, terror of townfolk by night and day, able to submerge tall buildings in a single hurl." He joined Whit across the room at the breakfront.

"We came to look at the house," Whit said loud enough for the deaf, or even the dead, to hear. "Do you know about it?"

"Your mother wears army boots," Casey said.

"Eoooworrrinnnssshawwwrrrlll," the gardener wailed.

"My sentiments, exactly," Casey said in mock civility. "Care for a spot of tea, old shat? So nice of you to bring joy into our lives. Do come again, and don't let that doorknob hit you in the ass on the way out." Casey nudged Whit. "Come on, let's go while we can. Oops, spoke too soon."

Whimpering softly, a bedraggled, once-white poodle trotted into the room. Water dripped from the dog's matted fur and puddled on the immaculate tile.

"The gardener probably left the door open," Whit said.

The poodle stared at the floor, whimpered.

"I can't bear it," Casey said. "Call the Animal Cops."

Casey pulled Whit through the door. "Do you suppose the dog's injured or sick or anything?" Casey asked.

"Let the gardener take care of Fido during his hangover. Don't trip over the rug." Whit flicked the rug over with his toe. In a few seconds, unseen, the rug's corner flopped back again, as though spring-loaded.

Whit puzzled. "How did that dog get wet? The sun's shining."

"Nice to be spared the usual olfactory offense of a majorly putrid drunk," Casey said. "But blackberry?. And maybe the dog fell in a puddle. Maybe he–" Casey pointed to the front doors, still closed, latched from the inside.

Whit dragged him forward. "I know this latch only works from the inside. I checked it when we came in. And the only other way in is through the door we were sitting beside. So the gardener came down a chimney? With the wet dog? And now that you don't mention it, the dog dripped on the tile, but there's not a drop of water on the floor in the room he came through to get there. Don't ask about that, okay? Promise you won't ask."

Casey gulped. "Chimney," he muttered, broke for the car. "Poodle." He hurried to lock the door of the open convertible.

Whit made sure the house locked behind them and pocketed the key. "Just don't ask."

CHAPTER SIX

Disappearing Stuff

In the darkened recesses of his kerosene-scented station, Phil dropped with a thud into his massive wooden chair. Except for spots accustomed to frequent wear, grease and stove soot darkened the whole area. With the real estate agent out for the count, Whit collected himself, hnmphed, and hnmphed again.

"Phil, the only spirits I believe in come eighty or a hundred proof. I don't buy any of this ghost crap, but I do want to buy your property. For cash. We came here to meet Bundrick to make an offer to purchase—with stipulations about title and rights of way. Do you want to sell? With or without the ghosts, doesn't matter."

"Son," Phil said. "I wouldn't mind gettin' a little piece of change out of that prop'ty after all these years. All m'daddy and Uncle Jeb ever got was a straggle of scared-ass tourists an' a burnt silo and boo coo of bad luck." He resettled his cap. "I done tol' you 'bout it, right here in front Bud an' Reb. So, I reckon if'n y'all want t'buy, it's durn tootin' fer sale."

"Y'all-a-buyin' it?" Reb's treble tone said "I dare you" through and through.

"May be." Whit cast a look at Casey, who smiled sheepishly.

"Ain't no maybe, Son." Phil heaved his chair off the wall.

"Mr. Tra–"

"Ever body calls me Phil."

"Phil." Whit looked the man in the eyes. "We walked through yesterday. The gardener. And his dog? Some things spooked Casey and we left. Mr. Bundrick said there were sixteen-something acres? I want to walk the property lines and see if the title checks out. I'm not interested in buying a courthouse full of hassles."

"Ruther'n a house full of haints," Reb warned, unasked.

"And what of the furnishings?" Whit spoke to Phil, not Reb. "I'm not out to swindle you. Those artworks? The antiques? You do know what that stuff could be worth?"

Phil adjusted his cap. "I reckon them's fine pieces of stuff worth a pretty penny, 'specially after all these years. But it don't matter none. C'ain't none of it ever be took out of there and sold. Them ghosts've never let anything leave their place. My daddy tried it and my uncle, and they both had nothin' when they got home, and no explanation fer it happenin'. The stuff somehow snatched itself back to where it was b'fore, purty as you please, right back where they got it—that is, when somebody got up nerve to go back again and look fer it."

"We don't want to remove anything," Whit said. "The market value isn't what interests us."

"Well," Phil said almost to himself. "Y'won't have no sons to leave it to." He ignored Whit's bristling gaze. "If'n it brings the same luck to you that it's brought to the rest of this town—well," He stood up. "I reckon that's all I'm a-sayin'." Phil pulled his sweaty blue work shirt away from his back as he made his way around the desk.

Whit and Casey exchanged puzzled glances. Reb spat. Bud lit another cigarette off the nub of his last one. He flicked the smoldering butt into a sunlit puddle that shimmered with rainbows from a floating oil slick.

"Eighty thousand, Mr. Bundrick said, is that right?" Whit stepped over the puddle. Casey circumnavigated. "You're aware that's an extremely small price, even for just the art?"

Phil said. "I done tol' y'it's hainted."

"I don't believe in 'hainted,'" Whit said, firm. "Unless you mean burdened down with judgments and estates that branch fifteen ways every generation. In that sense I've seen property that was thoroughly 'hainted.'"

Casey stood near the door, eyeing the station regulars who propped against the station's front wall, and studying the cobwebs that lined the yellowed plank ceiling. He alternated staring at the freestanding oil-fired stove with its triangular soot mark above it, and at the dark-green wainscot of beaded boards. He polished with his toe a recent scrape on the wide-plank floor, worn smooth by years of scuffling steps and, in years past, diurnal scrubbing with sand and kerosene.

Phil winked and smiled. "Well Son, the taxes ain't paid the last few years but that ain't much. Th'assessment for fire protection ain't much either, and anyhow I'm the fire chief so the town better not try'n collect. My daddy got the heirs and estates clean before he died. Had a deal of trouble doin' it, and if that ain't what put'im in a early grave, I don't know what was." Phil shifted his weight summarily. "I reckon y'all'll need to git y'selves a big city lawyer to see about anything that don't suit you."

"Why didn't Mr. Bundrick tell us all this? Or any of it?"

Phil flung his Braves cap onto a stack of Braves-monogrammed headwear that teetered on a narrow, bare wood shelf high above the clutter. "I git me a new cap ever' game we win. Course that ain't been often enough this season. Whit, let's set something straight. 'Mister Bundrick' is Bryson's town drunk. One of 'em, anyway. He ain't sold nothin' in a bunch of years—unless you count the land transfers us farmers do to keep ahead of the tax collectors, banks, and other blood suckers. 'F't'weren't fer 'is wife bein' a nurse an' commutin' t' Antioch Springs to work, they'd a-starved years ago. He's brought every no 'count tourist in here and tried to tell me they was up t'buy the place. Next thing, ol' Bundrick's drunk and that's that. Even if he don't ruin the deal a-drinkin', the people take a look out yonder and it's off to Milledgeville with 'em, never t'be seen or heard tell of again. If old Abe ever draws a sober breath it'll be a town holiday and we'll all go ridin' in the firetruck like the Fourth of July."

Phil sat down. He rustled through a stack of papers on the desk, sending a few sailing to the floor. "I've got a letter from a fancy lawyer over t'Atlanta about that durn title." He probed deep into the stack, sending more papers floating floorward.

"Don't bother," Whit said. "I'll get a new title search and survey."

Phil looked Whit in the eye. "I doubt you'll find a surveyor in these parts that'll set foot on the place. My daddy's done had that problem."

"I won't use one from these parts," Whit said. "Do you have the full legal description handy?" He flung the challenge despite strong let's-get-out-of-here looks from Casey.

"Yep." Phil reached into the middle drawer of the desk without following with his eyes where his hand went. He pulled back the grubby paw clutching a thin, yellowed piece of paper folded into a clumsy rhomboid. "This here's m'daddy's plat. Go do yer looking around with this and come on back. Unless y'bluffin' me?"

"I don't bluff," Whit said. "Let's see that plat."

"Whit, can we just forget it?" Casey shuffled his feet. "I don't know a soul in Milledgeville."

"That's good advice." Phil unfolded the crisp, fragile treasure. "Let' see. Nineteen an'–" He peered at the map, pulled his chin, squinted, wrinkled his brow. "–Sixteee–" He flipped the document around to Whit. "Eight. Ain't old at all."

"That ain't, uh, isn't old?" Casey chuckled.

"Son." Phil smiled at Casey. "Bryson's people ain't in as much'f a hurry as over t'Atlanta. Besides, ain't nothin' changed out there in a mess o' Sundays."

"Okay, Phil," Whit said. "We have the keys Mr. Bundrick sent us, so we'll go look around for a couple of hours. If it checks out, we'll sign a conditional offer. Land, house, outbuildings, and all contents?"

"And the clock," Casey chirped.

"For what good any of it'll do you," Phil said, nodded.

"And all the ghosts." Whit said.

"Durn shore, Son." Phil guffawed. "Them's free fer nuthin', all you can eat. I jes' wish you weren't a-foolin'."

"Me, too," Casey said.

"Ghost doin's aplenty," Reb said. "Y'git drove plumb crazy." He bank-shot an empty Yoo-Hoo Chocolate Drink bottle into a battered oil barrel that teetered against the far wall.

"Go on back outside, will you, Reb," Phil said. "This here's serious business."

Whit stuck out his hand for a shake. "Deal."

"Agreed." Phil wiped his fingers with his denim shirttail and shook Whit's hand. "Son, most anybody'll tell you, as far as Phil Trane's concerned, that handshake's worth a lot more'n any lily-livered lawyer can write up papers for."

"Same here," Whit said. "Come on, Casey, let's motor."

"Yonder comes Amos from the barber shop," Reb said. "I can smell that cologne he likes 'em t'use on 'im from half a block away."

At the abrupt dead end of a lane overgrown with thick woods, Casey stared into brambles that a rabbit would avoid. "We missed the turn."

"No kidding." Whit put the car into reverse, revved the engine, spun the tires. He twisted in the seat to back the open Fiat toward a space wide enough to turn around. "But how?"

"Ghosts." Casey folded his arms.

"Hnmph!" Whit bat-turned the car.

"Ohh-ohhhh." Casey whistled at the dust cloud that spread behind them. "You're ticked."

"You're the one who's miffed."

"Mmm," Casey looked at the speedometer. "Any faster and we'll miss the turn again, plus all of Bryson and half of Helen."

Whit braked. "Help me spot that imitation road. Please?"

"We just passed it–Ghost Villas is the other way from that burned-up brick chimney. The one we just warp-nined past?"

Whit bat-stopped the car. "Caustic, but correct."

"Buy the place, Whit, and ten more like it if you want. Annex it to Lenox Mall or build a convent for unwed caterpillars for all I care. But let's just get out of here."

"Due diligence, dear."

"The water glasses are worth the price of the whole place. Buy it. Use my plastic and get a two-hundred-percent share of the Brooklyn Bridge to go with it. But let's go-oo-oo hoh-ohh-ohhhm." Casey refolded his arms.

"You heard Phil. There's things about this place he won't tell."

"So give us an out in the contract. And let's GET out."

"Principle," Whit said.

"Okay, while Mister Principle explores, I wait in the car."

"Not. If you face up to your silly fear of non-existent ghosts, you'll be able get over it." Whit stopped at Vita's gate, looked over at Casey. "Now I *know* you're ticked."

"Very! I ought to smack you right in the kisser."

"*Frappe moi,*" Whit quoted-dared, squinted his eyes and jutted out his jaw. Casey kissed him.

"I most humbly apologize for any offense." Whit said. "Am I forgiven?"

"I'll think about it." Casey folded his arms.

CHAPTER SEVEN

Marking Time

The party wasn't bad. The food was good, the waiters scrumptious to gay eyes, and the drinks plentiful. The attraction, however, was the lifetime collection of one Efram Terwilliger Burnberry, late, formidable hoarder of the kind of rarities seen in museums. By dint of Mr. Burnberry's last will, his bereaved beloved (well, questionably so) family was permitted to keep none of his favorite things, only to share the substantial cash those delectably collectible items would bring. The event attracted an international crowd of bidders, wishers, posers, collectors, and hangers-on. And Whit and Casey. Their gazes met for the first time over one of the lesser known lots: *Tastes of a Connoisseur, the Estate of E.T. Burnberry, Session Two, Important Timepieces and Periphery, Lot 1721.* Casey wanted the unusual root burl boxes. Whit wanted the clocks. He already had the unusual Italian bevel-sided range covered, but not the "important" tall clock that dominated the lot.

"Heyyy," Casey inspected the goods. Meaning Whit.

"Hey." Eye contact. Gaydar. Bells and tingles.

While Ranger & Smith, Auctioneers & Appraisers, LLC, peddled the exquisite goods to other people, Casey chatted up Whit, who chatted up Casey in the foyer. Their shared interest in the late Mr. Burnberry's trinkets gave way to intense interest in each other.

"What do you do?" Whit posed the standard question.

"I'm a stripper."

"Lovely. What would you like to do for dinner."

"Eat."

"With me?"

"Certainly. Stripping is only an occasional part of my act. I'm stage director and an entertainer in one of the sleazier clubs in the French Quarter. It's nice work if you can get it."

"Can I get it?"

"I never kiss on the first date, but for you I'll make an exception."

Over coffee and pastries they explored immediate territory. Availability: Whit, recently re-single, just returned from unrequited sometime boyfriend in Paris, smitten; Casey, never non-single, always in the mood, lost in Whit's eyes, ready all of a sudden to retire from performing and explore the joy of mutual adoration.

By dinnertime, Whit and Casey had found out all they needed about each other. Family history: totally dysfunctional and mildly so, respectively, gay-supportive, all of the above. Health status: non-problematical on both counts. Likes and dislikes: Whit didn't like green beans and hated hummus; Casey claimed an aversion to crawdads and onions. Whit preferred single malt Scotches older than dirt; Casey picked Valpolicella, Beaujolais or Pepsi, liked milkshakes for breakfast, favored cream soda with pizza, and disliked wearing clothes. Atlanta native Whit, temporarily transplanted to San Francisco after college, returned to work with his father's architectural firm. Casey called Louisiana home–the tiny village of St. John d'Oro fifty boring miles north of Baton Rouge and ten miles west of nowhere. The locals affectionately (well, somewhat so) abbreviated it "St. Jack."

In a month of Wednesday lunches, Friday night dinners, and long phone calls during the week, it was no longer Casey and his hot friend Whit, or Whit and his cute new squeeze Casey. Just Whit and Casey. Inseparable. In love.

That was eight years before Whit and Casey gazed through Vita Sempre's ornamental (to say the least) iron gate. "Admit it's gorgeous?" Whit coaxed. "In the French sense of the word?"

Casey put on his best Bankhead. "Pahzzz-itively, dahhhling. Reallly it is, evahhh so, simply tooo tooo gawww-geous."

"You'd think whoever's keeping up the house would fix this road. I'll bug Phil about easements when we get back."

"If we get back," Casey said. "Did we make out our wills? Do we get double indemnity for being eaten by ghosts?"

"There are no ghosts," Whit said. "And nobody collects indemnities while dead. There are no Swiss banks or ATMs in graveyards."

"I'll haunt those deadbeats from the next world if it kills me!"

Whit laughed, handed over the gate's key.

After fiddling with the lock, Casey tossed the keyring back to Whit. "Won't work. Let's leave in a huff."

Whit flipped the ring back. "It worked last time."

"I didn't need the key last time, remem–This marker? The letters point out. I'm certain they pointed in yesterday." Casey tossed the keyring to Whit.

"Vandals," Whit said, returning the keys. "Keep trying."

"That rock weighs more than your fancy Fiat. Besides, it doesn't look tampered with. Key fits now." Casey moved aside for Whit to see. "But the lock's stuck." He blew a tuft of hair from his forehead and applied himself to the task. "Whit," he said in mock anger, "you just better get your cute butt over here. Pity this place if I break a nail."

"That's the spirit." Whit hopped out of the car. "The lock just needs a little convincing," he said. "Get tire iron from the car, please."

"Break the lock?"

"It's our house, or will be in a couple of hours. We'll get a new lock in town. The tire iron?"

"You want the phone number of your dad's lawyers, too? In case breaking and entering is illegal out here in the boonies?"

"The cops'd break every spring in their cruisers on that access road. The tire iron?" Whit held out his hands and wriggled his fingers.

Casey perched against the car's fender, wrist to forehead, face skyward. "Why, whatevah could ya'll do with that implement of destruction? Oh, wawwuh, wawwuh, wawwuh!"

"Thank you, Scar-letta, for that analysis. The tire iron, please, if you're not too busy with your screen test?"

"Now where would those Italians put such a thing?"

"Quit stalling! It's in the trunk–that's the space in an automobile dedicated to the storage of makeup cases and extra Yankee corpses."

"Oh wawwuh, wawwuh–"

"Get me that tire iron before I make 'wawwuh' on your ass!"

"Promises, promises." Casey tromped heavily around the car.

"Never mind," Whit said. "It opened."

"Does this mean you're going to make wawwuh on my ass?" Casey hopped over the car door into the front seat, folded his hands and put on a cherubic grin. "And what's a tire iron?"

"Hand me Phil's plat, please," Whit said.

"Come right to Bearing 321, all ahead full."

"Another movie?"

"Same one. The U.S.S. Constitution shells Atlanta with Scar-letta in a balloon over the battlefield knitting booties for Rhett's cute mustachioed self. The whole scene went to the cutting room floor before the cutting room even got wind of it."

"Why's that?" Whit screeched the Fiat to a dramatic halt just past the house.

"That was before your dad built his swimming pool, so there was no place in Atlanta for the Constitution to park. Whit PLEASE don't make me go in this horrid hacienda again!"

"Okay, I saw enough earlier. Too bad I left my digital camera in your car. See if you can find a barn and a gazebo. Maybe down this slope?"

The white cat peeked around the end of the house.

"Beautiful day." Casey skinned his shirt off and flung it into the open car.

Whit hnmphed. "I hope that oaf gardener isn't still around."

"Speak of the gardener, in he crawls. He's right over there. HELLO!" Casey waved a sock at the gardener, who leaned on a garden hoe amid a sloping expanse of lawn.

Whit flipped a thumb.

Casey paused mid-strip. "Don't, Whit, he's like a sewer--smelly but necessary. Do *you* want to trim all these trees?"

Whit hnmphed.

"Maybe it's just a fat scarecrow, not the gardener. It hasn't moved a sinew." Casey tossed his jeans into the car.

"Probably stoned out of his Purple Martin gourd. Maybe the spooky hoopla about this place is only a ruse to hide ten acres of Mary Jane plants."

Nude, Casey stretched and twisted in the sunshine, like a ballet dancer warming up for a performance.

Whit chuckled wickedly, grabbed Casey sideways around the waist and led him toward a pecan grove. "Let's give Scarecrow P. Sewerrat something to stare at."

"He's so drunk he won't see a thing, or believe he saw it, whichever." Casey returned Whit's hug. "Look, there's the white cat. If you hold me a little tighter, I promise not to say let's get out of here for a whole minute."

"Grapes," Whit said, pointing. "We can make wine!"

Casey cut a cartwheel and returned to Whit's side. "Sunshine! We can make hay!"

"There has to be a wine cellar," Whit teased. "Where they store the ghosts between marijuana harvests? Oops, sorry." Whit unbuttoned his shirt. "Come here, Cutie."

Casey purred. "Am I going to lose my virginity again?"

CHAPTER EIGHT

Peel Me A Grape

"M r. Trane, I mean Phil," Whit said, agitated. "You have some explaining to do."
"No barn, right?" Phil smiled, confident. He creaked back in his desk chair,
clasped his hands behind his head over a bald spot on the wall.

"Why didn't you just tell me there's no barn?"

"Son, sometimes it's there, but other times it ain't. Them's the facts, like it or no."

Whit held up his palm like a traffic cop, casting a sidelong glance toward Casey, who
had sidled into the station and perched against the doorframe.

"Howdy, Son. Did y'all see a grape arbor? Right past th'driveway?"

Whit winced.

"Oops." Casey sauntered out, whistling a melodyless tune.

"Yes, we saw the pecan grove."

Phil fixed Whit's gaze with a cool blue-eyed stare. "That barn's between the pecans
and the grape arbor, where the driveway turns into clay. It burnt to cinders fifty-odd
years ago. Wasn't no Bryson fire department back then, an' it burnt slap to the ground
an' ever'thing in it. Several fine horses, sad to say. Some folks 'round here claim it burnt
up th'original owners, too—maybe accountin' fer the ghosts. Ever since, sometimes it's
there bright as new–I've seen it m'se'f. And sometimes it ain't. Some folks even claim
they've seen horses in the stalls and hay up t'the rafters, but I don't reckon many of us,
me included, has got nerve enough to go inside a barn that sometimes–" Phil fluttered
his fingers. "--ain't nothin' but thin air."

Whit cleared his throat to speak, but Phil interrupted. He leaned around Whit and
shouted into the open door. "Reb! Get me one of them Nehi grapes, will ya!" He looked
at Whit. "Look at the plat, Son. It's dated ten years after that barn fire. Sworn to and

certified. Only, they ain't no barn, like I said. Not then, not now. And Mister, them roof timbers was big around as this here desk."

Whit whistled.

"I done tol' ya that place's hainted."

Whit tapped the air with his index finger. "I don't believe in ghosts, and I don't believe in ghost barns, ghost cats, ghost vegetarians, or ghost–or ghost *ghosts*. All the hocus-pocus in Georgia won't make a barn disappear."

Phil sat, fanning gnats with a new Braves cap.

Casey handed a grape drink to Phil. "Reb sent this."

Whit cleared his throat. "We still want to buy Vida."

Casey grimaced.

Phil lurched forward, scattered flies that buzzed figure-eights over the desk's littered surface. "Well, I reckon I underestimated you a mite."

"More than a mite," Whit said. "Cash, with some conditions."

Phil bellowed through Casey as though he weren't there. "REB! REB!"

Sounds from outside: tobacco juice kerplop on the ground, the weary creak of slat-back chairs.

"RRREEEBBB!"

Reb appeared at the door, grinning. "Phil, I ain't deef!"

"Take my ol' blue pickup and run over to Ol' Abe's. See if he's passed out an' if he ain't clean 'im up best y'can an' git 'im over here. Hurry up, before this feller changes his mind."

"Y'mean b'fore 'e loses it," Reb muttered. He shook his head in disbelief, took Phil's heavy key ring from its hook on the doorjamb and ambled out. "I don't know whatcha'll'll do with a house fulla haints."

"Before you get too excited," Whit said, "conditions?"

"Name it," Phil said. "You said cash money?"

"Cash. Asking price with the usual stipulations. Who owns the road to the front gate?"

"Smart question, Son," Phil said. "There's two roads. One goes up t'the front. A longer one goes behind the property, and ends at the old back gate that's been bricked up. I own the front one. That was my Uncle Jeb's cornfield. Nothing there but a row or two of collards when I feel like puttin' 'em in."

"Permanent easement, first refusal, unless you want to sell it outright." Whit made meticulous notes in his pocket notebook. "Fair's fair. I'll pay you extra for that. We want that road passable and presentable."

"Done." Phil grinned. "That's mighty careful dealing. You ain't some kinda lawyer?"

"My father's an architect in Atlanta. Garrett, Thomasee and Smith? Condos mostly. We did some of the new glass towers in Buckhead. Several more under construction, or about to be."

"Which is why we're looking for a place away from there," Casey said.

"We ain't got no architect in this town, or much need for one," Phil drawled. "We got a mess of farmers, some preachers for what that's worth, a good tractor dealer on the edge of town, and–" He looked up to see Reb backing the pickup into its place by the street. "AND A DAMN DRUNK REAL ESTATE MAN!"

Whit and Casey jumped at Phil's outburst.

Reb moseyed toward the station, tossing Phil's key ring in the air and catching it palm down. He shouted as he crossed the gasoline island. "Old Abe's–"

"Shoulda knowed." Phil slapped the desk sharply.

"–drunk." Reb reached around the doorpost to hang the ring on its nail. "He's got two big jars o' shine. Nothin' I could do."

"No problem," Whit said. "I'll write out something that will do until you can get Mr., er, Abe sobered up."

"I don't need no piece of paper." Phil took a long pull on the grape soda and stuck out his hand for a shake. "This here's how us farmers do business," he said with pride. "Nearest lawyer's thutty miles, an' that ain't far enough."

Whit pocketed his Koh-I-Noor technical pen and shook Phil's hand. "Deal."

"Whit!" Casey shouted above road noise of a loudness that visits open convertibles driven extremely fast. "Are you trying to get us a speeding ticket?"

"Just me." Whit slowed the car slightly. "You want one?"

"I've already had my year's quota."

"You've had your quota for the whole century," Whit teased. "Is that the exit for Bryson? Hold on!" Whit whirled the car into the ramp. "So, Cutie, do you have a date tonight?"

"Why what-evah could you mean?"

"Well, Scar Letta, I hope you'll join me in celebrating the purchase of our new plantation. We can have the finest old time in Atlanta. Wine and dine, go to all the best places."

"Do tell?"

"We'll stop by Pitty's for cocktails, and I know a perfectly fine barbecue house in Midtown. Afterward some coffee and cakes on Peachtree Street among the richest pimps and ho's in town, and then––"

"Oh, Mistah Garrett, how you do go on! But, go on." Casey fluttered his eyelashes. Whit slowed for the town limits. Casey enthused, insincere. "'Bryson. The Beautiful. Welcomes. You All.'" He quoted the dilapidated, Burma-Shave-esque signs that greeted all comers. "Have you developed a fetish for Phil's Texaco, or dirt? I bet even the motor oil they sell is grubby."

"Come on, Casey, perk up!"

"I'm perked." Casey groaned. "Visiting here twice in two weeks after I promised myself I'd never come back to this haunt–I mean, you-know-what-ed burg."

"As new property owners we should get acquainted with the local people. I bet Phil's a prime mover."

"He's a mover, all right." Casey commandeered the rear-view mirror to inspect his hair. "Look, he's coming out to welcome us. They ought to 'cue a pig or something neighborly like."

"Thank you, Miss Sarcastic 2001," Whit said. "Heyyy, Phil!" He shouted across the wide expanse of grease stained concrete.

"You're hollering like a country cousin," Casey accused.

"We're IN the country," Whit said. "Besides, there's no use whispering in this town."

"Tell me! Gossip travels fast, but in this burg it breaks the sound barrier."

"Even I was shocked," Whit agreed. "And I lived in San Francisco."

Casey tossed his comb to Whit. "Here, do something with your hair."

"It looks like I just drove for an hour super fast in an open convertible, right?"

"Smartass. I'll comb it for you."

"Uh, better not," Whit said softly. "We have a very unappreciative audience. Sneak a discrete peek at the Shell's angels across the street."

Casey glanced over while pretending to fiddle with the glove compartment. Three rough characters postured, menacing, at the gasoline island.

"Hellooo." Whit waved the pink comb.

Casey surveyed the hulky men. "Are you crazy? They look like they'd love to come over here and stomp us."

"They'll get stomped," Whit threatened, confident. "The skinny one on the right is a closet case for days," he said under his breath. "The red-headed one looks like a Tower Burgers cook. Only twice as greasy."

"I thought I'd never go willingly inside this palace of Phil's, but that Shell crowd makes bar bouncers look friendly."

"What's with them?" Casey asked Phil after bestowing howdyhowreyadoin nods all around.

Enthroned at his desk, Phil rummaged through his papers, looked up. "Roberts' crowd? They're a-standin' out there t'scare ya. Durn bullies. Them chickenshits're curious about y'all, like most folks, 'cept they're bigger fools. If y'don't let 'em know y're scared they won't dare bother ya."

"They're in for quite a surprise if they do," Whit said. "Are they dangerous?"

"Wellllll," Phil drawled thoughtfully. "I reckon I wouldn't advise you to rile 'em, any more'n I'd recommend teasin' a rattlesnake. But they ain't gonna fight'cha, 'cause that ain't Roberts' way. He'll sneak around and pull dirty tricks, and with him a-leadin' the others will too." Phil snorted. "They's school yard bullies that never growed up. I've always bullied 'em back, so they don't much take to my side of the street. None of 'em's dangerous any more'n a sleepin' rattler. Roberts is that tallest one on the end, leaning on the gas pump. He ain't got much nerve to y'face, but he's a firebug behind y'back."

Tall, built. Coal-black hair, bushy black beard. Permanent snarl etched into a Marlboro-man face.

"Roberts'll run people off if'n they let him," Phil said. "That bunch of ninnies with him, swaggerin' aroun' like stud lions, them toothless ol' pussies ain't got guts nor glory an' never had. Roberts is behind just about all the mean doin's in Bryson, includin' Vidah's ghosts, and he pays a price fer it, too. I don't know of any human that's had s'much bad luck. Payback fer his dirty tricks, and the way he treated his little brother and his helpers too, I reckon. My daddy hated him and his daddy before 'im, and 'is granddaddy, too. I reckon us two families ain't spoke a kind word since before the Creation."

"Why?" Whit prompted.

"Corn I reckon. Especially lately."

"You mean moonshine?" Casey perked up.

"Shore do, Son. But if y' take to moon, don't you be drinking any of Roberts's. His stuff'll get you blind drunk, if you know what I mean. Not even ol' Abe'll drink it."

"Quaint," Whit said.

"Them other fools over yonder, they's from out in the county. They he'p 'im run his stills and he keeps 'em in moon an' pays 'em a percentage to haul it aroun'. Ain't a one of 'em got a lick of brains left. Or liver, either."

"Doesn't look like they started with much," Casey said.

Phil laughed. "Reckon not, Son. Don't y'all be telling nobody any of this nor where you heard it from, either. But if I was you, either one of you, I'd stay clear of Roberts' licker, and him too."

"No worry," Casey promised. "I won't even drink Shell gasoline, much less Mr. Roberts' moonshine."

"Right smart, Son," said Phil, triumphant, seizing the paper he'd been searching for.

CHAPTER NINE

Rights and Passage

Phil waved the document, shooing flies. "What's this?"

"That means I've taken care of the liens," Whit said. "It's not a small amount, but you're underselling, so we'll call it even." Whit turned the paper over. "However, the whole sale is off, this section here, without a signed release of rights from someone named K. A. Plunk."

"Hmmm," Phil said. "You still don't understand about this town, or you'd know how glad I'll be to get rid of that place, undersell or not." He unrolled the papers. "Them liens are a right smart piece of change."

"This is the bottom line amount." Whit pointed. "There can't be a sale without that release. Whoever this Plunk guy is, his rights sailed through untouched, so until he's satisfied nobody can sell or buy."

Phil picked up a fanbelt off the desk and tossed it toward its place on a nail high above the front door. It bounced, and he caught it, dropped it back on the desk. "Son, I reckon you know what kind of financial condition I appear to be in?"

"I can surmise," Whit said.

"Appearances is deceivin'."

Whit picked up another piece of paper. "You understand these easements."

"Shore, Son. I live in the country 'cause I like it out here, but I've been to the Big City. More so than anybody roun' here knows about. What I don't understand is why y'd want a place that scares Casey half t'death."

"Me too." Casey muttered something about thirst and ambled out to where Phil's cronies propped as usual against the station's peeling clapboard. He selected a Yoo-Hoo Chocolate Drink from the ancient drink box and sauntered over to a rickety chair. Careful to prop at the same angle as the rest of the gathering, Casey leaned back.

"Howdy!" He stared into space-time in the time honored tradition and let the cold elixir bubble in the sweating bottle as he drank.

Inside, Whit took out his pocket notebook.

"That map your surveyors drew up?" Phil spoke softly. "I didn't want to say anything in front of your friend. I figured you didn't tell 'im.'"

Whit lowered his voice. "He and I stood in the middle of that pecan grove, but the surveyors measure and draw off and swear to a red barn within smelling distance of where we were standing. And big enough for half the horse population of Kentucky. Thanks for not mentioning it just now. There's no doubt the surveyors saw a barn. I still refuse to believe the impossible."

"Son, if y'stay 'roun' here long, y'got t'bleve somethin', and if 'tain't them ghosts I don't know what it might be." Phil contemplated the bare lightbulb, paused. "Ol' Mrs. Plunk?" He tapped the papers with his Bic. "Last time I worked on her old cars she tol' me she'd sign off if I ever got a buyer. She moved to this town when my daddy ran this station. They became friends, her and m'daddy. Him and me've kept them fancy cars of hers running all these years. I learnt it from him, and I still take care of her old jalopies." Phil shooed a fly from his desk. "Them's *some* cars. It's a miracle t'get parts, ever' time."

Phil took a breath. "She come t'Bryson back in the hard times. Had family money, plenty of it. Us Tranes weren't downright starvin' 'cause we growed our food, but nobody around here had a penny."

"It wasn't often somebody with family fortune still had a nickel of it left. If it wasn't the farms a-going bust an' folks gittin' foreclosed, it was something else again. We all got wiped out, one after t'other–especially when the bank closed and ol' Bud Trumbull up and left with who knows how much of our money.

"Ol' Mrs. Plunk's how a lot of people in this town survived without actually starving. She started a one-woman building boom. Had that big ol' house of hers built, and then got them boys, friends of hers, to build Vydah. She added onto hers several times. If it hadn't been for that money a-bein' spent we'd all've been far worse off.

"She and them Simple boys always had plenty, and they didn't mind partin' with it. Folks said one of them boys was hooked up with gangsters up Chicago way, but I ain't shore I b'lieve that. They was stage actors. Musicians or some such. Couldn't've been a nicer bunch, and they never hesitated to help a body in need."

"I wondered about the previous owners," Whit said, craning his neck to catch a glimpse of Casey, carrying on like one of the boys with the "boys" out front.

Phil followed Whit's gaze. "Looks like your friend's getting along right fine with m' friends–Amos in particular."

Whit said nervously. "Uh, you were saying?"

"I done said too much. 'Cept for me, nobody in Bryson's seen her in ten years or more. She sends somebody to town for anything she needs.

"Years ago, her and them Vidah boys had a hand in ever'thing that went on. We had an opera house, they called it, right yonder where the café is now. Most of it before my time. Concerts and ballets, jazz and dances. People say we had silent movies here after most everybody else had talkies, but I reckon that's exaggeration." Phil warmed to his subject.

"They stopped the movies altogether when Old Man Ramunsky built the Rosemary-Patricia Drive-in over at Antioch Springs. Years later, Old Mrs. Plunk and them boys started theater plays again. They had the old opera house painted up inside like it was in the Twenties, and it was lookin' right fine, too. Then a few of the local boys got hot to be actors and whathaveyou. Old Bob Roberts' little brother Bret was among 'em, and that didn't set well with them Robertses, not at all. I reckon that's what brought on a lot of this mess."

"Mess?" Whit prompted.

"You'll find out. That Mrs. Plunk, she's got to sign these papers anyhow, so go ask her." Phil looked Whit in the eye. "I 'preciate you payin' off them liens, Son, but I ain't got all my resources where a bunch of lawyers can find 'em. So, if y' do need out of this here contract I can reimburse ever' penny."

Whit shrugged. "We'll deal with that if we have to."

"Your friend, there, them ghosts or maybe them cats got 'im scared. But I see his name's on ever' one of these papers."

"Casey and I always put everything in both our names, so if one of us dies the other has legal rights that our families can't dispute. Do I need to explain why?"

"I reckon I know." Phil, held eye contact, lurched up from the desk. "Y'all go see ol' Mrs. Plunk an' tell 'er Phil sent you. I'll tell 'em you're a-comin'. Land sakes, Ernestine'll get calluses on her tongue a-spreadin' all this gossip."

Whit found Casey propped against the station's front wall, sipping a second Yoo-Hoo and carrying on in his best Cajun with Amos, Reb, and Bud. Casey exchanged wide grins all around and vaulted his empty soft drink bottle into the trash barrel. "Y'all take 't easy now," he drawled.

CHAPTER TEN

Kings and Queens

Casey hopped into the car, smiling wickedly, as Whit bat-turned the Fiat and peeled out. "Friendly folks," he said with a sly smile as Bryson receded in the car's mirrors. "I was telling them all about New Orleans and Mardi Gras, and they were suckin' it up–as Amos himself would say."

"He wouldn't say that. He hath no teef."

"Reb's the one with the gums, Whit. Don't make fun. There's a reason his tooth fairy doesn't visit any more."

"There but for the grayth of dental floth go I? Did he lose his choppers in a cockfight?"

"Amos wouldn't fight a fly, much less a chicken. There hasn't been a dentist here since before dentists were invented," Casey said. "No one to harp about flossing or keep cavities in check with poisonous heavy metals."

"Okay, I'm thorry I made fun of Amoth."

"Whit!"

"Okay, that was tacky. What exactly were you telling Amosss and the otherzzz about your old ssstomping groundzzz?"

"Just about Mardi Gras. The shows, the Krewes and all." Casey winked, grinned.

"And ALL?"

"They couldn't believe grown men can dress up like women so nobody could tell otherwise. I tell you–"

"You hung out for an hour with three rednecks in the middle of nowhere in the middle of Georgia--talking about *drag shows*?"

"Amos brought it up."

"I'm sure! But now who is making fun of who."

"Whom, Whit."

"Okay, yoummm are now the one making fun of themmm."

"Well," Casey confessed. "Goddess will surely punish me for it. But they asked where I was from, so I told them New Orleans, with the hurricane disaster. And Reb–he's the one with no choppers–naturally said I must have seen plenty of Mardis Gras, and I naturally started telling them all about it."

"Naturally."

"Then Amos asked if it's true men dress up like women. So I naturally told him all about that, too, and–"

"You told them *all* about it?"

"Sure," Casey said with a grin. "You and Phil came out and interrupted right when I was about to invite Amos to take in the early show at Peonies' Garden, since he was so interested in the subject."

"Oh sure! I can see them wearing their Sunday overalls, dropping by your Aunt Beatrice's condo for a drink without an engraved invitation. And then the lot of you head out to a drag bar for the evening." Whit swerved the car into a gravel road.

"Only Amos wanted–Whit, where are we going or do you know?"

"Notwithstanding the lack of your expert navigation, my map-hoarding, GPS-enabled friend, I have actually found the home of the mysterious Mrs. Plunk all by myself. We're going there to get her to sign this paper so I can buy Tara for you."

"Whit, my sarcastic friend, I so hate to bring this up," Casey teased, looked around. "But you have found exactly nothing but a corn field and a cow pasture. Not even any cows."

"How many cow pastures do you see?"

"Mmm. I can count them on one hand." Casey held up his middle finger. "One."

"Correct. That's where this Mrs. Plunk lives." Whit slowed the car to a crawl.

"Then Mrs. Plunk is either a moo cow or a mad cow, or maybe she's an old cow. She lives in a cow pasture?"

"No, she lives in a mid-evil castle on the other side of the pasture like a good old girl. There's supposed to be a dirt road. Aha! *Le rue dirt*." Whit wrenched the car into a right turn down a bumpy clay track. "And farther down this, the Arnold M. Dirtclod Memorial Parkway, there's a grove of pecan trees–*voilá, les nuts*–in the middle of which the Old Cow lives with her eighty-two cats and a pet fireman."

"You didn't warn me we're going calling." Casey dug through the glove compartment for his comb.

"No need to fret. The Old Cow's blind as one."

"One cow?"

"One bat. There's her cottage."

"Cottage? That place makes the Parthenon look like a privy. Whit, we should buy this one. It's way Southern, and it doesn't look half as haunted."

"Casey, there's–"

"–No such thing as ghosts. You told me. Fifty times just today. I'll bet this Mrs. Bat knows our Vita Sempre spirits personally."

"No doubt," Whit said. "That's Vita's back fence just past those live oaks. Remember the bricked up gate in the serpentine wall around our place? It connects the batgardens, or once did. Back when Napoleon was in diapers she sold her friends the land and got them to build on it, or so Phil said. You can ask her *all* about it. But how about not bothering her with drag shows?"

"Drag shows my ass."

Whit wriggled his fingers. "If you're good."

"'When I'm bad I'm better,'" Casey quoted in his best Mae West. He adjusted his clothes for an assault on the front door of the enormous Greek re-revival mansion a bit worse for several-score-and-some years' wear. "Wonder how this palace escaped General Firebug."

"They had the slaves bury it before Sherman got here, and then dug it up after he went by."

"I doubt it's ante-bellum," Casey said. "Twenties, earliest."

"Very astute. Late Thirties according to Phil. Built to Old South standards using non-Union labor." Whit chuckled at his pun, but Casey ignored it.

CHAPTER ELEVEN

Welcoming the Wagon

Mrs. Katharine Plunk's stately mansion had three-story columns that supported a heavy, classical entablature. Casey leaned backward to study the distant soffit. "All right for the cute curvy-outie balcony over the door. Echoes the arches over the windows, see? Way Greek. Eyebrows for days."

"If she runs short of drachmas–" Whit pointed to the unkempt shrubs that encroached the red brick porch "–she could open a flower shop. Those azaleas are as big as oaks, and that dogwood by the front window would keep Nome in firewood all winter."

"Oh, Rhett," Casey mimicked. "Can I put Tara back like it wahzzz? I mean before the wawwuh?" He fluttered his eyelashes.

Whit operated the tarnished brass door knocker. "Shhh!" Unsteady footsteps approached from inside.

"Hello." Whit handed his card to the somewhat elderly woman who opened the door. "Are you Mrs. Plunk? Phil Trane sent us."

"I'm not. Please come in. *Monsieur* Trane telephoned just now." The woman spoke in a soft voice with a Parisian accent. She led them through cavernous, richly appointed rooms with cracked plaster and faded wallpaper, to a spacious sitting room dotted with pristine white wicker that sported bright yellow cushions.

"Dust free," Casey whispered, pointed to a table. The woman had barely cleared the door. "Unlike the rest of the place, which hasn't seen a cleaning cloth since She Liked Ike."

"They gave the maid the decade off. This room is spotless, and it's ginormous so that's no small feat. What do you bet those bright squares on the wallpaper didn't happen from over zealous polishing?" Nodding approvals, Whit looked around at oriental rugs that splashed colorful pools on the pegged cherry floor. Glass and bronze sculpture adorned every available flat surface. A gleaming Bosendorfer grand occupied one corner. Around it, sheet music teetered on low tables and stacks of music manuscript spilled into piles on the floor nearby. "Way serious about music."

"The piano?"

"The manuscript. Somebody here writes music by the score."

Casey groaned.

Mrs. Plunk swirled into the room with a delicate whiff of Chanel and a rustle of old silk. "How do you do. Katharine Plunk." She offered her frail, pale hand.

A stern-looking woman of advanced years, Mrs. Plunk carried herself with a timelessness that transcended the cut of her Forties fashion. As aristocratic in manner as she was in dress, Mrs. Plunk seemed a figure on whom designer silks would be customary. She led Whit and Casey to a cozy chat corner that looked through wall-sized windows into a jungle of flowering trees long unchecked by gardeners' shears. With a flourish, she indicated a wicker settee for Whit and Casey, taking a rocker for herself.

"Thank you," Whit said, waiting for her to sit down. "Nice of you to receive us on no notice, for which I apologize."

"I *adore* this time of year." Mrs. Plunk stared intently at the space between them and spoke softly in a cosmopolitan manner tempered with Georgia drawl–Dom Perignon in a jelly glass. "I added this sun room so I and my guests could enjoy this season." Her arm made a sweeping gesture that took in the broad expanse of tall windows which formed three sides of the sitting room. "C'*est bon*?"

"It's truly lovely," Casey said. Densely appointed with palms, ferns and cut flowers, the room looked like a well groomed greenhouse amid an unkempt outside garden.

"My companion says you're an architect?"

"Not exactly." Whit smiled at Casey. "I'm an engineer in an architectural firm in Atlanta, and–"

"Excuse me," Mrs. Plunk broke in. "I'm so familiar with this old house it probably doesn't show. I'm nearly blind."

Whit coughed. "Phil told us."

Casey stared silently at a white ceramic cat that captured a delicate, feline preen on the piano.

"I do okay. Now, you were saying? An architect? This old house could use a good architect, not to mention a horde of gardeners. It's probably a good thing I can't see any of it very well. It must be getting as shabby as I. Beyond time for a renovation. On both counts, I expect."

"It looks fine," Whit said. "A little paint and some– But that's not why we're here. My friend and I are thinking of– We're buying the property next to yours, 'Vita Sempre' it's called. There's a matter of some deed restrictions that you control?"

A cloud moved over Mrs. Plunk's visage. She thought for a long moment. "Well, Mr. Garrett, I'm afraid that's going to be a problem." She leaned forward in her chair, not changing the direction of her gaze. "That land belonged to me. I still own property on two sides, and when I sold it–in, let's see, '38? Or '39 I think it was–I made sure it would revert to me under certain circumstances that I thought and hoped would never come to pass." Mrs. Plunk sat still and silent, as if weathering a storm.

Seconds ticked by.

"I suppose I could have asserted that clause," she continued as though the silence hadn't happened. "And I probably should have, to keep down trouble. But, well, regrets won't mend anything, and everything the place meant to me, everything those two boys meant to me–it's all gone in the wind, as they say in Atlanta."

Whit cleared his throat. "Uh, we are–"

Mrs. Plunk raised her wrist to stop him. "I'm a doer, always was," she said. "But I've kept silent because I hit my limit. I grew tired of doing, tired of causes, of fighting, and of being fought." She sighed, turned toward Whit. "I suppose by this time that deed is in quite a mess?"

"A tired mess." Casey smiled broadly.

"Phil's family cleared up most of it, and I've invested considerable resources to get it quite tidy." Whit prompted, "except for your original deed restrictions."

Mrs. Plunk tapped a slow tango rhythm with her forefinger on the arm of the chair. "*Trés désolé*," she said. "I'd rather not stir it up again. The memories that I and my friends–" Her voice trailed off.

"Mrs. Plunk," Whit stammered.

"Mr. Garrett, I'm sorry to disappoint you and your friend. I don't wish to surrender my rights. Not to you or anyone else."

Casey turned to hide his grin from Whit.

"I didn't mention––" Whit cleared his throat. "We're prepared to pay a fair price for release of any rights you may still have. It could be worth quite a sum."

Mrs. Plunk dismissed the idea with a summary wave of her hand. "Oh, Mr. Garrett. Give me my youth. Or give me back my Tonio and Paul, or my beautiful Dmitri. Give me back my eyesight, sure. Then we'd have a deal quick as a cat's whisker. But I don't need money." She sat back in her chair, crossed her hands in her lap and rocked gently.

"Forgive me," Whit said. "I thought–uh, those missing paintings?"

Mrs. Plunk smiled faintly. "What's missing from the wall behind me is one of Man Ray's early nudes," she said. "I've lent it to the museum through summer. I can hardly see it anymore, and it's shameful to hide it where no one can enjoy it. There's a companion sketch for it, a gift of the artist to the model, in my sitting room. A later one from the series hangs at Vita—perhaps you've seen it there? Do you know Man Ray's work?"

"Indeed." Whit chuckled. "I see what you mean about not needing money. But I do wish you'd reconsider. The rights you have aren't easily enforceable through the tax sales, heirs and estates. It could be costly to assert—"

The younger woman stepped into the room. Mrs. Plunk inclined an ear to her approach.

"Well," Whit said, resigned. "I apologize for troubling you. Mr. Trane told me you had agreed to release your claim. He said he had spoken with you."

The younger woman approached Mrs. Plunk's chair, nodded to Whit and Casey to stay seated. "Kath." She placed her hands lightly on Mrs. Plunk's shoulders. "Phil telephoned again just now," she said, "and we had a little talk."

Mrs. Plunk covered her companion's hands affectionately. "Allow me to introduce Miss Lovelle Truesdale. Everyone calls her Miss Trudy. This is—"

"We've met. Whit and his *bel ami* Casey. I do wish you could see them, *ma cherie*," Miss Trudy said with a tranquil smile. "I've never seen anyone more like Tonio and Paul. *Vraiment*." She leaned over and whispered something into Mrs. Plunk's ear.

Mrs. Plunk turned her face up to Miss Trudy's. "Oh, these old eyes." She sighed, leaned forward in her chair, fell back and squeezed Miss Trudy's hand. "I and Miss Trudy," she said with more of a challenge than a statement, "we're lovers."

CHAPTER TWELVE

Peonies on Parade and Other Amenities

Whit donned his aviator sunglasses, gunned the Fiat's engine and peeled onto the blacktop. "Are you scared of those mean ol' ghosts or Sappho's temple full of superannuated Lesbos?"

"Yes, and yes, and everything from here to the I-75 onramp."

"I felt at ease at Plunk's place, in spite of the initial friction with the reigning *reine* of the castle. I'll hurry so we can catch the AIDS benefit at Peonies Garden. I know you don't want to miss giving away some capital gains."

"Even a sassy drag show seems tame after Mrs. Punk," Casey said.

"'Plunk,' dear. Bohemian or whatever. Plaunikoitocschnackoverowsky shortened to Plunk when grandpa immigrated to the Old Country from the Even Older Country."

Casey made a thumbs-up gesture. "The old girl 'doesn't need money.' Hasn't bought a new dress since Franklin Delano, and those bright spots on her wallpaper—I still think they're from stuff she sold to pay her Tara tax."

Whit shook his head. "She could pay taxes on half of Atlanta with an original Man Ray."

"I doubt Miss Arrogance Nineteen Forty would admit being broke."

"Probably not," Whit said. "But she signed away her rights on Vita and didn't mention the handsome sums I hinted at paying."

Casey tsk'd. "Wait till the closing. She'll show up on her Harley with a bill for four million smackers and a new iron lung for her Yorkie. Bet we haven't heard the last of Punk dyke."

"Plunk dyke."

"'That's Plunk of the Chateau de Plonkère in Montmorenci, France,'" he mimicked. "'Most of my family fled during the French Revolution and changed the name to avoid discovery, but I'm a Tylah on my mother's side–from the Horace Bedford-Samuels Tylahhhs? Of Savannnah, you know?' Do you think she's really a drag queen? She talks molasses and bullshit like one."

Whit laughed. "Excellent imitation, and impromptu. What a talent. For that, Imp, I'll buy dinner. "

"Keep talking and I'll *be* dinner."

From the all-business hustle of downtown, through its teeming burbs' soccer-mom bustle, Atlanta sprawls in directions Descartes could only imagine, and spreads into ever more slumbrous bedroom communities peppered as far as a gasoline fill-up will reach. Urbia, suburbia, exurbia. Tributaries like creeks, to streams to ever broadening rivers of traffic.

The commuters' aorta, Interstate Seventy-five, doesn't go through or even near Bryson. You have to give up controlled-access periodicity for miles of quaint, narrow lanes that meander through the red clay hills. The ill kept road bisects Bryson and heads into the woods, gives off a few smaller lanes, and then stops, dead, without so much as a warning sign.

Bypassed by prosperity on its way through the Twentieth Century, Bryson is a farming community, home of a simple hardware store, an antique shop, a tiny bank, a tourist home-slash-bed-and-breakfast, a two-chair beauty shop, a one-chair barbershop, and two gas stations.

The town has neither newspaper nor radio station and little need for either one. With some fine tuning of antenna position and direction, Atlanta's broadcast media enlighten locals, but fifty-seven-channels (and nothing on) entails a satellite dish, of which Bryson boasts few. No loss. What local news or other misinformation the gas stations, barber and beauticians don't disseminate, the café does. Indeed, the townspeople stay better informed about purely local issues than anyh journalists–even electronic ones–would dare fit into print. For entertainment, too, gossip and religion generally suffice. And merge.

Except for a few edifices from the last gasp of the Twenties when farming was last profitable, most of Bryson dates to 1900. Except the bank. It had to rebuild after the local bonfire celebration of World War II's end got out of hand. The town's newest building, a pre-engineered structure with beige steel siding, was built in the Seventies with a federal grant for a volunteer fire department. The water tower, a few years older from another federal grant, is the only thing in town not shaded by trees.

The Twenties and Bryson did that "roaring" thing contemporarily. Just in time for the beginning of the Depression, the Georgia and Tennessee Railroad Company decided to build a freight and passenger station for runs from Atlanta to Chattanooga. The railroad quietly bought the old blacksmith property that was foreclosed after the shop burned down a year earlier, and laid plans for a spur through town, along with a train station. Bud Trumbull, the local banker, pressured the railroad to build at the other end of town on land he was willing to sell at a fair price. When his plan didn't work, he used the bank's money to speculate on much of the property that the tracks would have to cross, even paying real prices for it.

The project sparked an old-fashioned Southern Fuss. Some locals including the Roberts family nearly lynched the railroad's surveyors. The new railroad bypassed Bryson in favor neighboring Antioch Springs. Shortly after, when bank closings were commonplace, and conveniently before the shenanigans surrounding the railroad misdeal could be exposed, Trumbull's bank closed. No surprise: Trumbull left the night before, never to be seen or heard from again. Some said he took their money with him. Some said maybe there was no money left to take by the time he high-tailed it. Everybody said he better not come back.

The Farmers and Merchants Bank of Bryson was built over ashes that some said were the direct result of Old Man Roberts' fury over losing his money. From its outset, the new bank's state charter gave it credibility that Trumbull never had. Even so, it floundered along making crop loans and well-secured mortgages to farmers who had more faith in the weather than in any (choose an expletive) bank. There would surely have been a riot if ever a foreclosure were necessary. The farmers harbored serious distaste for banks and bankers. Truth told, most kept their money in whatever "Mason Jar" and "Mattress" might be metaphors for. Mattresses don't pay interest, but they don't cut a shine by moonlight for parts west when the auditors stop by.

Between fading Coca-Cola emblems, the sign on Phil's place said "Gro & Ser Sta." After Phil's father died, Phil concentrated on "Ser Sta." Attrition and appetite took care of the grocery stock, but the sign remained. The part of the building that had contained the grocery housed an ever-growing collection of tools, truck parts, Atlanta Braves hats and other treasures.

The station's ragged screen door, which slapped shut with a bang when anybody went in or out, still had "Claussen's Bakery" etched into its wire mesh in deep yellow and faded white. The candy counter, its plate glass sides and top perpetually grimy, displayed

AC spark plugs, oil filters, and empty Hav-A-Hank dispensers, plus a dwindling stock of penknives.

The general store atmosphere lingered, though pork rinds and potato chips constituted most of what Phil maintained of the "Gro." Tins of pipe tobacco adorned the counter, along with the ancient, mechanical cash register whose function had for years been limited to ringing a bell when its drawer opened. Giant vanilla cookies, sold by onesies out of a huge glass jar on the high, linoleum counter, yielded their space to Otis Spunkmeyer. Local gardens provided okra, peppers, tomatoes, corn, black-eyed peas and melons, each of which stood watch by turns in weathered wooden crates propped against the wall under the station's canopy.

In two cramped and cluttered service bays, Phil and his part-time helper washed, serviced and repaired automobiles, trucks, tractors, combines, harvesters, tillers, ditchers, loaders, bush hogs, mowers and most anything mechanical. Phil reigned as the county's guru of tractor repair. What he couldn't fix either wasn't broken or absolutely could not be fixed anyway. Besides, he had an uncanny talent for finding scarce parts. All in all, Phil made up quite well in the Ser Sta department what he gave up from the grocery. To hear him tell it, he couldn't change a dime.

Phil lived where he was born, in a huge blue two-story house a respectable distance behind the station. The house was Victorian, to say the least–a bunch of embellishments with a house attached. Phil's family once farmed much of the acreage between the house and the county line, but most of that ground to a halt in the Depression. Where milk cows, chickens, pigs and goats thrived, only a few pets remained. The older Trane always said he'd to return to farming, but never did.

Phil took little interest in clawing a living out of clay. After his father died, Phil planted most of the land in hardwoods, yielding valuable timber after decades—except the four or so acres that burned and had to be replanted. Nobody could prove anything, but Phil always blamed that wildfire, along with other blazes that warmed Bryson's history, on his nemesis, Bob Roberts.

Directly across from Phil's Texaco, Roberts' Shell station, much newer, sported curves of enameled steel. The station's hydraulic lifts made Phil's dug-out pits seem old-fashioned. Roberts opened the place after being booted out of the Army--rumor said for killing a man in a fight over liquor, but Roberts wouldn't talk about it. Ever.

The station came courtesy of his Roberts' new wife Ginny, only daughter of a well-off tobacco farmer down south Georgia way. Ginny was as well fixed for money as she was for coal black tresses. Sufficiently supplied, at least, to put up the new station and a rambling house behind it. When "our boys" got back from tidying up 'Nam, Roberts was ready with "Shell and Shine." Folks tittered that the slogan's latter term had little to do with wax and much to do with the family's long experience in the distillation arts.

Roberts boasted that he built his house for a brood of children. "Eight or ten of the bastards," he put it. However, Roberts' wife never troubled the stork. Folks said it was a good thing for the kids he didn't have. Roberts called it a curse.

Roberts' family never quite recovered, financially or psychologically, from the Trumbull bank's closing. At the Shell, Roberts accepted cash only and stashed it in his pocket. Anybody who stole a dime from him, Roberts made it known, would not live long enough to spend it.

CHAPTER THIRTEEN

The Clock That Could—And Did

The knotty pine interior of the Bryson Café has changed little since Ellen and Gary Mendels built it, adjacent to their bed and breakfast, in the Nineteen Fifties. At its front corner, the building adjoins the massive, brick clock tower beside which the turn-of-the-century opera house stood. The clock's bronze bell was sacrificed for scrap after Pearl Harbor. Its wooden ladders and works burned out when fire gutted the opera house. In front, a bronze plaque on a granite block proclaims the clock's history and promises, someday, a restoration that so far has only braced its walls with steel and put on a new face and lifeless hands.

"On the / Fourth of July in 1978, / This clock," the inscription concludes, "strangely kept time for twelve / hours and chimed the noon hour, by means no investigation / has ever explained."

Not much investigation occurred. The only entrance to the tower was sealed off by the partial restoration, and no one ever tried looking inside. No one was willing to.

As word spread of its "miracle clock" Bryson, particularly the café, got busy. The tourism boom didn't last long. The clock stubbornly silent, people lost interest, and some locals, namely Bob Roberts and the derelicts that hang out at his Shell station, made great sport of taunting them.

Gertie Mendels set a cup of lukewarm coffee in front of Phil. Glasses of ice water for Casey and Whit. "Phil, yer pie'll be hot 'n a minute and y'all's two milkshakes'll be up 'n a spiffy jiffy." She leaned close to Phil's ear but didn't lower her voice. "Did y'fare well in that land deal or do I hafta wear m'ever'day dress to our weddin'?"

"Git on, Gertie!" Phil slapped his knee. "I got plenty out'f it t'buy you any dress in Atlanta, and another'n f'y'Ma."

Gertie's family ran the café, as well as the bed and breakfast behind it. Known as "Bryson Tourist," the Victorian house rambled four confetti-laden stories through live oak trees that propped up the sky. Its many rooms were carved up in leaner times to house a gaggle of locals, along with any tourists who happened by. Old Man Mendels, who had a knack for keeping its antiquated heating and plumbing systems running, managed the place. His wife Ellen, Gertie's mother, took care of the café cooking. Gertie took care of the customers.

Gertie's wide aura of tight, chemical curls spewed forth from her round face like a sunhat, its frizzyness sufficiently crimson to pale any fire engine. Her pink-checked work dresses came, perpetually on sale, from Sky City Discount in Antioch Springs. The pink-striped apron that hugged her narrow waist showed worn patches at her hips. Gertie stored her hands in the apron when they weren't needed for talking. Her figure made hourglasses jealous—a full hour on the bottom, multiple hours on top. From long practice, she held her shoulders back so that her abundant bosom thrust forward, shading her white waitperson's shoes from the café's harsh fluorescent light.

Gertie's mother often predicted that with bosom so plentiful, Gertie would have no trouble landing a husband. Nonetheless, pushing fifty though grudgingly admitting to thirty-one, Gertie remained unclaimed. Since turning fifteen, she brazenly flirted with every man she served in the café, which was most of the men in town at one time or other. Old, young or in between, she brought them eggs and grits, liver and onions, fried chicken and cornbread, all accompanied by a winsome smile, a quick wit and a double order of double entendre.

"Ohhh." Gertie leered at Whit and Casey in turn. "New men's come to town and good-lookin' ones at that! Phil, you better snatch me up quick, or I'm liable t'be swept right off m'feet."

"Git on, Gertie," Phil teased. "This here's Whit, and that's Casey."

"Howdy y'all." Gertie tap-tapped Whit's shoulder with her order pad. "Look at you! If you ain't the best lookin' man I seen in this town in years." She winked at Phil.

Whit blushed. Casey grinned.

Gertie went on without stopping. "Mama! Looka here at th' new men! Handsome ones, too, an' this'n's done got marryin' on his mind." She tapped Whit's shoulder again.

"I seen 'em when they come in," Mrs. Mendels said from the grill. "Quit y'dawdling, girl. Pick up these plates."

Gertie squeezed Whit's shoulder, tap-tapped the table with her pad. "I'll be right back, handsome." She strutted away.

"Don't mind Gertie, Son," Phil said. "She ain't a bit serious. Gertie's a big churchgoer."

"That's not all she's big on," Whit said.

Phil nearly drowned on his coffee. "I reckon y'got that right." He blotted his face with a napkin. "Y'all planning on moving out here, now?"

"No way," Casey said.

"Way definitely," Whit said.

Phil looked Casey in the eye. "Ain't much t'interest young folks. Ain't been no kids in might near fifty years. Not a one."

"You mean no one paid pie to the piper and they all left for the big city?" Casey pressed his foot onto Whit's ankle. "Or people don't believe in sex in this county?"

"Son, it ain't that." Phil cast a glance to where Gertie was standing. "Plenty o' believers, I reckon." Phil lowered his voice. "And y'all own prop'ty now, so I reckon our ol' curse'll apply to you, too." Phil fixed his gaze on Casey. "This town's had th'evil eye put on it. You jus' read about our clock a-chimin' out there. There's more to it. Gertie! Where's m'pie!"

"I'll bring it," Mrs. Mendels said.

"Oh no y'won't." Gertie hurried to grab the pie. "Them men's mine!"

Whit shifted in his seat. "Phil, I've told you--"

"You don't b'lieve in ghosts," Phil interrupted. "Jes' listen. I'm a-tellin' truth y'c'n check at the courthouse. Ain't been no child born to anybody in this town in nigh on fifty years. Gertie was the last one."

"Last what?" Gertie delivered pie and shakes. "Phil, I know what you're a-tellin'. I'll come back in a minute. Mmm-hmmm!" She tap-tapped Whit with her order pad and rushed off.

Whit peeled the paper wrapping from a pair of straws. "I know clocks," he said. "Chiming requires gears. Either your clock had help from some practical joker, or there was an episode of mass hysteria." Whit sipped his milkshake. "As for the childlessness, I'd suspect ground water. Insecticides from farms? Runoff from an abandoned mine? This part of Georgia had a lot of gold mining before California stole its thunder. My point is: look for the real cause."

"Never mind him." Casey said, impish. "Just tell us about the ghost."

CHAPTER FOURTEEN

The Curse of the Stricken Stork

"It's a curse, not a ghost, but the two's related." Phil held up his hand to keep Whit from interrupting. "Son, we checked all that stuff. Ol' Bob Roberts did. Check, recheck, check again. The water, the soil, the food, the garbage dump, the creeks, ever'thing. Background radiation, fertilizer, radon gas, and genetics. There's folks here that breed chickens. Old Man Richards has a herd of Guernseys, and there's horses, pigs, and goats. Cats and dogs and even some ferrets. They reproduce fine, ever one of 'em. But ain't one woman got pregnant in this town for fifty years, married or no, and t'ain't no coincidence, it's a curse." He looked at Casey. "And a ghost."

"What trash're you tellin'?" Gertie plopped a second piece of pie off a spatula onto Phil's empty plate. "I knew y'd want 'nother piece, this bein' a special occasion."

Phil nodded thanks. "I'm talking about the curse, but I can't get these two t'believe me, partic'lar Whit."

"Handsome is as stubborn does." Gertie put a hand on Whit's shoulder. "Y'all'd best b'l'eve ol' Phil," she said. "There's stuff 'roun' here th' devil don't like–" she jerked her head toward the far end of town "–or maybe does. Hol' on." She put a smile on and hurried off to deliver a food order.

Whit insisted. "There has to be a logical explana–"

Phil punctuated his points with jabs of his crumb-crusted fork. "People from here move out and get married or stay here and live in sin, and ain't one of 'em ever had so much as one single child, dead or alive, or even got pregnant. Some of 'em's been mighty hot-assed, so it ain't 'cause they ain't tried. Ol' Bob Roberts'll tell you, if you catch him willin' to talk about the sorest spot in his head. He went off and got him a hot-tailed bitch down Swainsboro way. Sayin' he'd bust the curse and git her pregnant or wear her drawers plumb out a-tryin'. Well, he ain't got squat, and that girl left him. Bruised up to boot, but she got her licks in b'fore she left, bless 'er heart. Put Roberts in the hospital fer nigh on t'a week.

"He got every high-falutin' g'v'm'nt official over here a-pokin' an' a-proddin' and askin' personal questions. Health officials, medicine officials and nukular 'ficials. Pollution 'ficials. Water 'ficials. And ever' one'v'em's gone off stumped. Won't none 'em admit the town's cursed, but they all admit they don't know what's wrong."

"Well," Casey said. "I simply won't get pregnant."

"No, Son." Phil laughed. "I reckon you won't." He skidded his empty plate against the knotty pine wall. "I got t'finish up that John Deere before Old Man Wilbert worries 'ise'f t'death over it. Y'all finish y'milkshakes–Miz Ellen makes a good'n, don't she? Get to know Gertie, too. She's good people, none finer in these parts." Phil shook hands quickly all around and picked up the three grease-stained tickets Gertie had scooted under the coffee creamer. "This'n's my treat."

Gertie approached with coffee pot in hand.

"Gertie, you treat these boys good," Phil said. "They're from the big city, so they won't leave no tip." He handed her a folded hundred-dollar bill with the three tickets. "Keep the change."

"Goodness!" Gertie pushed the money into her bosom.

"Goodness," Casey said, "had nothing to do with it."

"You imp." Whit said. "Just watch out you don't get us into more trouble that you can charm ourselves out of."

Gertie took Phil's seat. "How's them shakes, fellers?"

"Excellent," Whit said. "Reminds me of downtown Atlanta with my father."

"I remember it like yesterday," Casey said. "Oh, wait, it was yesterday."

"Y'all from Atlanta, hunh?"

"Whit is. I'm from Cajun Country," Casey bragged, "St. Jack, northwest of Baton rouge, which is north of New Orleans."

Gertie looked from Whit to Casey. "Phil's right about Bryson bein' cursed, y'all. Somebody or some thing put the devil-eye on everybody. Wha'd'y'all do, anyway?"

"I'm an engineer," Whit said.

"I'm an entertainer."

"Really? Are you famous?"

"You might say that," Casey said. "My name's Casey DePaul, but on stage I was known as–"

"Here comes the bank manager," Whit interrupted, urgent.

"Land sakes!" Gertie propped her hands on her hips. "What's he doing here this time of day?" She raised her voice to a high-pitched shout. "Mama! Yonder comes ol' Ed Beasley, but he's early so I don't reckon y'oughta fry his liver yet." Gertie turned to Whit. "He always gets liver 'n onions on Wednesday. Mama makes it special. He says he don't even like it, but he wants it ever' week 'cause his ma, bless her heart, always told 'im it was good for 'im t' eat it before she passed."

Casey grimaced, stirred his shake in its steel container.

"Mama always has it hot and waitin' for 'im when he gits over here from the bank," Gertie said. "But it ain't even eleven-thirty, and he's never missed a minute bein' here at one-fifteen sharp. That's right after the bank closes for the afternoon." She lurched from the table, adjusting the frilly shoulder straps on her dress. "Ed Beasley!" Gertie challenged. "What're you a-doing here s' early?"

"Well, er, 'm, uh, came fer a cup of coffee, uh, with Bryson's uh, New Property Owners. How 'bout it?"

"I reckon," Gertie said. "But it ain't like you t'be s'friendly. You've got money on y'mind."

"How'd y'do again?" Beasley stuffed his hands in the pockets of his brown, three-piece suit as he approached the table. "Er, 'm not uh, intrudin'?" He looked from Whit to Casey, who fixed a steady gaze on the balding man's grey eyes.

"Sit down," Whit said.

"How do," Casey said as Beasley broke eye contact.

"Er, 'm might as well confess Gertie's right. Uh, wanted to ask y'all. Uh, Mr. Garrett–"

"Whit," Whit corrected.

"Er, Whit, uh, 'm just wanted to ask you, er, seeing as how y'all might be, uh, moving to Bryson? 'M mean, uh, owning property here? And all, er. 'M thinking was, well, y'all might, er, open an account?" Beasley took a long breath and pressed on. "The Farmers' and Merchants' Bank of Bryson could, 'm mean, would like to be of service to y'all? If y'all want. Errr?"

"Sure," Whit said. "In all the stir of closing the sale just now, it's something we forgot to do."

Beasley twirled Phil's abandoned coffee mug, casting quick, furtive glances at Casey, who answered with knowing smiles. "'M, yes, 'm was sure, uh, almost sure y'all would. Uh, y'all don't have to come back over to the bank. 'M your card's got the address." Beasley patted his breast pocket. "Just, uh, y'all sit right here and 'm a-bring the papers, er, in a minute. Errr?"

"Here's a check for the opening deposit," Whit said. "Take your time. We're getting acquainted with the pie and Gertie. Put all but five thousand of this in a CD, longest term you have. Highest return. The rest in standard checking. Both accounts in both of our names–like on this check–either signature required, not both. I assume that's no problem?"

"Of course." Beasley reached out for the check.

Whit pushed the instrument across the table and capped his engineer's pen.

"Money market account," the banker noted gleefully. "First 'm seen around here. Errr, no problem of course. Uhhh, 'm'll be right back. Errr?"

As Beasley hurried out, Casey blew him a kiss, but only Whit caught him doing it. "Beasley gives me the creeps."

"Creeps? Fresh out. The creep's just left." Gertie flopped down in front of them. "I didn't like Ed Beasley when I was a little girl, and now that I'm a big girl." She wiggled her shoulders. "I like him even less." She placed her hands on the table palms down. "I didn't bring 'im no coffee so he wouldn't set here a-saucerin' 'n blowin' it. Now y'all listen to Gertie a minute." She stretched her neck to check for food ready to deliver. "I got the *power*. I mean, I *know* things."

Whit took a breath, ready to speak.

"Hear me out," Gertie said. "I got t'say m'peace before Mama gets that ham steak ready. Then y'all do as you will, but at least I'll've told you." She dropped her voice to a deep-throated rumble. "That place you bought's got the devil power, an' I don't want y'all a-gettin' hurt."

Mrs. Mendel uttered a stentorian *tsk*. "Gertie, pick up this ham steak! Reb's a-settin' there starvin' t'death."

"Comin' Mama! Fellers, if y'all want to come to Bryson, buy y'self a piece of land in town or outside it, and build you a house. Leave that Sempre place to the devils that haint it."

"Gertie!"

"Hold On To Your Pantyhose!" Gertie skipped to the counter.

CHAPTER FIFTEEN

Milk Shakes and Meanies

"Whit, can we go?" Casey flicked crumbs off the table with his pinkies.

"Definitely. This ghost crap is tiresome. Should we take anything with us? A certain Man Ray?"

"Nah, it looks fine where it is, and great art is like a gay bar."

Whit puzzled. "I'll bite. How is great art–whatever?"

"Only a drunk whips it out just to show off." Casey smirked. "Besides, we're in a convertible. What a shame if it got ruined."

Whit put his checkbook away. "I'm proud of you."

"I'm proud of me, too." Casey checked the milkshake containers for remaining tidbits. "For what?"

Whit eyed him suspiciously. "You don't believe in 'Devil doings,' in Gertie parlance?"

Casey shrugged. "Same stuff, different drag, but I do not want to visit Spirit City now, if that's what you're suggesting."

Whit snapped his fingers in the air. "Okay, we'll blow a ton of cash to buy a dream castle in the country, and then leave without even going there. How decadent."

"Very. Now I'm really proud of ourself." Casey used his straws to chopstick a small clump of ice cream that had clung to the bottom of Whit's glass.

"In that case, let's go look for stuff in the antique shop down the block from Phil's."

"Talk about eccentric. We just bought a place filled with enough antiques to redecorate Tennessee, and you want to shop for antiques?" Casey moved another chunk of ice cream into his mouth.

"I know you want to. Besides, they might have an old clock I can't do without."

Casey pushed the empty milkshake glass away. "They might have an old clock, and you definitely can't do without."

"Admit you want to explore it. I saw that twinkle in your baby blues as we walked past it on our way to the bank."

"I'm not into clocks, you are."

"Okay we'll go home. Hmmm?"

Casey grinned. "All right, I admit it. Wild hippopatami couldn't keep me out of there, but I'm getting escape vibes, and–here comes the human douche bag again."

"Ed Beasley!" Gertie shouted from behind the counter. "You back a-ready? I'm gonna start chargin' you rent."

The banker smiled feebly, sidled by Gertie, nodded as he made his way past the sunlit booths spattered with customers.

"'M here's the, uhhh, certificate, errr, two signature cards? Uh, you can order printed checks, uhhh, but nobody does. 'M these are all we use." The banker fixed his gaze out the window, handed Whit a packet of papers. "Errr?"

"Counter checks?" Casey laughed, eyed the pale green pads Beasley edged onto the table. "No account number?"

"'M, yes, uh, but everybody knows everybody around here. 'M mean, uh, just your name is enough."

Casey smiled. "So, if I want to know our balance, I just call and ask?"

The question brought puzzlement to Beasley's face. "'M, ask Ernestine for Mrs. Hughes' desk–she does the posting."

"And no internet banking?" Casey beamed. "No voice mail system where you press '1' if you want to stay on hold another half hour. Press '2' if you prefer to stay on hold another half hour, or '3' to stay on hold another whole hour."

"No, uhhh, 'M see what you mean." Beasley emitted a laugh. "Errr, we're small. Everything used to be this way. Or maybe you're too young. Errr?"

"Much," Casey said.

Whit handed the completed forms to Beasley and dismissed him with a nod. "Okay, Casey, let's go blow tons of money on an antique do-whoppy at the junk shop."

"We already have an antique do-whoppy."

"I know, but do-whoppies work best in pairs. We need another one to round out the set."

"Okay, Mr. Charmer, since you put it that way. Later, Gertie!" Casey waved bye as he and Whit headed out.

"Y'all come back soon! I'll tell the preacher t'git set up f'r a weddin'."

"Which'n y'marryin', Gertie?" Reb snickered as Gertie delivered his sweet tea refill. "Don't look like either one'm'd be much in'er'sted in women."

"You mind your tongue, Reb!" Gertie set down the glass with a loud knock, sloshing liquid onto the Formica counter. "Hesh up, before you stir something up again after all these years."

Treasure Chest Antiques accounted for almost all of Bryson's tourism. Its Depression glass, Deco bric-a-brac, old lace, dolls and furniture brought dealers and collectors far removed from the Georgia foothills. The memory emporium occupied four storefronts starting two doors from Phil's Gro. Ser. Sta. and abutted the tack and tractor shed of Laurel's Feed Seed & Hdw at the other end of the block. Every square foot stayed packed to the pressed-tin ceilings with memories, jumbled from one estate sale to another, one chic fashion to the fad that replaced it, one century to the next.

Isabel Franks presided over the mélange of styles gone passé. Ask about almost any object in history and she could tell you not only who made it but where in her store you might find one showing very little wear, and at a fair price compared to market value. Attractive and mysterious, Isabel wore long, coal black hair. Her ice blue eyes pierced your gaze through to your soul, and her preference for gold jewelry—new or antique—caused her to jangle as she moved, like a handbell choir tuning up. Pendants, baubles and necklaces competed for space around her slender neck, and bracelets twinkled and tinkled in clusters at her dimpled wrists. She wore more rings than she had fingers, and even her ankles sported multiple adornments.

Isabel favored low-cut tops with built-in frills and flirt, always light blue. Her radiant, wavy tresses swept her shoulders, mostly owing to frequent shakes of her head calculated to accomplish the effect.

As Whit and Casey walked up, Isabel flounced out of the store. "Hello." Casey fixed Isabel's blue gaze with his own. "You're not closing early, are you?"

"Not until four o'clock. I'm Isabel." She stepped aside to let them pass into the store. I always have a late lunch at the café." She moved her eyes to Whit's. "You're the new folks Ernestine told me about?"

"That's us." Whit fished in his pockets for a card.

"I'll only be forty-five minutes. Cecil's in charge." She stashed Whit's card in her bosom without looking at it and hurried off, a-jingle, in a flurry of blue frills.

"Let's go see what's new in old clocks," Whit said. "Ooo, from first impressions, we might as well go rent a truck. Neat stuff here, and plenty of it."

"I see one item I want." Casey put his palms on the cold Italian marble top of a large buffet. "You."

"Imp. I bet there's lots of things you want here. Are you looking at stuff or just flirting?"

"Yes. Ten cents and a piece of ass says the 'Cecil' who's supposedly watching this place is that large-in-charge gray pussycat in the front window."

The cat curled on a cross-stitched chair pad propped between a framed sepia photograph and a tin drinking cup. "You win," Whit said. "Wow, this place is stuffed with goodies. We'll be hours exploring a tenth of it. What are you doing for dinner?"

"I've got a date."

"Who, might I ask, with?"

Casey plucked a dulcimer. "You if you ask me."

"Want this neat little jewelry box?" Whit held up the treasure.

"Definitely! Do you like any of these mantel clocks?"

"Not a one," Whit said.

"You of the galaxy-class clock fetish? I bet you're thinking they'd all look wonderful in our den."

"We don't have a den."

"We would if we had all those clocks. Can't you hear them just cry for a den. Tick-den-clock-den-tick–" Casey spotted a distant trunk. I'm going to the next section."

"I'll look over the rest of these clocks."

At length, Casey sneaked up behind Whit. "Tick Tock Tick Tock––"

"Sounds like a Casey. A genuine DePaul if I've ever heard one. Rare. Unique in the entire world."

"–Tock Tick Tock–"

"Freshly wound, too." Whit turned around. "These models have great pendulum bobs."

"–Tick Tock–"

"And well timed mechanisms."

Casey giggled. "Ticktockticktock. Put me down, here comes the other pussycat."

"Right on time." Whit squinted at the Regulator behind the front counter and sneaked a pat on Casey's posterior. "The finish on this model is way fine."

"Besides all forty-leven of the clocks, is there anything else you want?"

Whit lowered his voice as Isabel flounced through the door, ringing its engraved Swedish cowbell. "You."

"Hello, again," Casey called to Isabel. "We're over here under the silver."

"Sorry it isn't better organized." Isabel perched at a mahogany Queen Anne desk behind a jeweler's showcase of walnut and beveled glass. Silver lions at its corners, the showcase held business receipts, invoices and other papers, in neat stacks on velvet shelves. "Gertie told me all about you guys."

"In under an hour?" Casey moved toward the desk. "She doesn't even know *all* about us. I hope."

"Gertie knows more than you think. She's got the power."

Whit hnmphed.

"So she told us," Casey said.

"She really is clairvoyant," Isabel said. "I am too."

Casey picked his way closer to the desk. "Takes one to know one? Okay, what do I have in my pocket?"

Whit hnmphed, examined another clock.

"I don't do parlor tricks, but just this once. Come 'round here so I can see your eyes." Isabel caught Casey's gaze and held it while he fidgeted, transfixed. "You're an easy subject, so let's see. Left pants—your left—key chain, three keys, one is... Apartment key? But it doesn't go to where you live. Comb. Wait, comb's in the back pocket. Left side. Other back pocket. Wallet. Inside that..." Isabel looked more intently into Casey's eyes. "Pictures. Lucky penny? Picture of a woman. Older woman. Not your mother, an aunt? Cards—credit cards not business cards. Some membership cards. Cash. One bill is Monopoly money—I only read this, I don't explain it."

Casey's mouth gaped. Whit put the clock down.

"Other front pocket, coins, two pennies. One's Canadian." Isabel smiled, inhaled deeply, and broke eye contact. "Dates and mint marks? Or have I convinced you?"

Whit moved closer to the desk. "Is she right?"

"Way close. Too close," Casey said. "I'm spooked again."

"No reason to be afraid, Casey," Isabel soothed. "You're in tune to the psychic plane, so you're easy."

Whit smirked.

Isabel played her fingers in her necklaces, keeping them tinkling. "You have the power, if you let it through."

"You got stuff I forgot I had, like the Monopoly money."

"As I said, you're easy. I couldn't do the same with Whit. He's putting up a block."

"No, I mean—" Casey looked at the cat.

"Can I tell you're gay?" Isabel grinned. "Yes. Cecil read you like an Edmund White book."

"Are we that obvious?" Whit chuckled.

Isabel smiled, winked. "It takes one to know one."

"All right!" Casey congratulated. "Then you and... Gertie!"

"Correct. See? Now you're communicating on the psychic plane yourself. We've kept it so secret no one in town would even suspect, so there's no way you'd know otherwise. You won't breathe a word?"

Whit propped an elbow on a massive armoire. "Rainbows abound. Mrs. Plunk wrecked us, too. Miss Trudy told on us. In French, yet. Is anybody in Bryson hetero? Not that we care."

Isabel shelved some papers. "Depends on which closet you rattle skeletons in. People who put up the gruffest front hide the gayest old bones. Casey, I didn't mean to scare you."

"If I were scared I'd be making for the door."

"Or jumping over Cecil through the window." Whit approached the front of the store.

"You can't hide it from me, Casey." Isabel set her necklaces jangling. "I indulged in that silly trick just now to get your attention. That place you bought has the spirits of its former owners connected with it, and maybe some others I haven't been able to identify. The curse on the town is from them."

Whit interrupted. "I don't believe ghosts. Or curses."

"Keep going," Casey said. "I believe all of it"

"Whit," Isabel said, "there hasn't been a baby born–"

"Big deal. Everybody's queer, like I said."

"Point taken," Isabel said. "But if there were an explanation, Roberts would have found it. He's obsessed with this thing. Y'all look out for Roberts. His skeletons are what I alluded to earlier."

"Phil and Reb warned us about his moonshine," Casey said.

"If you see anything on fire in this county, check Roberts for warm matches. There's plenty more. Your new place–that house was built by two guys a lot like you two. You can tell they had plenty. Just like you two–that's the town gossip."

Casey snapped his fingers in the air. "Hey, we're hot news on the local grapevine!"

"Those boys were famous, and they had hearts of gold." Isabel pulled a faded theater program out of the bottom of the showcase and pushed it to Casey. Autographed "Best wishes, Tonio," it detailed an all-Rachmaninoff recital, September 13, 1947, eight o'clock, to benefit Bryson Opera House.

"Bob Roberts' daddy had two sons, the second a good many years after the first. They're rough, back to the great-greats, but Bret–that's the youngest–Bret was never like the rest. All Bob did was torture dogs, start fires–all kinds of mean tricks. Bret liked books and music. Likely he was the first one of the Robertses to ever read a book, and that sure includes their family Bible. Although, I'm not one to talk on that score."

Cecil shifted position on the window sill, clanking the tin cup next to him against an iron kettle.

CHAPTER SIXTEEN

Moon Shine Mayhem

Casey opened and closed a drawer in the dresser he leaned against. "If Roberts is that bad, why isn't he in the clink?"

"He pulled two years for shooting a man in a brawl after his wife left him. Prison made him meaner–he had a real bad time of it, we heard. Not a day off for good behavior, so that lets you know, right there. He's tangled with the feds about his stills a few times, too. Spent time as a guest of the taxpayers on account of it, but he went right back to moonshining."

Whit cleared his throat. "So Roberts rigged this phony ghost to cover up his liquor still. Or the extra bodies from that serial killer thing he's got going."

Isabel laughed. "Bryson's too small for that big a secret. If you look for reasons this town is cursed, Roberts is where to start, but it has more to do with his firebug tendencies than liquor. The precipitating incident goes back fifty years. I promise you those ghosts are real–wait, Whit, hear me out."

"Good ghosts or bad ghosts?" Casey asked, intent.

Whit hnmphed, puttered through a steamer trunk, examined aging doilies, porcelain dolls, pocket watches.

"I've demonstrated that I'm in a position to know. I came here in the Seventies." Isabel waved away Casey's objection with a jingle of her wrist. "Time's been good to me." She smiled as Casey nodded. "I was brought here by Bob Roberts."

Whit looked up from the trunk.

"I was a pretty well known reader of spirits with some successes–helping catch some jewel thieves. Roberts hired me to find out why no one could have children. He'd given up looking for a scientific explanation.

"He paid me cash in advance, drove me to Vita's iron gate, broke the lock, and pushed the gates open. He wouldn't go an inch further. I walked into the grounds, but it was extremely threatening. I can't describe how strong the impressions were. Burned barn, tortured animals, images I can't stand to remember even now. I screamed and ran, right past Roberts, still standing at the gate. I ran through the woods, and eventually stumbled back to town. Those horrible visions dogged me every step. The spirits forced me to look, using me to make their anger known. I saw the fires as they had happened years before. Vita's barn and carriage house. And the old Opera House.

"I saw Roberts running, chasing Bret, yelling obscenities about sexual services. People said that happened, exactly as I saw it, before Bret disappeared." Isabel shuddered. "That place—your place, now—is the center of the spirit energy, and that fire, especially the barn, is where the curse originated."

"Why did you stay in Bryson?" Whit examined a pocket watch.

"The simple answer is: Gertie. I was young. I hadn't learned the trouble I could get into looking into the past or future. I nearly collapsed, and I stayed at Bryson Tourist trying to recover. The Mendels helped me a lot, particularly Gertie. We clicked. The heart doesn't yield to logic. I went back to Indianapolis and brought my things. I had to close my mind to the spirit world because I couldn't face it. To keep afloat and stay close to Gertie, I opened this shop on the stuff my family could send me to get started."

"You've done well," Whit said. "This is an amazing collection." He brought several items to the counter.

"I don't collect, only buy and sell. Jewelry is my weakness. Yours is clocks."

Casey and Isabel exchanged glances.

"Excellent choice, Whit. This watch was made by, or maybe for, a small company here in Georgia—there's one of their tall clocks at your new place. I've got a book if you want to look up the design." Isabel caught Casey's quizzical glance. "Yes, I did go back to Vita. Eventually."

"Weren't you afraid? I am, just thinking about it," Casey said.

"Fear is something you control so it won't control you. Actually, I went back many times, but alone. When Roberts wasn't there, the spirits were communicative, rather than threatening. Mischievous, sure, but not violent. That's why I'm telling you this. Those spirits have potential for evil, but it's all centered on Roberts. They used me to focus on him, and they've dogged him all these years. Growing up, he bullied the other children. Some say he molested every child in town, boy or girl, at one time or another. That's why the curse.

"Young Bret hung around out there, taking care of the horses for the owners at first. When the Opera House got going again, one of the volunteers saw marks on the boy where Roberts and his old man beat him unmercifully. That led to a major town stink, with Bret admitting Roberts constantly abused him sexually. A crowd of thugs torched the Opera House. Not long after, the barn went up, and the guest house."

"Barn?" Whit hnmphed.

"The one that isn't there sometimes." Isabel grinned. "The stress of the Opera House fire so close to their home sent Gertie's mama into labor–fortunately only a little premature. And that kicked off the curse."

"No offense, Isabel, but I've had enough hocus-pokus." Whit plunked items on the showcase. "We definitely won't invite Roberts to tea, but I still–"

Casey chanted with him in unison, "don't believe in ghosts."

"–don't believe in ghosts. Thank you, peanut gallery, for your support. How much for these treasures?"

"What do you think, Cecil?" Isabel jangled an arm at His Imperial Greyness.

The cat stretched a paw against the window.

"Cecil says fifty bucks–gay guy discount."

"Thanks. The stuff's worth ten times that," Whit said. "This watch looks like it was shipped here in a time machine."

Cecil stretched two paws forward.

"Ha!" Casey exulted. "He's upping the price to a hundred bucks for you being a smartass."

"Okay, I'll quit while I'm ahead," Whit said. "We'll talk about those mantel clocks when Cecil's in a better mood."

Casey sighed. "More clocks."

Isabel scribbled a receipt. "Yes, Whit, I'd be glad to ship the doilies to your sister– Asheville, is it?" She looked up from the pad. "He let down his guard."

"He does that sometimes," Casey said.

"Now *I'm* spooked," Whit told Casey. "It made me very uneasy for someone to read my mind like that."

They approached the Fiat, still angled into the curb in front of the Phil's Gro & Ser Sta. Casey hopped into the car. "Isabel reads minds so well I'm surprised she didn't have a blushing fit."

Whit teased. "Were you thinking sleazy thoughts?"

"Always. Right now, for instance."

"To the hot tub!" Whit turned the key to start the engine.

"Do it in the car all the way home?"

"Who's going to drive?"

Casey pondered. "We need a chauffeur, don't you think?"

Whit switched off the engine. "That chauffeur has let us down, and we didn't even hire him yet."

"How's that?"

"Chauffeurs do preventive maintenance. See that little red light? Great color for convertibles, and for J. Crew sweaters some seasons. Not good for lights in the instrument panel of a vintage Italian sports car fifty miles from an *Italiano* mechanic."

"Light years from a cell tower," Casey lamented. "Pray, Mister Exotic Car Fancier, what does that little red indicator light indicate? Another bifurcated doframmus gone bad?"

"Worse."

"A parsnipped portobello?"

"Even Worse."

"Not a flat Italian soda!" Casey gazed at the panel. "If not a pneumatically challenged Pirelli, it's a...?"

"Fanbelt."

"Fans wear belts? We *are* talking Milan here?"

"Fiat fanbelts have never seen *L'Uomo*. Casey, my entertaining friend, the gravity of our situation escapes you, so let me explain. We, that's you and me, are sitting on the outskirts of nowhere in an exotic automobile which won't go anywhere, not even into the middle of nowhere, without a replacement part that isn't available anywhere, especially not where we are, which is here."

"Ewww."

Whit hopped out of the car. "Pull the bonnet latch, please."

Casey studied the car's controls, whistling "Somewhere over the Rainbow."

"Pull this thing, Dot." Whit peered into the car's innards. "Sliced fanbelt *Italiano*." He displayed the part's remnants.

"Can we get a taxi back to reality?"

"Maybe Phil has a replacement." Whit led the way into the station.

"Figures," Phil said before Whit spoke. "Cut half in two while we was lollygaggin' up at the café. I might have one that'll fit, but length is critical on them Fiats. Follow me to my Hope Chest." Phil opened a dreary back room stacked with parts. Empty toilet paper boxes held a confusion of fan belts and radiator hoses. Many more hung from nails pounded at odd angles into the beaded wood walls all the way to the ceiling. With Whit's assistance to hold it taut, Phil measured the Fiat's belt. He puttered around in the car's engine compartment, proclaimed a narrow range of acceptable sizes, and set Whit and Casey searching the jumbled stacks while he peered at the specimens on the walls and measured any possible matches.

"Fellers," Phil said. "That's all the belts I got. I can send Reb or Amos over to old Roberts' Shell to see if he's got one, but if he had fifty he ain't likely t'cooperate. It's him that's cut this'n in the first place, fer shore."

CHAPTER SEVENTEEN

Stay for the Night

Whit grumped. "Can you just get me a new belt?"

"Sure," Phil said, "but it cain't be here till tomorrow. Y'all can borry m' truck. Reckon you can drive a dualie?"

Whit thought. "Drive it, sure. Park it? No way. I doubt it would fit through the parking gate at our condo, much less maneuver into our parking spot. Order two of those belts for me, please. I'll keep a spare from now on. Uh, Casey, let's talk."

As Whit led him outside, Casey took a longing glance over his shoulder toward the Fiat. "Whit, before you suggest it, I'm not staying in that ghost-ridden house?" Casey shivered.

"I know better than that," Whit said. "We can call my dad and fight off his cute chauffeur for an hour–and you know the family politics that would cost."

"Been there, didn't do that, not because he didn't try."

"Me too." Whit grumped. "Anyway, Isabel recommends the local Tourist so highly, I suggest we stay for the night."

"Night!" Casey sang, quoted.

"Then we can spend tomorrow rummaging in the antique store until Phil gets done with the car. It'll be an adventure. That place is carved intact out of the Age of Dinosaurs."

"Probably run by a Tyrannosaurus, too. I'm not sleeping in the closet, if you know what I mean and I'm sure you do. I don't do separate rooms. Muss up a bed in the morning so they'll think it was slept in? Too much like your Aunt Beatrice's. And your father's. And my Aunt Inez's."

"Fun's more delicious when illicit." Whit winked.

Casey grinned. "Okay, let's go."

"Fellers." Phil tossed his empty Nehi can into the outside bin. "I got two of them belts coming tomorrow, first thing. Let's push y'all's car in the bay, out of harm's way. The station stays bolted, and I always leave my meanest hound in there to take care of any trouble. B'sides, ol' Roberts knows fer shore if 'e messes with me he'll get his ass whupped. I done had t'remind 'im of that once er twice't over the years." He took a breath. "Won't take long t'put a fanbelt on, so y'all'll be on your way by eight or nine in the mornin'."

"We'll be on our way after lunch," Casey corrected. "I know nothing of that *other* nine o'clock."

"I reckon not, Son," Phil said. "But I don't know about that nine o'clock y'all're familiar with, 'cept on Braves nights.

Towering into live oak trees that shaded half of town, Bryson Tourist occupied a nineteen-teens mansion built board by ornate board under the brooding supervision of Gertie's great-grandfather. Once prosperous cotton gin owners, the household survived the impoverished Thirties, the fighting Forties, the Superficial Fifties and the Decade of Big Hair by enclosing ever more of the house's copious full-wrap porches and octagonal sitting rooms, walled in or walled off to make rentable space. As the Seventies stumbled by, the Mendels converted odd crannies to bedrooms and hung the simple wooden sign–"Tourist"–over the balusters of the much-diminished front porch.

For Ellen Mendels, her husband and Gertie, the house's generous proportions still afforded ample living quarters–all of the bottom floor that wasn't in an unpresentable state of disrepair. Ellen Mendels ruled house and household.

On the second floor, Isabel called a former porch and sitting room home. At the rear, Ed Beasley rented a small sunporch with a bathroom and kitchenette patched into one corner. Looking like it was thumbtacked on as an afterthought, Beasley's room had its own entrance, a rickety, homebuilt stair that crisscrossed the back of the house. The house's second and third floors comprised a gaggle of odd-shaped rooms with gable windows that peered through or into the oaks' umbrella. Furnished in mismatched veneers, those rooms hosted travelers.

Whit and Casey stepped into the dim front hall. Its sky-high ceiling dripped ornamentation over elaborate transoms, thence to the wide chair rails, ending in a flurry of darkly wooden artifice at worn wood floors peppered with threadbare woolen rugs. The hall's expansive glass-paned pairs of doors stayed curtained off from the inside. A simple writing table beside the stairs held a guest register, a huge Tiffany lamp and a tiny, hand-lettered sign that read, "Ring Bel Sin Regster."

"How quaint," Casey said.

"How French!" Whit clanged the bell. *Conciérge*," he mocked.

"Wha'd'y'want?" A gravelly voice drawled through curtained doors slightly ajar opposite the desk. The smell of alcohol wafted from the room.

"A room for the night," Whit said.

"Sign in," the voice said. "Key's in the jar on the table. Who's that out there–Mr. Robson again, auditing the bank?"

"Nope." Whit signed with a flourish worthy of a famous Hancock.

"Gotta be Porter, the antique man–no 't ain't, cause he talks Yankee. Well who is it, then?"

"Whit Garrett."

"Don't bleve I know ya but no matter, just sign. Rooms're up at the top. Third floor. They's a elevator end've the hall, but it's a hand cranker an' it's less work t'climb th' stairs. Pick any room y'want, but the ones on th' front side look over t' the fire station. Them's the A numbers."

Whit tossed key 3A to Casey.

"You're new to town. Café shuts at eight sharp. Ain't much left after seven, so y'oughta git over there soon. They's Nabs and Pepsi in the machines."

"Does this key fit the front door, too?" Casey asked.

"Front door?" The voice puzzled. "Why in thunder would anybody lock the front door?"

"No reason." Casey nudged Whit. "Burglars, maybe?"

"Town's too small for that. Say, if you get a hankerin', I keep a little corn."

"No thanks," Casey said.

"Suit y'se'f. There's a Pepsi machine behind them stairs. Ice's in the Frigidaire in the kitchen. Just he'p y'self, an' be shore t'refill th' icetrays."

"The room has a waterbed and a jacuzzi?" Casey peered around the stairway to admire the aging soft drink machine.

"Nothin' like that 'round here. We don't allow no hanky pankin'." The voice warned, stern. "Is they one or two of ya?"

"Two," Casey said.

"Married?"

"Certainly," Whit said. "Toronto in style," he whispered to Casey, "and France, and–"

"Well, that's all right, then. I'd catch hell if I rented a room to two people an' them not married."

Silence.

"Wait a minute," the voice said. "I don't hear no woman out there. They's two of you?"

"I don't have a woman with me," Whit said.

"Me neither," Casey said. "I mean me either."

"Then how can you two be married?"

Whit reiterated, firm. "We are both married. Several times."

"Y'all men or women?"

Casey put a finger to his cheek in mock contemplation.

"All men," Whit said. "And all married. Problem?"

"Don't see none. Whew! You had me confused for a minute. Y'all'll need two rooms. The rooms ain't got but one bed. Two men'd have to bunk up in one bed."

"We do it all the time," Casey said.

"Y'do?" Sounds of a Mason jar lid being unscrewed. A pause, some spluttering. "What'd you say your name?"

"Garrett."

"Look here, Garrett, y'all ain't-er-'funny,' are you?"

"Hilarious," Whit said.

"Well, I reckon th'ain't a thing wrong with it, m'self, but my wife–she's the religious kind, nigh onto rattlesnakes, an' I'm talking mostly 'bout the preacher. Got it real bad. She'd give me preachin' hell if she know'd. So, you and your friend'll need different rooms. They's plenty of rooms. Always is."

"Men room together in college," Whit said. "And in the military. You wouldn't say the Marines were 'funny' would you?"

Casey joined in. "John Wayne himself would rise up out of his grave and slap you with his horse!"

"I reckon," the voice said, reluctant. "Jus' th' same, y'all take two keys. One price, so ain't no different."

"One. Room. Is. Sufficient." Whit pronounced firmly. "Two men. One room. One bed."

"And one woman madder'n wet hornets if she finds out. I cain't allow it."

"Let's go," Casey whispered. "Your dad's chauffeur. Ack."

Whit squeezed his arm to reassure him.

"I get it," the voice exulted. "Y'all're them city fellers that bought the Vidah place. Folks was sayin' y'all two was–chummy. Joint bank account 'n' all? Makes sense, now."

"What does?"

"Bein', uh, you know–"

"Funny?" Whit admired the ancient drink machine. "If we don't sleep here tonight, on *my* terms," he whispered to Casey, "I'll buy this dump and turn it into a home for wayward crack whores with hot and cold running drag queens."

Casey giggled.

The voice dropped to a serious tone, apologetic. "Like I tol' ya, I don't mind one bit, but my wife bein' s'religious, I advise you not to let on to nobody–I mean, about bein'–"

"Funny." Casey chirped.

"Y'all're welcome as can be to stay, but *nobody*–and that means my wife–cain't nobody ever be the wiser about two men of the same sex a-sleepin' in one bed. No offense intended. Folks 'round here don't much care 'bout people bein', er, funny."

"You asked," Whit said, firm.

"I did, and I'm glad I did. So's I can head off trouble if I have to. There's a good chance she won't find out, if y'all don't mention it."

"No ask, no tell, no problem," Casey said, icy.

Whit plucked a single room key from the jar. "Come on."

CHAPTER EIGHTEEN

A New Trick for an Old Relic

Whit sat up in the bed, rubbed sleep from his eyes with the back of one hand and, with the other, rearranged Casey's limbs, which intertwined his own.

Casey blinked one eye open, closed it, stretched. "Mmm."

"You're awake?" Whit kicked a flowered quilt to the floor.

"Nope."

"Did you sleep well?"

"Not a wink," Casey said. "Some man kept me up all night making mad passionate love."

Whit wadded his pillow into a ball and propped on it. "Hnmph! Same thing happened to me."

"I couldn't see who it was, because I had my eyes closed." Casey stretched, languid and lascivious. "But I sure hope he happens again."

"Then close your eyes."

"Ellen Mendels, I never seen the like," Bud Speaks accused. He sipped fresh steaming coffee at the counter of the Bryson Café. "You done cooked them eggs wrong again. What in the world?"

"I got here late fer once in twenty years. If's any bi'ness of yours." Mrs. Mendels had been singing-whistling-humming a Gershwin melody all morning.

"Well, I reckon the extra sleep ain't done you no good."

"Who said I was sleepin'?" Mrs. Mendels turned to face him, stirring the bubbling eggs sidewise.

"What'as y'doin', then? It ain't likely you was out paintin' the town, 'cause that wouldn't take two minutes, much less all night."

"Maybe I got me a new boyfriend, replacin' th' ol' relic I'm married to." She frammed two slices of bread into the toaster. "Or maybe that ol' relic was a-treatin' me good fer a change. Y' grits ain't done yet." She clattered the plate of eggs onto the counter.

"Ellen Mendels, you're acting like a school girl."

"You want to eat them eggs or wear 'em?" Mrs. Mendels resumed humming the perky tune.

Casey, nude, bounced toward the door of the room.

"Hey you with the buns," Whit said.

"*Moi?*" Casey stopped, shifted his weight onto one foot, bent his knee slightly, put a hand on his shoulder.

Whit threw him a towel. "Put this on. This is the Motel 2 of Bryson, not the Roman Baths."

Casey folded the towel to half its width and hooked it low over his slender hips. He stepped into the hallway just as Gertie pulled the opposite door closed.

She quickly put a finger to her lips and glanced up and down the hall, then up and down Casey. "Mama'll come up here to clean after breakfast. I turned down a bed f' one o' y'all t've slept in," Gertie whispered. "Messed up the room a little an' hid a extra key. Y'all come on down whenever y' ready." Before Casey could protest, she sneaked off, tiptoed around a known creak in the ancient floor.

"One set of plumbing, down the hall." Casey grumped as he bounced back into the room. "Your turn." He let the towel drop from his waist as he closed the door behind him with the sole of his bare foot. He strolled to the window and eyed the tree-lined street below, the fire department just beyond. "Great view."

"Sure is," Whit said.

Mrs. Mendels' favorite relic yelled up the stairs and slapped the wall to punctuate each phrase. "Folks!" (*Knock, knock*) "Y'all're 'bout t'altogether miss breakfast." He chuckled at the creaking of bed springs and the bumping sound the ancient maple headboard made against the bedroom wall. He opened the French doors in the bottom-floor hallway. "With that banging last night," he muttered, "I had to do something to distract her, and I reckon it's got her in a good mood fer once. Good thing Ellen's busy a-cookin' now an' cain't hear that racket," he said to the empty stairs behind him. Mendels selected fresh squeezings from his sideboard cache, but put the jar back and settled into the well-worn couch.

Whit held the room door open. "Casey?"

"I'm checking for incriminating things left behind. Dirty socks? Coupons clipped out of the Gideon? Oranges, fried eggs." He bounded after Whit, yielding right of way to Ellen Mendels halfway down the second flight of stairs.

"Goodness!" Mrs. Mendels tsk'd. "You boys just now up?"

Whit replied with a grin.

"Y'all go on over t' the café. Gertie'll take care of ya."

"Howdy!" Gertie exulted. She tap-tapped Whit on the shoulder with her order pad. "Glad t'see ya, darlin'. Mama didn't, uh, Wake Y'all Up just now?"

Casey's wink brought relief to her face.

"Plate lunch's done over," Gertie apologized-bragged. "But I c'n make y'a hamburger or somethin' on the grill."

"Great," Whit said. "Cheeseburger all the way."

"No onions," Casey corrected.

"How 'bout you, Hon?" Gertie flipped a mint green page in her order book.

"Give me two cheeseburgers and a grilled cheese sandwich on the side with a double order of French fries, a salad with blue cheese dressing, and a milkshake," Casey said. "No onions. Chocolate. And apple pie. Heated."

"*Ala mode*," Whit added. "Casey always wants ice cream."

"Anything but vanilla."

"Gracious!" Gertie scribbled. "You expectin' a famine?"

"It's these early mornings." Casey moaned.

As Gertie took away empty dishes, Whit passed Casey another napkin. "Do you want anything else," he teased, "or do you mind leaving something for the rest of the country?"

"I'm okay," Casey said, cat-level contented. "For now."

"Finally. Now, what's our agenda?"

"We already did that," Casey said, demure.

"That was Column A. Pick something from Column B. How about: 'Scour the local antiques emporium for old clocks?'"

"Possible."

"Rescue the car? And check for clocks at the antique store?"

"Is there an echo in here, here, here?"

"Okay, let's go dig through the antique store for clocks, clocks, clocks."

"You've already mentioned that. Twice, twice, twice."

"Three times, but who's counting? The clocks are conveniently located on the way to Phil's for the car, car, car."

CHAPTER NINETEEN

Oyster Dinner for Four

Casey vacuumed his milkshake glass with his straw. "Climb the water tower and toss pennies onto the street, street, street?"

"And risk damaging the store full of clocks?"

Casey grinned. "Is that it for Column B? You skipped: 'Get gloriously naked and make mad passionate love till midnight.'"

"That's Column C, but I did leave out one possibility: Go check out our new house."

"Column Z in my book. Ghosts!" Casey gazed into the street. "Can't it even rain, drizzle, pour, cloudburst?" He pleaded with the sky. "A little snow? A thunderstorm? Boom, boom?"

"I'll compromise. Come with me to Vita and I won't hassle you to go inside, or tease you about the ghos–you-know-whats. You can make warruh on your tanline while I look around."

"Okay, since you put it that way." Casey crossed his hands in his lap. "I'll expect a reward–give those you-know-what's something to titter about."

"Deal," Whit said.

"Mmmmm," Casey purred. "Does May have an 'R' in it?"

"Is a fever goin' around? Papa was buggin' me fer oysters, too."

Whit stuck out his hand to shake.

Phil held up his grimy palms and apologized. "Them tractors ain't shiny on the inside."

Casey waved a high five. "How's the repair going?"

"Still waitin' for th' parts t'get'ere." Phil put down his wrench. "They had to send for 'em t'other end of Timbuktu. Sorry, Whit, ain't nothin' I can do or I'd've already done it. I'll git Amos t'go call 'em."

"No problem," Casey said. "Whit wants a few dozen clocks from Isabel's, anyway."

"And Casey would rather buy me all the clocks in Georgia than go to you-know-where," Whit said.

"Casey's stalling, yes," Casey said. He pleaded with the sky. "A typhoon?"

Phil laughed. "Son, I reckon y'cain't stall much longer, 'cause yonder comes the parts truck. Won't be more'n half a jiffy and y'all'll be on yer way."

"Don't hurry on my account. Clocks, Whit. Clocks even you don't have."

"My helper ain't comin' in, so I'm goin' t'need somebody t'keep tension on th'alternator while I tighten th'idler." Phil turned to Whit. "You won't even get your hands dirty. Let me git my ol' hound out of there."

When approached, the locked bay shook with ferocious canine threats. "Yikes!" Whit jumped back. "Is that dog dangerous?"

"Damn shore is," Phil bragged. "They don't come any meaner'n'at'n, 'cause if they did I'd have whatever's worse. I call 'im 'Mister Hyde.' He gnaws railroad spikes t'keep 'is teeth good 'n' sharp. Y'all stay right here till I chain him up around back."

Casey whistled. "'Mister Hyde' sounds like he got expelled from the Hellhound School of Dog Obedience."

Phil strong-armed the growling beast around the building, led Whit and Casey into the dim work space, switched on overhead fluorescents and plugged in a fat orange extension cord that set a huge fan groaning in the far corner.

Whit popped the Fiat's hood and peered inside. "It's done."

"The parts just now drove up." Phil pocketed the bay's padlocks and yelled at the delivery driver. "In here when you get th'other stuff unloaded."

Whit stood aside and pointed. "Thanks, Phil."

"Y'all're welcome as c'n be, but I didn't change it."

"Uh-ohhh." Casey sidled over to the car and glanced inside.

Phil lifted his Cat hat and resettled it. "It's durn shore fixed, or I'm not a-standing here."

"I'm not standing here, either. Catch up with me at Isabel's." Casey galloped out.

Phil put his hat on top of the drink box. "Sorry, Whit. I shoulda kept quiet." He pushed coins into the slot, slapping the panel as each one rattled through the machine's works. "Ain't no way anybody come in here last night, 'cause if they did, Mister Hyde woulda eat 'em up. That's 'xactly what I got 'im fer. You want a Yoo-Hoo, a Nehi or something?"

"No thanks. Your helper, then?"

"He ain't even got a key to this side, nor suicidal tendencies to tangle with Mister Hyde. It'd have to be somebody my ol' hound wouldn't eat up, so it was either me, which it wasn't." Phil made eye contact and held it. "Or one of them ghosts I sold you, and that's who I reckon it was."

The parts driver pressed a clipboard into Phil's grip.

"Took y'long enough," Phil teased. He juggled his Yoo-Hoo, the clipboard, his cap and the sack of small parts as he initialed the invoice.

A vintage Fiat 124's fanbelt traces a circuitous route past most of the car's innards, all of which depend on its integrity. To avoid premature failure, it must be installed to factory specifications for tautness, a factor that is severely limited by the amount of available working space (none), the amount of clearance (even less), and the obscurity of its intended path from view (bigtime). Replacing the belt is a delicate job that can be accomplished with difficulty by an experienced juggler, contortionist and magician if the phase of the moon is just right and Murphy's in a good mood.

Whit tested the belt's tension. Perfect. He snooped around under the hood for signs that the car's engine dirt had been disturbed. Nothing. "Not even a German mechanic could get this belt on without smearing grease, or smudging a fender or something."

"That's another reason I know your ghosts done it." Phil pointed with his hat. "No human could have."

"MY ghosts?"

"They're yours, now. I sold 'em to ya. You bought 'em, and I'm glad to be shed of 'em."

CHAPTER TWENTY

Parts Is Parts

"**Y**our ghosts done you a good deed," Phil said. "I reckon y'oughta take it as a welcomin' gesture."

Whit spluttered. "I'll have to admit *something* beyond comprehension happened here."

"Son," Phil said, "I ain't ever tol' nobody, an' I'd 'preciate it 'f y'wouldn't tell this around, but I ain't no virgin to ghost parts."

Whit stared at the car's engine.

"Ol' Mrs. Plunk. That ol' Dusenberg of hers? Them cars was custom made, and parts is scarcer'n plate glass windows in a outhouse. This here's happened more'n once on her buggies. Parts just appear, an' I put em on. This'n mighta had somethin' t'do with them ghosts hatin' Roberts and him the cause of the belt being cut in the first place."

"Phil, I–"

"Hol' on, now, Son. I reckon them Vita ghosts look out for people that was good to 'em when they was alive. I had parts appear out of nowhere–purty ones, seventy-leventy years old and crisp like just been pulled off a shelf. Beyond comprehension, like you said. But I ain't ever had 'em do th'installation."

Whit patted his pockets for the car keys. "I'm spooked. I'm really spooked." He stared into the car's engine compartment.

Phil put his hat back on. "You still lookin' for somethin' logical? Nothin' in there makes any sense, and that durn shore includes that toy Italian engine. Mr. Hyde was hongry this mornin' so he didn't eat nobody fer a snack during the night, which he'd a-definitely done, long before they'd've ad'ny time to fix a fanbelt."

"You could have picked up belts on your way to the baseball stadium?"

"I didn't go t'Atlanta last night, Son. The Braves played out of town. They lost, but at least I wasn't there to see it."

"Your helper?"

"You know y'self it takes two people to put that belt on—or a real talented three-armed man. Besides, he's been in Hiawassee a-drying out since last Monday, and he won't get out till Tuesday week. Face it, this here's a pure-tee miracle."

"'Pure Tee.' The Patron Saint of Imported Automotive Conveyances doles out grace. Where's the altar? I want to light a candle."

"I done tol' ya this ain't the first time. But, you ain't a-gonna tell that, remember."

"All things are logical. Even this. Somehow. And I won't tell anyone, because no one will believe it."

"All things ain't what they seem. Here." Phil pushed the exotic parts toward Whit. "Y'all'll want t'keep these extra belts in case Asshole over yonder gets another bug up his butt."

"I guess." Whit put his keys in his pocket and retrieved his checkbook. "Let me hold your pen. A whole disbelief system, world view and the Laws of Physics, dashed. In the middle of nowhere under the hood of a red convertible in a grimy gas station. Uh, no offense."

"C'ain't fix tractors in a parlor." Phil resettled his cap.

Whit shoved his hands in his pockets, rattled his keys.

"Your ghosts've got nuthin' against y'all, or they'd've fixed yore wagon, instead of fixin' yer fanbelt."

"Good point, and I'd agree with you if I believed there were any ghosts—mine or anyone else's."

"This side of the street, their doin's're to th' good. Across yonder—" Phil gestured toward Roberts' Shell "—they ain't been s'kind." He paused a long moment. "I reck'n this fanbelt thing's gonna get to your friend Casey even worse'n you."

"I should call and see if he's in shock."

"Phone's yonder." Phil cocked an eyebrow. "Mind there ain't no private phone conversation in this town."

"How quaint."

"Sometimes it's quaint a pain in the ass."

Before Whit could pick it up, the phone jangled. Phil handed Whit the handset.

"Phil's Station? ...Phil just handed me the phone... Just a couple of minutes." Whit hung up. "Casey's at the café. How did you know that was him? Please, no more psychic crap."

"I just knew. Happens all the time to just about ever'body. Probly even you."

"I don't want to think about it." Whit sighed. "Thanks for fixing, or *not* fixing my car as the case may be, and for getting these replacements." Whit poised his pen over the check. "Name your price."

"Say bye to Casey for me." Phil squinted at the parts receipt, handed it over.

Whit wrote in the amount. "Ummm, I had my keys in my pocket a minute ago."

"In the car, maybe?"

Whit scoured the area around the drink machine, the workbench, the front of the car. "I don't suppose Bryson has a locksmith?"

"Not since Old Man Hobbes retired. You got a spare key? Or Casey?"

"In Atlanta. Shit! *Excuse mon Français.*"

"Sometimes..." Phil chuckled. "Them Frenchies know just what to say." He closed the car's hood, took off his Cat hat. "Y'all just take my dualie an' go git th'other key."

Whit sighed. "This is not my day."

Phil led Whit to the side of the station and introduced him to Ethel. "This here's my sweetheart." He shouted over loud growls that echoed off junked vehicles at the back of the lot. "Mister Hyde! Shet up! Now shet up!" The hound grumped, harrumphed, growled, lapped some water, snarled, and eyed the activity suspiciously. Phil rubbed Ethel's sides lovingly. "I take her out most ever evenin'. She loves to go see them Braves."

Built long and tall, Ethel had an extra wide body, a high torque rear end, and a load-bearing figure that would make Rubens proud. She wore six radial road-grippers to support her bed. The newest, shiniest firetruck could only envy her high-gloss red paint, and a freshly minted mirror might, just *might*, achieve her polish.

"Your sweetheart's a pick-up." Whit laughed.

"Shhh! Ethel'll get offended." Phil soothed a gleaming, shoulder-high fender with a loving pat-pat-pat. "Three tons of eeeficient fffine-lookin' eee-go strokin' deeezell truck-in' powww-errr!" He walked all the way around the vehicle and tapped Ethel's front tire with his toe. "Twenty-four Valve Turbo, Son. More hosses than Kentucky. Here's the key. Stroke 'er easy an' sidle 'er up to that orange pump so I can feed 'er some go-juice. Ethel's got a big-ass Cummins. Diesel fuel only, and that means *only*," he warned. "If you were t'put gas in 'er she'd blow you sky high."

"I know." Whit assured.

"Wait. Y'got to get her warmed up 'fore y' git her goin'. Ethel ain't no mushy-ridin' soccer-lovin' lily-livered Ess-You-Vee."

Whit opened Ethel's door and peered into her posh black interior. "Does this thing come with dining room furniture and a fireplace?"

"She's a big'un. Reckon you c'n drive 'er, Son? I don't want her t'git scratched."

"I can handle it," Whit said. "I drive a delivery van as a volunteer for the food bank once a month. It's only key rings I can't be trusted with." He climbed into the driver's seat and looked down onto Phil's Cat-capped head. "I'll be extra careful with your girlfriend, I promise."

"Take y' time, Son." Phil took his cap off, rubbed the top of his head with his palm, replaced the cap. "Before you attack that big city traffic y'better wheel 'round these parts a minute or two. Ethel handles a whole lot different from y'all's Eye-talian wind-up toy."

Whit started the engine and let Ethel idle until Phil pronounced that her purr indicated travel worthiness.

"Take good care of m'girlfriend," Phil cautioned for the thirtieth time. "Mind she's right smart o' power."

Whit let the clutch up. Like an earthbound starship jumping to warp speed, Ethel blazed a crimson trail past the station. "*Now* you tell me." He stomped the brakes. "Whoa, Ethel! Save some rubber for Indianapolis." With some difficulty, he managed to "ease" the vehicle up to the diesel pump where Phil stood laughing and sweating.

At the Bryson Café, Gertie held forth on "devil doin's," while Casey polished off a vanilla Coke. "So, why don't our ghosts just scare Roberts into moving away? That's what I'd do if I were them and from what I hear I might as well be."

"They've tried." Gertie leaned across the table in the front window. "Ol' Bob Roberts is as stubborn as 'e is mean. They drove a lot of his cronies crazy, and might-say picked some of 'em off–or caused 'em to be. Scared 'em to death, scared 'em to suicide, or managed to scare somebody else into killin' 'em. Some of 'em accidentally. Others, well, folks suspect."

"Thanks, Gertie. I'm glad to know, in case Whit and I have to tangle with–whatever."

"I reckon y'all ain't got nothin' t'fear from them ghosts. Over th'years they've often been a-undoin' ol' Bob Roberts's mean doin's. Makes up in some ways for the curse. Y'all's car's a sure sign-–HOLY SPRINGWATER! What in thunder's that?"

Casey followed Gertie's gaze out the window. His jaw dropped. "That's not thunder, Gertie. It's a mirage!" He pinched his forearm. "Did you spike the vanilla Coke or am I seeing ghosts in broad daylight?"

"You ain't seein' no ghost," Gertie said. "That's Whit with Ethel, Phil's girlfriend."

"I don't see anyone with Whit. And I *better not*, either. If he's riding somebody's girlfriend around in a truck the size of Kansas, that boy's got some explaining to do."

"Honey, Ethel's the truck." Gertie lurched up from the table and propped her hands on her hips. "Somebody better go see if ol' Phil's still a-kickin'. He don't let nobody so much as breathe hard on Ethel's red paint, much less drive her. This here needs to be writ down. I wish I had a camera."

"I wish I had a television crew!"

CHAPTER TWENTY-ONE

Out Behind the Barn

At the mouth of Vita Sempre's woodsy road, Whit brought Ethel to a gentle stop. "What are we doing at Versailles? Is this a joke?" He scraped the transmission into reverse.

"You're driving this battleship, not me. Maybe Ethel's horny and wants to visit the grape arbor. Big ol' F-350 over there she wants to neck with."

"Ethel's an insentient truck."

Casey patted the dash gently. "No offense, Ethel, Honey."

"Very funny."

"Nervous yes, frightened yes. Funny no. But better to make a joke than to make for the county line. What county did you say Milledgeville is in?"

"Very not funny."

"Let's see if I understand. First–" Casey held up his middle finger. "We, that is you–" He pointed at Whit's chest. "–and Ethel." Casey swooped his hands to take in Ethel's interior. "Along with li'l ol' *moi*–" He circled his nipples. "–turned left." Finger point leftward. "Directly off of Bryson's Minus-Twenty-First-Century Main Drag, being mostly a *big* drag–" Casey threw his thumb over his shoulder. "I hasten to except its meritorious Home for Unwed Clocks, source of joy and inspiration for–" he pointed to Whit "–a certain boyfriend who is trodding very thin Icee at the moment, raspberry kiwi flavor." He jabbed the air with two middle fingers. "Second––" *Jab* "–We hung a left onto the–" *Jab* "–secondary road." Two fingers of one hand. "Which is correctamento, and three–" Casey extended a pinkie. "–we took another right." Point. "Onto the main highway, which is dead to rights again." Four fingers. "So four and counting, here we are right here, where we would be if we had turned right at the outset, which is wrong and we didn't do." Palms outward, fingers spread. "Therefore, we are not here. Even though it looks like we are." Casey took a breath. "Either that, or this is the whole other side of some alternate universe and we're rollerblading through time toward the celestial funny farm in a truck the size of the Pirelli blimp. I conclude that there can be only one, Kenobe, count 'em *one,* conclusion: We are here, where we didn't want to be, because?" Casey touched his cheek.

"Please don't say it," Whit said.

"No need. You just thought it. And now *you're* spooked?"

"Me? Either we've spent the last‐‐" Whit held up both hands. "‐ten minutes in a major time warp‐"

"Jump to the left." Casey bumped his hips accordingly.

"‐Or there's something going on‐again!‐that doesn't yield to the laws of physics."

"Out here, what applies are the Laws of paranormo-physics. Exotic fanbelts appear, keys disappear. Two men in a truck do the Transylvanian Time Warp and end up where we didn't drive, and are now arguing metaphysics instead of steaming up the glass of the world's biggest pickup. No offense, old girl." Casey patted Ethel's dash. "Anyway, I bet ten cents your keys are in there on the table like Isabel predicted."

Whit hnmphed.

"Obviously those you-don't-believe-in-'ems snatched your keys to lure us here."

"Isabel knows too much," Whit grumped. "And no imps besides you have had their hands in my pockets. This key thing, and the fanbelt thing, and particularly this Time Warp thing has me thinking of taking our things on a long vacation to another side of the planet."

"Grand idea! I'll pack our trunks. Your new pink-striped Speedo is sooo cute."

"Thank you." Whit put Ethel into reverse.

"Whit, uh, since we're here? Don't you want to step inside and check for certain lost objects? Those unnameable things-starting-with-a-'k' that you made me promise not to tease you about losing?"

Whit hnmphed.

"The things that brought us to this quaternian crossroads in the Old Granddad of time warps?" Casey jumped to the left.

Whit switched off the engine, then quickly switched it back on. "Phil said to leave Ethel running. Keep her warmed up."

"Inside? Keys? Oops, the 'K' word."

"I'm not sure. I wouldn't have hesitated before Ohm's Law took a beating from Plunk's constant and the continuum Humpty-Dumpty'd. The truth is, I'm afraid I'll find those you-know-whats exactly where you-know-who, and you-know-who-else-with-the-big-boobs predicted they'd be."

"Sooo..."

"Casey, my newly clairvoyant friend, it's not the objects I'm afraid of finding, it's the fact that their presence here will slap reality in the face. There's no scientific way–"

"Fooey! Science is an elaborate nomenclature to describe pure magic to the satisfaction of disbelievers."

"Good line."

"I adapted that one from Gertie. Except she ascribed everything to Pure Religion. If there were any danger, Isabel and Gertie would have told us."

Whit hnmphed.

"I'm not spooked, and I spook easy. Aren't you curious? C'mon. I'll hold your hand." Casey checked the door locks, his fingers crossed.

"Okay, but I still don't believe in ghosts–I think." Whit eased the truck forward. "But I do believe in dirt. Phil's not going to like this nasty road's red grit on his truck. I hope Ethel's makeup won't require a major touch up."

"Or plastic surgery."

After a nervous ride through the scrub, Whit pulled the truck into the wide clearing in front of the iron gates.

Casey pulled Whit's briefcase onto his lap.

"Don't bother looking for the gate key. It isn't locked."

The mysterious white cat peered around a brick column, bristled and dashed off. *Through* the column.

Casey took advantage of Ethel's immense side mirror to adjust his hair while Whit fumed at the gates. "Won't budge," he stormed. "Not an angry inch." He ticked off possibilities as his inspections ruled them out. "No locks, stops, rocks, or pins." He examined the gate closely. "Never underestimate Old Man Rust. Casey, bring Ethel's tire iron, please."

"Again with the tire iron." Casey marched around the truck, "Wawwuh, wawwuh, wawwuh. Wonder where Ethel keeps her trunk."

"Nevermind, gates opened." Whit swung them wide.

Casey hopped over the tailgate into the back of the truck.

"Another time warp. Those gates. Don't. Open. Out."

Casey looked around. "Funny, they look out to me. Way out. All senses of the word. Why are you standing there? Let's move."

"Last time we were here, they opened in," Whit said.

The cat romped across the lawn.

"So they're movie star gates. Swing both ways?" Casey ignored the cat.

"These gates have been innies every time. Now they're out like Friday nights when the Pride tourists hit town."

"Ohhh," Casey said. "They chunked into big iron catches. Like meat loaf."

"Meat loaf?" Whit paced.

"Thick and heavy."

Whit pointed with his toe. "*These* meat loaf catches?"

"The very. Maybe there are extra meat loafs. Like Thursday at your grandmother's— one with onions, one without."

While the cat watched from a distance, Whit poked the driveway's edges with the toe of his shoe, but he found no more catches, meat loaf or otherwise. He leaned on Ethel's neck-high fender and propped his chin on his palms. "This is funny."

"Funny peculiar? Or funny as in 'Will & Grace'?"

Whit frowned. "Funny as in I'm getting way tired of this Cattin' Mouse Whit And Casey Whodat's Antique Ghost game."

"This really is funny," Casey said. "Funny you, talking about ghosts like they're late for a bridge tournament. Blaming Non Existent Ghosts for stuff you can't explain." He took a breath. "There's our cat. Anyway, the ghosts have you believing in them, whether you admit it or not."

"I Don't Believe In Ghosts!" Whit chanted. Twice.

"Okay, then what caused the Time Warp that got us here? And the Meat Loaf Mystery? Just to name the most recent items."

"Mass hysteria. Malicious cats. Unclaimed bus tokens. I don't know, just unexplained phenomena."

"Old Man Ghost's ugly daughter Unexplained. Whit, lots of things are never explained or understood. Black holes, Nutella, muons, M Theory, and why Dorothy never knew about those silly shoes all along. There's probably a warehouse full of ghosts someplace known only to ATF agents and kooky colonels with steel plates in their skulls and the keys to Area Fifty-One in their pantyhose." Casey smoothed his hair. "Let's go. Inside or home, doesn't matter. Ethel's bored sitting here, and so am I."

Whit thought a long minute. "You're not scared at all?"

"Nope."

"Okay." Whit studied the open portal. "Then I'm not either." He threw Ethel into gear. "I'll think about these shenanigans—"

"Tomorrow, at Tara?" Casey prompted. "That's the spirit." He propped against the cab in the back of the truck and blew kisses to the white cat as though he were on a Mardi Gras float.

Leaves crunched in the driveway under Ethel's many tires. Whit switched off the engine, switched it back on. "We're supposed to leave Ethel idling." He called back to Casey, "Start sunning, Son. I'm going in among the Unexplained Phenomena to look for certain lost objects. If I see any ghosts, I'll stomp their diaphanous asses."

Casey bounded out of the truck, sailed his clothes around his head as he removed them, and tossed them into the cab.

Whit fiddled with the lock on the front doors.

"Clothes," Casey said, mostly to the sky. "Useless." Nude, he cartwheeled around a wide circle of lawn. "I don't know why the things were even invented."

Whit turned to smile at him. "To keep Calvin Klein from having to work for a living."

"Ohhh."

"Your butt's going to find out why sunblock was invented if you don't go get some from my briefcase."

"Thanks for reminding me. Ummm, having trouble?"

Whit seethed, the cat just out of view. "Lock's stuck."

"Let me see what I can do." Casey stretched his arms and arched his back from side to side as he pranced to the door.

"Mmm." Whit nuzzled Casey's ear.

Casey purred. "Join me on the lawn for a round of croquet?" The lock fell open to Casey's touch, and he flung the door wide with a gracious bow. "Odd, I don't get a smidge of the vibe I got the other times we've been here."

"With a naked man being smooched on the doorstep, those ghosts are way too scandalized for any funny stuff. Go tan. I'm determined to look around."

"Sunshine here I come." Casey went back to his gymnastics on the lawn.

Whit marched into the house. After a minute, he shouted from the door. "Want to know whether the missing objects are where Isabel and Gertie said the Unexplained Phenomena put them?"

CHAPTER TWENTY-TWO

Fun in the Sun

Casey basked and baked. The white cat meandered over, nuzzled Casey's hand for a rub on the head and curled up beside him. Meanwhile, Whit explored the house and jotted meticulous notes in tiny, studied print in his pocket notebook. He detailed heating, plumbing, door and window hardware and electrical services. He cataloged structural details, tested doors for plumbness and operated knobs and latches. With quick strokes of his Koh-I-Noor zeroes–pens for anal retentives and mechanical drawing fetishists–he diagrammed storage and utility spaces, all in the patient, thorough manner that an engineer insists on and an architect reveres.

In two hours, Whit emerged into the afternoon sun, pocketed his pens and notebook, and locked the twin front doors behind him. Ethel hummed her throaty basso continuo in the driveway. Near Casey, Whit stepped out of his clothes, deposited them in a heap, and tossed his reclaimed keychain onto them. "I'm all yours."

"No way I'd share you."

The white cat blinked.

Whit stomped the dualie's brakes. "What in my worst nightmare? It's the non-existent barn." He switched off the truck's engine, switched it back on. "A huge red one with white trim, straight out of a Madison County bridge book for the coffee table set. Casey, the world's biggest barn crash landed from Mars fifty yards from your nose, and you didn't see it?"

"Nnnope."

"You fell asleep."

"I drifted off like always. But most of the time I don't have Martian barns flying around while I nap."

Whit popped the truck into neutral. "My apologies. It's those pesky ghosts up to their tricks. Ummm, this Barn From Mars?" Whit peered at Casey. "I don't suppose you want to go explore it?" He stuck his hands in his pockets, rattling his keys. "I mean, aren't you curious?"

"Nnnope! Curiosity murderiferated the pussycat."

"Meowww. It has 'I dare you' painted all over it. I'm too curious to pass this up. You stay here and keep Ethel company while I go explore." Whit caught Casey's glance. "What?"

"Um, suppose that ghost barn re-ghostificates itself while you're in it. You'd disappear back to Mars or wherever?"

"The rules of engagement, like the laws of physics, are fractured. So who knows?"

"In that case." Casey scratched the air with curled fingers of both hands. "Meooowrrrh! I'm going with you. "

"If I get propelled to Mars somebody needs to stay behind to inherit my fortune and fritter it away on trips to Reykjavik and Lichtenstein."

"Pffft. We go together or No Go."

"Fine." Whit eased Ethel over the lawn's edging toward the barn's wide open doors. "Gangway, ghosts! Company's calling!"

"Those Martians will get the thrill of our lives if they transport us. Ummm, you don't suppose that bit about the anal probes–oh, never mind."

Whit reined Ethel to a dust-cloud stop just as her tailgate moved into the cool, calm space under the barn's tin roof.

Casey locked the doors. "We're not in Nebraska, anymore, Tonto. Heyyyy, hay! All those stalls. TeaBisquick is jealous."

"For a ghost barn that appears when it feels like it, this sure looks–" Whit whistled. "–and smells real."

Casey wrinkled his nose. "Smells like horseshit to me."

"Exactly." Whit kept his hands on Ethel's controls, his foot poised over her accelerator. "You were expecting Givenchy?"

"Hay I'd expect, but a barn that doesn't have any horses shouldn't smell like horsey do. You did notice there aren't any horses? Just our white cat, licking himself."

"I was *so* trying to ignore that fact. And the cat."

Whit revved Ethel's engine and poised his hand on her shifter. "Maybe the ponies are doing that chukker thing on the polo field. Or the ghosts forgot how to cast the horse spell."

"They got certain rearward parts of the horse down pat."

"Old Ghost Family recipe. Eyeglass of newt, hair of hellhound, vial of dragon sweat, tail fur of pussycat." Whit kept an eye on the rear exit. "At least now I know the surveyors were telling the truth. I'll send them an abject apology."

"Whit, I know you have a problem with all this, and it's making me nervous, too, sooo, ummm, if you want to zoom us out of here that would be way fine with me. Hint-hint?"

Whit poised a hand over the gearshift. So here we sit in a borrowed truck in a non-existent barn with bad breath but no Clydesdales. Unexplained paranormalities."

"Paranormalities." Casey put his arm through the crook of Whit's elbow.

"I feel like a character in those horrid horror flicks you like so much. The Vampire Gladiators from Ninja Ten are suiting up while we, defenseless Whit and his faithful sidekick Casey, prepare to face the Quaternian Doom Cats with only the Lesbian pygmies to cheer us on."

"Sidekick? And the Ninja Ten are after us too?" Casey's voice quivered. "We're Martian paté in the next reel for sure. Can we just catch the ending on cable."

Whit extricated his elbow and patted Casey's knee. "So! Gangway for the phone booth, and start clicking your red shoes. Our Hero Whit springs into action, exclaims Whit."

"Is that scripted?"

"Sure. According to the script it's at this exact point that Whit says something pithy and 'once again saves the proverbial day,'" Whit said.

"Go for it, Casey urged," urged Casey. "The script also calls for Casey to be grateful, and he is *ever* so. Whit's heroics will be rewarded. Totally."

Whit cleared his throat. "Something pithy!" He shouted at the barn's rafters. "'Oh no,' says Whit whipping out his pocket watch." Whit's pockets didn't contain a watch. "Will you Look. At. The. Time. Can't keep Ethel out after curfew." He frammed Ethel into reverse and stomped her accelerator. In a cloud of haydust, Ethel lurched backward out of the barn and swirled a wide red arc toward the lawn. Whit kept accelerating as Ethel hopped the edging onto the driveway. He yelled, "Whit cuts a wheelie on the way out of Dodge. Cue the cornets."

"Oh my," Casey mimicked. "My personal hero Whit 'saves the day' by invoking Ethel's fabulous talent for hauling ass. Yay Whit. Yay Ethel. Who was that masked truck, anyway?"

"Roll credits." Whit brought Ethel to a stop in front of the house. "The *barn!* Take a look. It's gone."

Casey locked the iron gates and climbed into Ethel. Whit maneuvered her gently along the unpaved road. Branches scraped Ethel's roof, and Whit ducked. "Oooh, I am sooooo cool with ghosts," he said. "I'm catching onto this ESP thing. The vibes are coming in loud and queer. Vibes cat's framming out an F-flat minor riff. Way modal."

"And?"

"The vibes tell me you're effen hungry."

"Fffamished, flirt."

"If we EVER make it into cellphone functionality, please ring up Petunia's and see if Eric can squeeze us in. Eightish?"

"Heavy on the ish. It must be past rush hour in Bryson now. How long have we been gone?"

"No telling. Ethel's clock is way off."

CHAPTER TWENTY-THREE

How in Heck

Whit paced under the canopy in front of Phil's Gro & Ser Sta. "This is beyond believable, beyond UN-believable!"

"Son–" Phil surreptitiously eyed Ethel for scrapes. "It's unusual for them ghosts to let anybody off that light. People come back from out there cuckoo as flinders. Ol' Abe claimed he got stuck f'r a whole night. Told tall tales about transparent cats, an' music a-playin'. When he got back his supper was still hot a-waitin' for 'im. Abe ain't drawed a sober breath since."

Whit hnmphed. "Can't say I blame him. No explanation makes any sense, not even one that makes no sense. Einstein's life work notwithstanding, Heisenberg more certain than ever, chaos OCD-ized, Tempus Fugit in every universe but a red pickup."

Phil took off his Cat cap. "Yep. I don't keep up with them high-falutin' principles– been a long time since I went to Tech—but t'ain't nothin' new in this town, whether Eisensteinberg likes it or no."

"We sat inside a barn-sized truck inside a barn that doesn't exist. The Fourth Dimension origami'd itself into a kite and flew." Whit studied his wrist as though it held a watch. "I could deal with it if time skipped forward. Backwards defies everything. I made drawings, lists, in this notebook." Whit held up the evidence. "Pages of it, see? Structural, HVAC."

"I don't doubt you, Son." Phil put his cap back on, squinted at the tiny lettering, neat enough to make Ludlow jealous. "But I done tol' ya, that place ain't of this world. I reckon y'all believe me, now."

"I reckon." Whit put his notebook in his pocket. "I'm baffled. And mad, and–" He kicked the pavement.

Phil pointed with his hat. "Downtown Milledgeville's 'bout a hunnert miles." He laughed. "Good program down there, so I hear."

"Very funny."

"Sooner or later y'all'd've made them ghosts' acquaintance, so I reckon sooner's just as well." Hat back on. "Once they pull their timeclock stunt, folks leave 'em alone, put puzzles together and make baskets and stuff." Phil pointed southeast.

Whit hnmphed. "Time can not stand still. For one thing, Casey got hungry, and that takes at least an hour."

Phil took off his hat and checked his watch. "Ethel's clock's right on the money. Didn't y'all look at it?"

"I figured it was off. Sorry, Ethel." Whit patted the truck. "I should not have doubted you."

"Like I tol' y'all when ya first drove up, my watch says it's fourteen minutes after y'left, don't count the twenty we been a-jawin' since. That's barely time to get out of sight and back–unless you done a drag race like I tol' ya not to."

Whit patted the truck's door. "I kept her running, like you said."

"Especially in that barn, I expect." Phil put his hat on.

"And to get out of there, I floored her into a drag race, as you call it. I confess."

"I don't blame you fer that." Hat off. "I bet Casey's a-shaking a higher number onto the Richter scale, hongry or no."

"He's having a ball. I'm the one who's shaking. He couldn't wait to go gossip to Isabel."

"I seen 'im light out." Phil combed his hair with his fingers and put his hat back on. "You okay, ain't you?"

"I suppose. Why? Do I look like I've seen a ghost?"

Phil grinned. "Reckon so." Hat off again. "Well, y'all's car's fixed, and y'got yer keys. How 'bout puttin' Ethel back where Mister Hyde can keep an eye on 'er." Hat on.

"Sure. Hey, Phil, thanks for listening. And thanks for the loan of Ethel. That road is pretty dirty. I'll buy her the fanciest wash in Atlanta, and a polish to go with it."

"Thanks, but it don't look like that's needed. She's still shiny as a new dollar."

Whit sighed deeply. "Wonders never cease."

CHAPTER TWENTY-FOUR

Denial and Then Some

"All right, Mister Burst-At-The-Seams-With-Stuff-To-Tell, what gossip gushes from your afternoon séance with Queen Never-titty, the Human Ouija Board?" The Interstate's on-ramp receded in the distance, and Whit put the red Fiat into overdrive.

Casey smirked. "You really want to know?"

"Fresh from the unsettlingest experience of my life so far, yes, laddie."

Casey tugged his seatbelt. "I love it when you whip out your Scottish accent. But you disapprove of idle gossip."

"There's idle and there is professional. YOU are world McClass."

"Thank you!" Casey bowed.

Whit took the fast lane into Atlanta's afternoon exurban rat race.

"I thought you'd want to be spared. That other issue?"

"Issue?"

"Denial, McWhit. Even after our unexplainable experiences of the last twenty-four hours, you still won't or can't acknowledge the ghost realm."

"Just as with kilts' contents, seeing is believing. But Casey, my catty friend, if you don't blab what you found out, and soon–" Whit cocked his index finger and pointed it at Casey's ribs. "Brackita-brackita and off to road rage history with you. Not a jury in Orange County would convict me."

"Violence will get you nowhere. If you bric-a-brac me, you'll never find out what I know. Ummm, were you planning to go postal before or after we eat?"

"Casey?" Whit stowed his imaginary weapon in an imaginary holster under his elbow.

"Okay, okay. I'll tell. But you have to admit our new house is haunted. Ghosts, not the imaginary types you don't have any trouble denying."

Whit sighed. "Given! Now dish, Dish!"

"You gave in so easy, I should hold out for a fast lay on a slow train near an Alp." Casey pointed to the speedometer and harrumphed. "Neither one of us has relatives in power out here. The cops won't just give ticket, they'll stow us in the whatever county this is hoosegow."

Whit slowed the car enough to reduce the startled looks of drivers he passed. He glared.

"I'm dishing." Casey smoothed his hair. "I found out that Isabel–Queen Never-Titty as you call her–knows our ghosts personally. And like everybody else in town with a few notable exceptions, they're queer."

"Stonewall South at Poltergeist Plantation."

"'Poltergeist' sums it. Those ghosts are way mischievous, a reflection of the lifestyle they had when they had lives to style with." Casey touched his palm to Whit's knee. "Story time! See, Paul's the one that looks like me. Paul Ghost. Picture if you will: Me! All decked out in wayyy retro threads–Forties silks with a Gatsby hat, and–"

Whit laughed. "You with hat hair?"

Casey grimaced. "Okay, the hat's a hand prop, for effect. Sooo, way retro double-breasteds–Italian, of course–fluffy silk cravats. You remember the classy duds we saw at Ghost Villa that first day? They're wearing it. And Paul's wayyy cute. They both are. This year's stuff, up to the minute, but you know how the years tick by, new fashion every season. So silk is in, with a jacquard weave in a delicate monotone, and come spring it's crinkly crepe with plenty of contrast, and then Egyptian cotton is the new jacquard but in eggshell hues and–"

"Fast-forward the fashion trends report?" Whit zoomed around a startled tourist.

"Paul looks like me. Well, I guess it's me who looks like him. Tonio is the other one. But Isabel says there are more ghosts than just those two."

"The more the scarier."

"Tonio–he's you! Well, looks like you. Not quite as *cute* as you. He does those retro fashions, unlike the geeky engineer thing you insist on–white shirts and khakis. But he's so you."

"I'm me, he's him. I'm here and now but he's–keep going."

"Paul, Tonio and Old Mrs. Plunk are–*were*–major-league pals from the theater or something. A ballet dancer–that's Paul. The other's a composer, musician, whatever. That's you. Er, Tonio."

"I play a mean CD."

"Tonio Ghost was a jazz dude. Mildly famous, mega-rich."

"Lovely couple the Haunted Duo."

"It gets dishier." Casey leaned across, tsd'd at the speedometer. "Please slow down. I don't want to finish this story in a paddy wagon."

Whit let off the accelerator and checked the mirror so he could move a few lanes rightward. "What cop in his right mind would be out here in this traffic? Ooops. Crazy one coming up super fast, like Krispy Kreme is about to open." Whit slowed, eyed the mirror. "Just in time. Casey, you saved us!"

"I had a hunch, like a little voice almost shouting." Casey shuddered.

"Okay, I'm grandpawing it the rest of the way. Especially with Officer Bluelightspecial hugging our tail. You were saying?"

Casey took a breath. "Anyway, they met–Plunk and the two ghost units–at the *théatre de whatever* in Paree. She's debutante material from a long line of bootleggers, politicians and other crooks. Her old man owns a sugar refinery. Brings the stuff over from Cuba–we were speaking to them then–refines and packages it. She gets sent to get educated on the *rive gauche* in the 'Propah Tradition for a Suth'n Lady.' Or so Daddikins thinks. But Plunk's blowing daddy's bucks in the *arrondissements des artistes*, and hanging out in the salons with girlfriend."

Whit held up fingers. "As in fingerquotes girlfriend fingerquotes? *Quel* scandal!"

"Exactly. The *beau mecs* are doing ballets, concerts and each other. The chicks are doing whatever it is that chicks do. And the whole thing's a major *menage à howevermany* in the *gaie* Paree sense of the word that dare not speak our names." Casey took a breath. "They're all living high on the proverbial porcine roast, as in *haut cochon*, hiding out from their fams far from the good ol' USA, which was way no good for being gay in."

Whit eyed the mirror. "Do-nut holder still on our tail."

"My little voice says he'll give up soon. Before any of them got promoted to ghosts, the four of them are hanging out in Paris, 'cause that's where on the planet it was okay for girlfriends to have girlfriends, as well as boyfriends having boyfriends of the same sex."

"Ducky."

"Quacked, actually. Plunk's fam, over here, gets wind of what's going on, over there, and threatens to cut her off centless over here. Mysteriously–get this!–they *croak* a month later in a sugar-plant fire of questionable origin. Plunk's got an alibi, being in Paris at the time."

Whit sighed relief. "Do-nuts gave up, as you foresaw."

Casey continued. "Only. She. *Wasn't!* She was here–in Bryson, that is–scouting for land to blow her trust fund on, remote enough to bring her 'girlfriend,' who was about to finish the Cordon'ed-off-Blue. Here they planned to do the happy-ever-after-fairytale thing away from prying eyes."

"Spicy. Do go on."

"She claimed she wasn't bothered about being cut off, because her old man couldn't touch her trusts and she didn't want his filthy old money anyway." Casey twisted in his seat. "The Savannah constabulary gets wind of where she is, which is here, or more importantly where she *wasn't*, which was touring the Eiffel. And they haul her off to the Tybee pokey. But Miss Sudden Heiress is rolling in sudden cash. The parental units didn't have time to cut her out of their wills before they went on to that big sugarcane field in the sky. Besides, in cobwebby old Savannah, Plunk packs a passel of *pouvoir*. She knows things about people's daughters that have read with her between sweet Sapphos' syrupy lines. Besides, her old man wasn't Mister Upright Citizen."

"Always the case."

"Plunk *gets off*–free as a Parisian piaf wingéd pigeon creature–and comes to Bryson to finish Xanadu. The lez heiress really needs a hideout–from family, the press, and the Camellia Society. Good thing tabloid TV hadn't been invented." Casey smoothed his hair. "And here we are."

Whit grumped. "Stuck behind the commuters."

"The story isn't done. Not even close." Casey crossed his arms. "Cost ya."

"I've already met your conditions. A deal's a deal."

"That was only for the first chapter."

"You didn't say anything about chapters."

CHAPTER TWENTY-FIVE

Going Nowhere, Fast

"Something wrong?" Casey asked.

"Nope. If this beltway muddle ever clears, I'm taking the exit." Whit weaved the open convertible rightward a few lanes.

"Did you forget your keys? Your Bvlgari charge card?"

"None of the *abvove*." Whit wedged into the line of vehicles that spilled down the long exit ramp.

Casey pointed to a tall orange billboard that adorned the ramp. "Awww. You're planning to shop till I drop at the Franklin Discount Mobile Home Parts Supply."

"Nope. Our condo's on the thirty-eighth floor, so we can miss their Pre-Fourth of July Blow Out on textured skirting. Besides, I doubt they have any clocks that I don't already have one of."

"Three of, six of." Casey smoothed his hair. "But Whit, my fellow time traveler of a mere fortnight ago, perhaps you could enlighten li'l ol' me as to why l'il ol' we are waiting here in li'l ol' Bumfudge Acres for these li'l ol' slowpokes to creep through that li'l ol' redlight."

"I'm using this exit to make an 'I turn,' as opposed to 'you turn,' since you're not driving. You're riding along, so it's a 'we turn—' in an inverted U-shape, pointy at the bottom a la Bvlgari." Whit edged three pickup lengths ahead—one change of the distant traffic light. "Translate: I'm turning around to go to Bryson. So now we have a destination."

"You need another ghost fix?"

Two pickups made it through the stoplight. "We can feed and water the pet spirits." Whit said. "Sunshine on your cute can."

"Nooo more ghost infested sun for me, Son."

"Why?" Whit edged forward another truck length.

"Two guesses, one has to be: 'I'm not crazy.'"

"Okay, then Guess Number Two: 'You're scared.'"

"Rightamento!"

"And Guess Three: 'You're scared?'"

"Right again. Three out of two."

Another pickup length. "So?"

Casey smoothed his hair. "Duh? When you get frightened halfway to morguesville by a ghost palace multiple times you don't drive fifty, no, eighty-from-way-out-here miles to go there. Maybe you drive a bunch of miles and a big wide river *away* from there. A much better idea, now that I think of it."

"According to you, those ghosts are us. We're them, whatever." Whit patted the accelerator needlessly. "And Isabel claims our ghost alterselves are dangerous only to the meanies."

"That's the overview. What does that have to do with going there? To scare me? You were no model of leonine fearlessness."

"The time warp thing? I was as creeped out as you."

"Then your ego wants you to prove–I can't imagine what."

Whit paused. "Kind of you to mention it, *Herr* Fraud."

"Speaking for myself, I myself don't have anything to prove to myself or to anyone else's self, not even to your self."

"Got it, Mister ESP," Whit said.

"Therefore I don't, as in do not, want to spend the afternoon or even two consecutive nanoseconds at our new palace. And Whit, you needn't bother proving anything to me."

Whit patted the accelerator.

Casey sighed. "Isabel says when we ventured inside the barn we fulfilled some cosmic imperative–her words–and are now a-o-k by our alterselves the gay-as-geese ghosts. I still don't want to go deal with them, and I don't want to deal with me, either."

"Awww."

Casey puzzled a moment. "It's my ESP thing. Isabel says it's a gift and a curse, both at the same time. I can let it through or turn it off, and for now I want it off."

"You do?"

"The 'power,' as Gertie calls it–I'm afraid of what I'll find out. About myself. About us. About existence? The future? The Meaning of Life? About your Uncle Giorgio's recipe for tíramisú?" Casey took a breath. "Things best not to know."

"Two weeks ago, your ESP saved us—saved me—from a serious traffic fine, maybe worse," Whit said. "So if the little voice in your head happens to tell you something else along that line, please don't blow it off, okay?."

"The voices in my head are quiet."

"To Vita, then?"

"Whit, you want to go prove something to yourself, or maybe to your pal Piotr the professor. 'A drive in country,' like we intended when we left Buckhead an hour ago, does not equal 'visit ghost-infested house to test Piotr P. Piddlewhiskers' Hypothesis of Provincial Paranormal Phenomena.' I'd rather drop in on Aunt Beatrice unannounced."

"Ooo, that's serious." Whit moved one pickup and a tractor-trailer rig closer to the intersection.

"I'm serious. For once."

"I'll notify the media. Green light and we're off."

"Hell no! I won't go!" Casey folded his arms, retrieved his cellphone from the car's glove box. "I'll hop out here and get a taxi. And you, Mister, can go it alone."

"Casey!"

CHAPTER TWENTY-SIX

Donna Mobile

Whit secured his seatbelt. "Casey, my heart, yesterday you got your cute blond dander up into the stratosphere when I tried to make a U-ey toward Bryson. You threatened to make me a gay divorcé, among the milder things you fired at me. Today you're driving, and you want to go–where?–not to my old man's lake cabin. Not just to Bryson but beyond. Beyond reason, beyond all sanity–out, and I mean OUT, to our country estate, manned by our altershades and a morph-o-matic cat." He checked the seatbelt again. "What's up with that?"

Casey screeched his sporty blue Saab into the perpetually dense traffic. "*La donna e mobile,*" he sang.

Whit pointedly gazed at a moving van as it whooshed within inches of the Saab's front fender. "'*Mobile*' isn't the word for it. Raise Verdi to an astronomical power and add a French countertenor. Want some pickles with your rhubarb ice cream?"

"*La donna* may be *mobile*, but *la donna* is not pregnant." Casey swerved, waved thanks at a motorist whose return gestures hardly conveyed welcome. "To be pregnant, *la donna* would need to '*mobile*' some sex, *olé*."

"I had a headache." Whit folded his hands in mock prayer. "Those trucks! The big ones eat Saabs for snacks."

"Headache indeed, Mister Sleep-on-the-Couch." Casey darted into a left lane. "And I missed those rigs by a mile."

"Guest room, not couch. As in queen size bed with politically correct rainbow embroidered quilt. And like: barely a foot." Whit re-aimed the air conditioner vent into his face.

"Bed, couch, whatever. And okay, a foot."

"I needed space to sort things out–like your threat to leave me. Devastating." Whit inhaled deeply. "And a Munchkin's foot, Mister Offensive Driving Course."

"I was furious. I've already apologized. Forgive me?" Casey pleaded with his eyebrows. "I like it better when your space and my space overlap. And a toenail's still a miss. If this car had a back seat, I'd invite you to go sit in it. Over my lap."

"Apology accepted, forgiven, looking forward to the makeup sex. But like I said last night, I'm having trouble dealing with the ghost us. The fanbelt, the keys? The barn? The time warps."

Casey bumped his hips. "And?"

"I 'vanted to be alone.' Yikes! And wherever we're headed, it would be nice to arrive in your comfy Saab, instead of an ambulance?"

"You're quoting movies now. Have we switched roles here?" Casey honked and braked at the same time. He blew a kiss to a passing commuter. "And sorry, I misjudged that one."

"Movies? Far be from me to encroach your territory." Whit hnmphed. "And you're driving like a maniac."

"You're my security blanket, my teddy bear, cuddle toy, co-dependent Ken doll, Erector Set." Casey applied the accelerator generously. "And I always drive like a maniac when I haven't had any in forever."

"I love being your security blanket, *et cetera*. But Ken doll? Anyway maybe this is the real problem–lately I'm the one who needs reassurance, comforting, Kendolling." Whit took a long breath. "And you've had plenty. Just not today."

"I enjoy being the nurturer almost as much as being the nurturee."

"This is a big change between us."

"Change is frightening–unless you need it for a parking meter," Casey said. "Change is useless at Saks, meaningless at Starbucks." He darted across lanes. "Your Teddy Bear role hasn't changed, we're just developing it in other dimensions–oops, bad word. This whole adventure, especially the soap opera conversation we're having, makes me want a security hug." Two lanes rightward, to the astonishment of drivers around him. "Dramatic organ riff on a major sixth–bahhh-deedle-eedle-eedle-dah-dah-deee–pregnant pause, cut to Tide." Casey grinned, impish. "It's been–" He sighed. "Almost twelve hours. A tonic ninth now returns us to our program. Whit frowns. Closeup on Casey. He smiles." Casey profiled for an imaginary camera. "Whit, please tell me our honeymoon isn't over. After only eight years, four months, one week and a day. What about our relationship? And the twins? How will Auntie Myrtis make it without her medicine?"

Whit held up an imaginary film clapper. "Tune in again for another excruciating chapter of 'As the Ghost Turns.' Roll credits. Casey, my favorite drama queen, we are not playing parts on a stage. We are having an argument. Isn't this our first one? I lost count." Whit covered his eyes. "People who are having an argument might have soap opera conversations off and on, but they don't have mad passionate sex. Off, or on." He peeked through his fingers. "And nothing is over till the station break—not the soap opera, not us, nor any voluminous ladies that might vocalize. We're far from 'over.' I hope. We're just adjusting. Yikes!"

Casey panic braked. "Why are we having this silly argument, anyway? You do think it's silly?"

"I guess we're having this argument—yes it's silly—because..." Whit thought a long moment. "Because I stupidly insisted on buying a houseful of spooks that I don't believe in, can't understand, can't control, and don't want to accept. Maybe to prove to you or to me—or to that bus you almost creamed?—that there's no such thing as—that rent-a-truck!—ghosts. I've seen and experienced things I can't explain. I don't need to detail any of it for you, since you're in on the spirit thing. Which is another problem."

"Okay, why should the silly ol' ghosts cause you to sleep on the metaphorical couch? My spirit thing is history if it bothers you. It bothers me, too, as I've already explained."

"That 'couch' was uncomfortable." Whit put his hand on Casey's knee. "And there was no Casey in it."

"I missed you, too."

Whit hmphed. "If you'd be kind enough to miss these large Saabivores, we might live to tell this terrifying tale to any wedding guests who happen along."

"I missed that SUV by an inch, easy. I'm back in your good graces? I hope." Casey braked. Fast.

Whit's fingers danced across an imaginary keyboard. "Organ riff," he explained. "You were never out of my good graces. I was afraid I was out of yours. If you want to visit Bryson, go for it, but can I hold onto your arm for security?"

"Hold anything you want." Casey dodged a bus. "Cool! Now, back to the sex issue? You know that lovely grape arbor behind our new palace? Hmmm?"

CHAPTER TWENTY-SEVEN

Tea with Mousse or Lini

Promptly. At three thirty o'clock, Post Meridian, having *repondient comme ils plaient*, Whit and Casey stepped onto the fine Southern porch of Mrs. Plunk's expansive mansion. Casey tapped the doorjamb.

Whit grumped. "With any luck she's not home and we can escape this stuffy party."

"Thank you, Auntie Social. It's afternoon coffee to get acquainted with our new neighbors-to-be. You *RSV-peed.*"

"Bryson's Welcome Wagon has square wheels. The phone call I answered sounded more command performance than invitation." Whit tapped an enormous porch column for solidity. "'Dahlings, you'll zohhh do me the honor of caffayyy Thurrrzzzdayyahhhftahnooon? Do be a deeeeeer and zzzay yezzz. You'll commm?'"

"Are you doing Plunk or Dietrich? Bryson or Berlin?"

Whit rapped the door. "That knock will make it past the front hallway." He inspected his knuckles.

"Thanks, Butch." Casey smoothed his hair.

"Rrrr. I took out my bad mood on the door. I can chill now."

Miss Trudy swept the door wide. "*Bienvenue!*" She beamed. "Nice of you to drive all this way at the last minute. Whit, Casey, do come in."

The woman led them through the long central hallway to a bright, air-cooled sitting room. "We'll be comfortable here," she said. "I'm off to the kitchen to finish up. Kath is on her way down."

As though on cue, Mrs. Plunk appeared in a delicate charcoal colored dress, plain except for its pearl studded bodice. Her entrance brought the subtle aroma of old Chanel to the spacious room. Casey nodded. "Hi."

"Hello, Casey," Mrs. Plunk said. "Whit. I know you're here, too, because I can just make out a second shape next to Casey's voice, and I heard your footsteps in the hall. Thank you both for joining us. I've been looking forward to this more than most of the events of the last decade."

Casey whistled. "My, don't we rate."

Mrs. Plunk made her way to a glass-topped rattan table set for six. A tall arrangement of purple lilies adorned its center. She stationed herself at the head of the table and gestured broadly, clutching a delicate silk handkerchief of palest blue. "Please take the seats facing the window, if you don't mind. My other guests aren't here yet, I'm sorry to say, though I'm not surprised. They are known to be–the current term is 'punctuality challenged.'"

She sat down. "Tru is bringing coffee and something delightful. She has a talent for liberating the palate from ennui." Mrs. Plunk lowered her voice to a near whisper. "She doesn't know that I know she's been baking since yesterday. The smell, you know. But I'll act surprised."

"Yummm." Casey sat down.

"Whit?" Mrs. Plunk turned toward Casey.

"I'm here," Whit said, hurriedly seating himself. "I was just admiring your garden."

"Well, I'm sure it's in a horrid state, though perhaps for someone with experience in such things its design peeks through."

"It's glorious," Whit said. "I mean, the plan still shows. A little pruning, and–"

"Everything needs attention around here, but after my old gardener's sons came back, some of them, from Vietnam–well, let that go for now. I want this to be a happy afternoon, free of time-worn unpleasantness. Excuse me if I change the subject."

Miss Trudy bustled in with a French press coffee service. "I have a surprise for you."

Casey hefted the delicate china cup, smelled the coffee, put it back down.

"The Blue Mountain Jamaican," Mrs. Plunk said after inhaling the aroma. "Mellow, with a full-bodied kick. Unless you prefer something else? Tru keeps a variety on hand. Decaffeinated if you must."

"This is great," Casey said. "But I'll take you up on the cream."

"I'll switch to Altura for the next round." A knock on the front door, and Miss Trudy stepped away quickly.

Mrs. Plunk tsk'd. "Always fashionably late, even when late isn't fashionable. And they know I can't stand tardy, fashionable or not."

Miss Trudy brought two attractive women of late middle age. Identical in appearance, they wore identical pale blue knit shirts and crisp-pressed jeans.

"Thanks for coming over," Mrs. Plunk said. "Late, but I'll excuse. Yvette and Yvonne Plunk, may I present Casey DePaul and Whit Garrett, our new neighbors. The Misses Plunk are my twin daughters."

"I think we've met," Casey said, confident, nudging Whit. "Or one of them, perhaps, at Vita Sempre."

Whit's jaw dropped. "At where?"

"Very observant." Yvette sat across the table from Whit. "I am, that is, *we* are the 'gardener' whom you encountered."

"I knew it," Casey boasted. "Don't mind Whit. His mind's stuck in a grape arbor."

Whit blushed brightly. "This gets stranger and curiouser."

Miss Trudy presented a huge silver tray loaded with brioches, fresh and perfect, stuffed and topped, and smelling of pears and clove.

"*Ma cherie!*" Mrs. Plunk said. "You've baked. *Quel surpris!*"

Whit gazed at Yvette. "A scheme to scare people away?"

Yvette nodded. "Only our part of it is a trick."

Mrs. Plunk cleared her throat. "It's time to tell all." She rustled forward in her chair and applied butter to a brioche. "Whit, Casey, I asked you and the twins to come over today so you boys would know what is and isn't going on. I feel responsible, since I could have prevented the sale. Perhaps also you'll understand the *why* of some of it."

Yvonne stacked dishes on the nearly empty silver tray while she and her twin spoke in turn. "The gardener is the only thing we account for," she said. "We do it to keep people from snooping around. Everything else, the dog, the cat, the piano, the balls of light, the rug, the barn–especially the barn. We've never had any part of."

As she left with the tray, her twin continued. "We've lived in Mama's groundskeeper's cottage since we turned twenty-four. You can see it from Mama's front porch."

"Towers over the sycamore trees? We saw it," Casey said.

Yvonne laughed. "That's us. Mama's always done things on a grand scale. Our cottage sits just in front of a bricked-up gate that once connected our properties. The two places share that portion of the serpentine wall."

Returning from the kitchen, Yvette took up the story. "Mama's wine cellar is underneath our cottage, and the wine cellar for your property is on the other side of the fence under the caretaker's tool shed. When the places were built, Mama and her friends were concerned about this being a dry county. Prohibition was over, but this part of Georgia didn't notice for years."

Mrs. Plunk interrupted. "We had other worries, too, as you must have heard."

"They might not have." Yvonne gathered items to take kitchenward.

Mrs. Plunk settled back in her chair. "Then I'll tell them. Tru, is there anything appropriate in the pantry, or do we have to send to the cellar?"

Miss Trudy smiled. "Patience. We have another surprise."

Yvette resumed the narrative. "For fear of the authorities, and what I'll save for Mama to tell, they built a tunnel between the two cellars. Vita already had a tunnel from its basement."

Yvonne passed a tray of glasses to Yvette to distribute. "Mama brought a crew from her sugar mills to put in the tunnels, so none of the local workmen knew anything. Since the lawns and gardens were under construction, nothing ever looked unusual."

Whit cleared his throat. "Secret tunnels. And twins. That's how you pulled off the gardener's miraculous appearances."

"Exactly. Excuse one sec." Yvonne bustled away.

Yvette continued. "Mama put us up to a stunt once or twice when people came nosing around asking too many questions. So we put on our act when needed to discourage intruders."

"Tonio and Paul disappeared the night of the fire." Mrs. Plunk pressed on. "For all I know they could be living it up right now in Athens, Greece, or Athens, Georgia. But let's not talk about that just now." She held up the empty glass Yvonne set in front of her. "Goody."

CHAPTER TWENTY-EIGHT

Two for Tea

Whit leaned toward Yvonne. "Um, that time at Vita? The gardener?" He glanced at the other twin. "Did you–?"

Yvonne exchanged knowing smiles with Casey. "The arbor? We didn't watch. Not our thing."

"*Les chats ne font pas les chiens.*" Yvette misquoted a French proverb: Cats don't sire dogs.

Whit looked out the window. "Mrs. Plunk, if you're interested, my father has a delightful Japanese man keep his gardens. I'm sure I could persuade him to come over. This is just the sort of challenge he loves."

"Thank you, but there's not much point. Maybe if my daughters take an interest in this old place someday."

"Someday," said Yvonne. "We like gardens, but not formal like this."

Yvette smiled at Casey. "You wanted to ask us something?"

Casey looked into Yvette's intense blue eyes. "Ohhh! You've got the power thing, too. It's all new to me."

"Go with it," Yvette said. "The energy around here is particularly abundant. What's your question?"

"Gardening–give Whit a thrill. You guys keep up the grounds so well next door. Why the poor state of the gardens here? Vita isn't so formal, is that it?"

"A good question," Mrs. Plunk said, squinting at the twins. "And for the answer, I'm afraid the conversation has now turned serious."

Yvette raised her eyes to the ceiling and shook her head.

"I educated the Misses Plunk in Europe," Mrs. Plunk said. "The best schools. I kept them away from here so they wouldn't be–put on the spot–by the lifestyle I and my companions chose. I also wanted them out of harm's way."

"Bob Roberts? Or the ghosts?" Casey asked.

"Both, and more." Mrs. Plunk took a breath. "Tonio had 'family connections' that weren't entirely peaceable. He wouldn't hear of adopting a stage name, and with the concerts and ballets he and Paul were in public frequently. We didn't know if they might have to escape, or at least hide out from a crowd of shall-we-say non music lovers–Tonio's family's enemies."

"You mean the mob?"

"Some business in Miami, which was just getting started then. Most of the stories you hear aren't accurate, but what's true is scary enough. They accepted Tonio's lifestyle, to their credit, but they were involved in–" Mrs. Plunk cleared her throat, stopped. "In the Forties and Fifties, things were unpleasant for us–meaning us third-sex people–on this side of the Atlantic. It came as quite a shock when we came home. We had missed a lot that we were fortunate to have missed.

"In Tonio's case it was extra bad because his family's enemies took such a dim view of anything they couldn't shoot. Just being–" Mrs. Plunk pronounced–"ho mo sex u al, or even looking like you might be. That wasn't safe or wise. The only places we could go were run by 'the mob,' as you so eloquently put it. We were an illegal vice fought over by various factions who exploited the fact that we were persecuted by our own government. Having fled the stranglehold taking over Europe, we came home to the land of the free and found ourselves not so free. Lady Liberty gave us the raspberries. We hid in the closet under constant threat of being accused of ho mo sex u al–synonymous with communist by some logic I fail to grasp. Some of that has changed now, but there's plenty of changing yet to do."

Whit hnmphed. "Some places are still Berlin 1940."

"I've read about those times," Casey said. "And there are movies."

Yvette chuckled. "We're still working on Question One."

Mrs. Plunk prompted. "Vita's gardens."

Yvonne picked up the story. "We traveled and studied, and traveled. When we came here, finally, Mama had an army of gardeners keeping up both places in the pin perfect style to which she's accustomed."

"Thank you." Mrs. Plunk nodded. "But that 'army' of gardeners was only Mr. Williams and his four sons."

"Mr. Williams lived just across the creek a mile or two down." Yvonne brought a numbered bottle of very old very cold very superior very French Chartreuse *Vieillissement Exceptionnellement Prolongé* liqueur. "Their house burned one Thanksgiving day, and Mama took the family in. The wife was killed in the fire."

"That was so nice," Casey said.

Yvette poured Chartreuse into Casey's glass, then Whit's. The liqueur's distinctive bouquet suffused the room. "Mama's always had a good-gal streak, in spite of herself."

"Herself rides a spotted horse," Mrs. Plunk said, swirling her glass and savoring the aroma of the liqueur. "You gentlemen will forgive if we skip the cigars with our brandy."

"Neither of us indulges that vice," Casey said.

"I do," Mrs. Plunk said. "Another bad habit I picked up in France. I quit when the twins came along. Motherly consideration."

Yvonne resumed. "We only scared the curious. We never did any of the actual gardening. Mama insisted we study horticulture and design, and we did, but it's not our thing."

Whit stared into Yvette's eyes. "Whose thing is it, then?"

Yvette shrugged.

"Noman," Yvonne said. "In the words of Polyphemus Cyclops. 'Noman is killing me by fraud! Noman is killing me by force!'"

Whit hnmphed. "Noman is quite the expert. *Horticultural Digest* for days."

"You guys first saw the place in early April. Spring. Did you see new growth on the trees?" Yvette shrugged.

Yvonne continued. "I promise you didn't. Add fifty years to Vita's plants, and you'd get the size Mama has. Huge. The ones over there are the size they were when the barn burned. They flower, leaves grow and fall, but Vita's plants never grow."

"Magic doesn't stop when you outgrow Grimm," Yvette said.

"After the fire, Mama fretted about Vita's burned grounds," Yvonne said, "thinking Tonio and Paul would return. After a few months, Mr Williams–he was a very shy man–asked Mama who was doing all that work."

Mrs. Plunk swirled the Chartreuse in her glass. "The poor man thought he was being replaced." Mrs. Plunk sipped. "That's when we knew there was something inexplicable. At first we wondered who. Then we wondered how. Gradually, we came to believe no one. Noman."

"In a big freeze, it didn't freeze. And then we noticed it never changed," Yvette said.

Whit hnmphed. "I don't believe it."

"I do. Also fairies, tooth and otherwise," Casey said. "And white rabbits, hatters and evil queens."

Whit studied the room's elaborate crown moldings. "Gnomes."

CHAPTER TWENTY-NINE

The Gay Ones Are the Best Looking

Yvette replenished Mrs. Plunk's glass.

"Do you think Paul and Tonio are still around?" Casey asked.

Yvonne said, "There's a block, somehow, which makes us think someone still alive is involved."

"We are both psychic, probably as much so as Isabel," Yvette said. "She originally came here because of the childlessness."

"We were next to last," Yvonne said.

Mrs. Plunk held up her palms. "Penultimate children of a decadent, careless past. But I did my share."

Yvette continued as though not interrupted. "Grandfather wrote into his will that Mama had to marry and bear a child."

"Just before the deadline, Mama's fairy godfather hooked her up with a gypsy ballet dancer, and here we are." Yvonne said.

"How crude," Mrs. Plunk admonished. "Dmitri was an absolutely gorgeous man. He wore shoulder-length wavy hair of purest blue and dense black, and he had ice blue eyes like Siam's housecat. Beautiful." She gazed at Casey. "And a ballet dancer's body that would best any movie star, then or now. Quite a catch, *mes filles*."

Yvonne winked. "The gay ones are always the best looking."

Mrs. Plunk snapped her head toward Yvette and Yvonne in turn. "Gay or not, he was obviously up to the challenge."

"All this talk of good looking men." Casey fanned himself, no-thanked a refill.

Whit hnmphed. "Shall I peel you a grape?"

"You guys probably haven't seen half of your new house." Yvette gathered glasses onto a tray. "There are some solid looking panels that open onto stairways to secret rooms Tonio built, in case his Godfatherish relatives showed up."

"We want to show you our secret entrance, the hidden rooms and such." Yvonne stood up.

"You mean now?" Whit put his napkin on the table, then replaced it on his lap. "I didn't intend to go there today. Maybe not any day, with ghosts doing the gardening."

"The 'G' word!" Casey chided.

"For you, we think the welcome mat is out." Yvonne refilled Whit's water glass. "Since you, you know... grapes, seems like the spirits want to know you better."

"We talk to them," Yvette added. "The spirits?"

"Not like cable television," said Yvonne. "Just in the hope Tonio and Paul, or maybe Dmitri or Bret can hear us."

Casey squeezed Whit's elbow. "Let Whit off, please. He's not comfortable with interdimensional communication. I'll go with you and show Whit around later. If he ever wants to."

"We've told them all about you two," Yvonne said. "Mama?"

"You girls show Casey around. I and Whit will speak of gardens, formal and elegant."

"Perhaps we could speak of antique clocks. And those delightful Man Ray works?" Whit said to Mrs. Plunk. He cheek-smooched Casey. "Thanks, Sweetie. Enjoy the vibes."

The throaty roar of a big Harley brought Bob Roberts to his feet. He took a look out the cracked front window of his tattered Shell station. V-Rod, VRSCA, fuel injected, liquid cooled. Sterling silver accents on black, mirror polished like Sunday candlesticks. Roberts watched the helmeted cyclist pull up to the gasoline island. He moved to the doorway.

Manly pump ritual: *Revv-revvv,* dismount hog, lean on kickstand, *revv-revvv,* remove gloves, doff helmet, shake mane, *revv-revvv,* balance helmet and gloves on black leather seat, *revv-revv,* shut off engine, and fill the tank.

"Who'n'ell's'at out 'ere?" Roberts bellowed, stepped outside and leaned back against the door jamb.

"Who d'f'ck'n'ell wants t'know, Asshole?" Mid-grade unleaded. Three point four gallons. *Major* attitude.

"I said WHO IS 'AT!"

"Fff'koff!" Wallet, leather, chained to belt loop. Folding money. "You th' clerk, Asshole? You git the greenbacks?"

"Clerk?" Roberts spewed steam and respect simultaneously. "I OWN 'is f'k'n place!"

"Sympathies, Asshole." Money between teeth. Engine start. *Revv-revvv.* Helmet on. Faceplate up. Gloves. *Revv-revvv.* Kickstand up. Walk the hog. Back. *Revv.* Walk. *Revv.* Forward. Around the gasoline island. Walk. Mount the hog. *Revv-revvv.* Roll. To... Roll. Just... Roll. Beside Roberts, leaning back, hands stuffed in his pockets. *Revvv-revvvvvv.* Money in gloved hand. Drop to pavement.

Roberts' jaw dropped. "Whuht-thhaaa–?"

"Keep the change." *Revv-revvv.* "Buy yourself some candy, little boy." Snap! Faceplate down. *Vrooommm!*

Roberts stared. "Yesss, ma'am!"

At the Bryson Café, culinary highlight of Bryson, Georgia, as well as being the only place to eat, Gertie stacked clean water glasses on the Formica counter beside the ice maker. "Lookayonder out th' front winderglass, Mama." She smoothed her apron and primped her hair. "They's a whole mess of new men a-ridin' up. Good lookin' ones, too."

"The street's plumb full of pickups. I hope I got enough hamburger steaks."

Gertie fluffed her hair, threw her shoulders back, and smoothed the bodice of her dress. "Mmmm-hmmm. I'll get 'em set up an' pick me out a husban'."

"Psshhh." Mrs. Mendels slid an iron skillet of cornbread into the oven. "Good thing I got plenty o' turnip greens."

Gertie moved toward the front door and arched her back straight. "Y'all come on in." She eyed the men up and down as they filed by, took out her order pad, riffled the pages. "Set where y'like. Lunch special's on the blackboard. Ain't no beet salad left. Never is. Ever'body want sweet tea? Best in these parts. Th' cornbread'll make ya slap your gran'maw."

The men took window seats, gulped water and iced tea as Gertie set the glasses down.

"Mmm-hmmm, look at you, Mister!" Gertie moved in on a T-shirted muscular man with dark, wavy hair. The last to enter, he wore a mammoth Stanley tape measure, a pager, and a cellphone on the wide leather belt of his worn-to-ribbons jeans. Gertie urged her prey toward the far corner. "If you ain't the best lookin' man I seen today! Come set over here, so you and me can git started on our courtin'."

Brazenly flirting at each table, Gertie wrote six copies of the same order: "hbrg stk, fries, t grns, g bean, T, cbrd." Then another for the man with the cellphone: "hbrg stk, fries, g bean, T, cbrd / no onions." She turned the pad so the man could watch her underline the word "no." And tap-tapped him on the shoulder with the order pad. "Got t'small good when ya courtin'."

"Seven specials! One no 'O' fer m'new fee-ahn-say. I done picked me out a good'n. I'll tell ya his name soon's I find it out." Gertie patted her red curls, rested her hand on the man's shoulder, and pretended to whisper to him. She said loud enough for all to hear, "You are some kinda built. What's your name, darlin'–Tarzan?"

"Stan."

"What's y'last name, Stan? I got t' get started on m' monogrammin' in time for the weddin'."

"Matthews." Stan patted his shirt pockets for a business card, grinned, and handed over the small treasure.

Gertie held up the card by its corner. "SM Construction?"

CHAPTER THIRTY

Call Waiting

A Cadillac hearse glided into Bryson. It crawled past the Farmers and Merchants Bank in a stately ooze of gleaming black and polished chrome, playing glints of reflected sky onto the squatty building's locked doors. Hurrying across the street on his way to work, Ed Beasley, branch manager, loan officer, chief financial officer and head teller, froze in mid-stride. His customary to-go cup of Bryson Café's boiling hot coffee sloshed perilously toward his starched white cuffs. Beasley managed to steady the liquid–and himself. He followed the hearse with his gaze, hardly breathing as it crept past the Volunteer Fire Department.

Beasley took a few steps, stopped, looked back, steadied his coffee. The hearse crept through the deep shade of the huge oaks next to the café. He took another step. Gawked at the hearse, stepped again, stared. Halting, reluctant, the black behemoth moved on as if deciding where, or maybe whether, to collect or discharge the dead.

"Mama! Yonder comes a hearse! Somebody's done passed in the night." Gertie love-tapped another potential fiancé on the shoulder with her order pad. "There goes ol' Ed Beasley t'open the bank, but you finish y' ham biscuits 'fore ya gallivant over there. I tol' ya them was good 'uns. Mama! You got that fried baloney?" She turned back to her prey. "Don't stay gone too long, Hon. We got t'plan the weddin', less'n you just wanna elope. Mama! I ain't heard of nobody sick, much less a-dyin'. What's a hearse a-doin' in town? I just hope it ain't a-huntin' me s'close t'm'weddin'."

"Here's the baloney. Hush, child. Your palaver's liable t'bring down the bad. Take these grits b'fore they git cold."

The hearse moved on. Beasley unlocked the bank's door, snapped the lights on, raised the window shades on the glass doors, flipped the cardboard sign around to "Open," and lunged for the phone.

Ernestine plugged in Beasley's call. "Number please?"

Stuck in a time long past, Bryson Phone Company worked only slightly newer than what Alex Bell and the Deity hath originally wrought. Dating to the Thirties and the hardware store's patriarch, Hiram Laurel, the tiny system depended on human-assisted connections. Pick up a handset, and a panel lit up at the "central office" on Main Street. Hardware store, second floor. An operator handled the call by plugging in a wire and pressing a blinking button. "Number please?" The actual connection entailed physically hooking up the appropriate jack and pressing another button. Exactly one call could be answered at a time. One had always been sufficient. Rarely in Bryson did two people make calls at the same time, and if that happened, the second one waited till the operator connected the first, often after considerable chit-chat.

Laurel's system was top drawer when rural phone service was rare. However, population and progress passed it by. Outlying areas seceded to join Atlanta's Southern Bell–later renamed BellSouth, then re-eaten by AT&T. An ice storm brought down so many lines that Laurel gave up trying to restore them and didn't oppose the move. To maintain outside connectivity would have required modernization. Laurel opted to cede that service to the neighboring Baby Bell. After that, his operators could only connect local calls.

Laurel negotiated clever deals with the communications giants that allowed his tiny system to co-exist. He agreed not to connect any new customers, and never published a directory. No one bothered to challenge him for such a tiny market. No one expected him to last.

In all of Bryson, three dozen loyal subscribers remained. Some, like Phil's station, still had only local service, since they rarely needed to communicate with the outside world. Or wanted to. The big companies would only supply shared lines–four subscribers per "party" line. Laurel's lines stayed as private as the operators, Ernestine and Louise, chose to make them.

Fact was, the whole system amounted to a gossip fence. *Soandso's soybeans came in early, so he'll be spittin' in high cotton this year. Miz Hmmm's got herself a newfangled hairdo, and she bought one of them bikinis to wear to the beach. Suchandsuch family's got relatives visitin' from down Augusta way.* To a small town, the lack of privacy was more perq than problem, and few complained.

Laurel boasted that his operator-operated system provided the comforts of modern software-driven marvels. The decrepit wooden console sat near a huge window that overlooked most of the town. With a sidelong glance, Ernestine or Louise could tell where a subscriber's vehicle was parked, and for how long. They knew when a phone was busy, because they had to disconnect a cable when a panel light went off at the end of a call.

Where else but H. Laurel Phone would you get *intelligent* call-forwarding?

"Number please? Randolph?" Followed or preceded by considerable catching up on any local news. "He ain't home. I'll ring Moody's Barber Shop. I see his pickup out front."

And call waiting.

"Phil's on the phone yappin' about his infernal Braves. I'll buzz you back when he gets off."

Conference calling.

"June's at the beauty shop right now, and Vonice's on that line with her sister as usual, but I'll connect y'all together and you can try to get a word in edgeways."

And automatic directory assistance.

"Bert? He's back home now. One sec, Hon." You don't need to know that Bert's number is 306, that his address is 3130 Mist Drive, or that his last name is Harmon with an "o," not an "a." Just ask for Herbert, or Bert. And get connected.

Eighties exigencies took out the phone company's twenty-four-seven operation. At the end of the evening shift at eight o'clock, the operator—usually Louise—plugged the whole switchboard into a "red line" phoneset with an actual rotary dial at Bryson Tourist. It had three incoming lines and an outgoing forwarding button that thunked and popped and made other joyful noises which most of the time connected the caller to the asked-for number. To make a call, you had to wait for "number please" from Laurel himself. His living quarters occupied the front side of the second floor at Bryson Tourist. You had to ring till the Red Phone's buzzing awakened him—several ringy-dingy's, minimum. Klutzy, but few complained.

By virtue of such customer satisfaction, Laurel enjoyed immunity from usurpation by larger phone companies. With little promise of growth, the cost to serve so few subscribers kept the biggies at bay. Laurel didn't care about profits, or need to, and the system broke even, a little better some years.

"Number please?"

"Somebody's, mmm, number is UP! Uh, look outside," Beasley said. "'Mmm, did you, uh, see the hearse just went by? 'Mmm, who might that be?"

"Hearse? Nobody's even sick that I've heard of. Let me look out the win—Well, if that don't beat all!" Ernestine tsk'd. "Ed Beasley, you go look again and tell me if you see anything out th'ordinary. Do you want to call somebody, or you just foolin'?"

Beasley rattled the buttons on the bank's ancient black desk phone. "Ernestine, mmm, did you, er, hang up on me?"

"Go. And. Look." Ernestine dispensed with the "number please" formality. "Ed Beasley, that hearse's done gone down the street. Go to the door. You can't see it from where you're a-standin'." *Disconnect.*

The funereal juggernaut paused ominously in front of the hardware store. On the sidewalk, Reb and Bud examined galvanized pails, enameled steel tubs and wooden-handled lawn implements. Bud spotted the hearse, nudged Reb. Reverently, they came to parade rest, doffed their caps and bowed their heads, exchanging looks of alarm, questioning, and concern. They watched, nervous, glaring into the gathering clouds reflected in the hearse's deep-tinted windows.

The vehicle made its way past Isabel's antique shop. In the store's front window, Cecil looked up from his ablutions, winked both eyes, and went back to washing himself.

At the end of the block, the hearse turned into Phil's Texaco Gro & Ser Sta. Reb's look changed to frantic. "Is'at'n comin' fer Ol' Phil?" He dropped the trencher shovel he'd been considering. "Not Ol' Phil!" Caps clutched to their hearts, Reb and Bud set out after the vehicle. The hearse rolled to a stop.

"Have. You. *Ever?*" Reb swatted his knees with his cap. "I done see'd ever' thing, now."

"Yep." Bud put his cap on, sighed relief. He took the cap off, scratched his head with it, stared.

Reb put his cap on. "A hearse, a-pullin' a trailer! I figgered ol' Phil fer tryin' t'take it with 'im, but this here's somethin' *else.*"

Four women got out of the hearse and stretched. Black jeans, black denim shirts, black work boots. Big smiles. They looked around and yoga-stretched.

"A doozey, ain't she?" The hearse's driver kicked the trailer hitch with her boot. Twice. She waved a high hello to Bud and Reb and patted the corner of the black and chrome trailer. Its curves mimicked the 1960 hearse that pulled it.

Polished silver lettering on the trailer's side: "Four Broads Landscaping & Irrigation."

"Ed Beasley, stop ringin' this phone. That hearse ain't comin' to get nobody. Didn't you see it was a-pullin' a trailer?" *Disconnect.*

Beasley turned to the door. "'Mmm, yessir! Well, uh, what can I, 'm, do for you this morning? Er, you're new here. Welcome to Farmers &, uh, Merchants. Er, Beasley. 'M, uh, the manager."

As he came out of his station, Phil laughed heartily. "I didn't know my time was up. Figgered I'd've'ad till dinnertime, at least."

"We get that all the time," the hearse's driver said with an amiable smile. "My name's Drusilla. Everybody calls me Cilla." She stuck out a hand to shake. "That's one reason we drive this old hearse. People pay attention."

"I don't doubt it. What can I do for you ladies? Cilla?"

"Looking f'a place called 'Vita Sempre.' Are you Phil? The owners said to stop here and you'd direct us."

Phil moved closer to Cilla, looked her over. Excellent figure, short but impeccable nails. No makeup and none needed. Engaging eyes. "That's Whit and Casey's place." He gestured. "Yonder way, not s'much's two miles. They bought it offa me a little while ago." He looked into her eyes again. "Y'all're who they sent to do th' landscapin'?"

"That's us. Four Broads, see? We're supposed to work on a long driveway. Turn scrubby woods into a suburb of Eden." Cilla bestowed amiable smiles all around, lingering on Phil.

"Well, I must say y'all're not what I expected." Phil backed into the station, beckoning Cilla to come with him. "But with them two, it ain't ever what you'd expect, anyhow."

"Ain't that the truth." Reb chimed in, resumed staring into the space between the gasoline pumps.

"Cilla," Phil said, "come on in my office. Whit left a map and some papers with me."

The other women moved toward the drink machine, digging in their jeans pockets for coins.

"Nabs machine's broke," Reb warned. "Just open the front, git what ya want and pay Ol' Phil fer it." He looked up. "Ed Beasley! What in the world're you doin' here during bankin' hours?" Reb stared at the stranger beside Beasley. "An' who's this feller?"

CHAPTER THIRTY-ONE

Nabs on the House

Phil nodded at the stranger. "How do. I'll be right back." He led Cilla to his office. "Y'all're clearing scrub. I don't care if you get some of my side, so don't worry 'bout property lines. Just don't take down any good timber–theirs or mine."

"Anything under five inches we leave alone." Cilla smiled.

Phil checked Cilla's eyes. "Plenty of ten and twelve inchers in these parts, so maybe eight's a better startin' number. Stack anything good for cord wood, an' I'll send m'helper t'git it." He looked up, waved the women's money away. "Y'all don't worry 'bout them Nabs. My treat."

He turned back to Cilla, waited for her to accept a drink and a pack of crackers from one of the women. "Now, right here." Phil pointed to the map. "I'm Phil Trane, by the way. Ever body calls me Phil." He searched her eyes. "Right here, you'd have to take down a good sized sycamore to straighten out the road like this plan says, but it's a real nice tree, so me and the boys've agreed we want to leave it be."

"That's here?" Cilla gently nudged his arm with hers. Pale peach against tanned leather.

Phil made no effort to break the contact. "It's way over the eight-inch mark. So split the difference and move the roadway. That ain't what's in the papers, but we all shook hands on it an' that's gooder'n any gold. Let Whit know which way you take the road so he can change the legal mumbo-jumbo." Phil left his hand on the map, took off his Braves cap with his other hand and laid it on the desk. "Cilla, if you don't mind my askin? Well never mind. I ain't gonna."

Cilla smiled. "New Jersey, Eastern Shore."

Phil studied her face.

"That's where I was born. My parents were Swiss, so I speak Jersey with their accent. I'm the only one of the Broads that talks Yankee. The others are from around here. They're my business partners."

"If y'all're doin' work for Whit it's a safe bet y'all's workmanship is jamb up. Come on back and be sociable, if'n y'interested."

"I'll do that," Cilla said. "Nice weather like this, we camp beside the hearse, especially this far out." She rolled the map and drawings and tucked them under her arm. "I don't suppose–" She put a hand on Phil's forearm. "–you've seen someone named Erica? Tall? Long hair? Rides a motorcycle?"

"We seen her. A sight to bee-hold."

"Yesterday? Day before?"

"Both. Day b'fore that, too. Gittin' t'be a reg'lar thing. She gases up her hog at the Shell." Phil waved his hat toward the other side of the street. "Lays a cussin' on ol' Bob Roberts loud 'nuff f'th' whole town t'overhear. Yesterday she out 'n out coldcocked 'im by the front sidewalk. Roberts was a-kissin' asphalt. Fer no reason that anybody could tell, 'cept he's is a real ay-double-ess, 'scuse th'expression. Got 'im s'riled up, after she sped off on her Harley he commence t'flinging stuff out of the station. Took 'is helper a hour t'clean up."

Cilla nodded. "That's Erica. Roberts is bad vibe city, we heard from Casey."

"You heard right. He don't sell as much gas as he does licker. The shine's higher octane, but not nearly as good t'drink." Phil emitted a laugh. "When you see y'friend Erica, thank 'er fer all of us. Ain't often we see Roberts get his due, but your friend, she put it to him and made 'im like it."

Cilla joined Phil in laughter. "If I know Erica, she's not done yet. Roberts must have said something that made her mad. Either that or she's in love. Or both."

"You want a sack or somethin' to tote them papers?" Phil led Cilla to the front. He pushed the screen door wide and propped it open with his foot for her to pass through.

Reb twisted around. "Sounds like y'all're a-havin' a mighty good time in there."

"Mornin', Phil," Beasley said. "'M bringing–This is, er, Dan Richardson. He's, uh, come t'–"

"Yonder's Roberts," Phil told Cilla. He put his arm around her shoulders and gestured with his cap.

Phil glared at Beasley. "You come down here for a purpose?"

Beasley cleared his throat. "'M, Mister, er, Richardson, here, wants to, uh, talk to you. 'M, about your telephone."

"Local Calls Only, like the sign says." Phil pointed to the station's front room. "Just pick it up. Reb, how 'bout mindin' the station a few minutes while I take these ladies out to Vita."

"What?"

"Mind the store fer me."

"Okay, Phil, but this ain't like you at all."

"I reckon it ain't."

Beasley cleared his throat. Again. "'M, uh, Mister Richardson doesn't want to make a phone call. He, uh, wants–"

Phil cut him off. "Cilla, get one of your partners to follow us in the hearse. You and me'll take my red dualie and I'll show y'around. Tie a ribbon on that big sycamore."

Cilla tossed her keys to a companion and took Phil's arm.

"I'll be back in a few," Phil told Reb, nodded, stepped around Richardson. "Come on, Cilla. That'n yonder's mine. She's a big diesel."

CHAPTER THIRTY-TWO

Phoning Home

I n the window at Isabel's antique store His Regal Greyness looked up from a preening marathon devoted to his mid section. Across an aisle of highboys, dressers, and chests, Casey puttered through a steamer trunk packed with yesteryear's foibles, fetishes and frills. "You're buying the hardware store?"

"Not the whole thing." Two clogged aisles away Whit admired an unusual mantel clock. Definitively Deco. "Anyway, WE didn't buy either the hardware or the store. We're leasing two spacious office suites upstairs over the oval headed brass screws."

"Not even Isabel has that many clocks."

Whit held up the Deco treasure. "Ooo, this one is a must-must. Sweetie, *our* new office suites are for *our* new telephone company. It's an acquisition *we* made by buying out the common shares and forgiving some debt. Big company, too. Thirty paying subscribers, growing slightly less than zero percent per decade."

"It better come with some clocks."

"W. Garrett, co-CEO of H. Laurel Phone Company LLC, at your service." Whit bowed. "It's named for the hardware store, which is named for its founder. He's owned most of this end of town since his ancestors towed Main Street over behind the Santa Maria." He rubbed imaginary dust off the Deco clock and moved it to the glass showcase under Cecil's watchful eye at the front of the shop. "We own it, so we can rename it if you want. 'DePaul Communications?'"

"Land lines? These days? Let's name it Dumb & Bummer."

"Cute, but keep in mind, Cutie, *you* are the other co-CEO."

"In that case, 'What-a-drag Telephone.' I've got it. 'Tel-A-Queen Telecom.'" Casey put a finger to his chin in mock contemplation. "Clocks, cars, antiques, *objets d'art,* haunted mansions. And phone companies. Do you have any *other* fetishes I should know about?"

"Blonds."

"Oh? How many of those do you have?"

"One. But mine is the *definitive* unit."

"Cute. Uh-oh. Here's a glorious old pocket watch you're going to have to have. I'll put it on the counter, and when Isabel comes back, I hope Cecil charges you twice price."

"Ouch," Whit said. "How do I deserve such wrath?"

"Nothing. Cool clock, Whit. Quite a find."

"Thank you. Great find on the pocket watch, too. Thanks for rescuing it from that ratty old trunk." Whit opened the watch, turned it over. "A railroad watch that I don't have the definitive model of. Excellent. Okay, give."

"I have but one clock to give for my country."

"Not clocks, information." Whit pleaded with his eyes.

"You first."

"Okay, here goes. I wanted to get Vita's phone turned on." Whit held up a hand against interruption.

Casey crossed his ankles, propped on his elbows against the glass showcase. An ancient ceiling fan stirred his hair. "Is this going to take very long?"

"Long version, but you asked." Whit cleared his throat. "I called Laurel while you were on your cell counseling Billy through his weekly ex-boyfriend crisis."

"And?" Casey prompted.

"And Laurel said Vita already had a line. Ghosts don't need phones to gossip, so no calls in decades." Whit took a breath. "Laurel said pick it up, and if we get number-pleased, it works."

Casey drew circles in the air with his index finger. "Local Calls Only, like the sign says."

"If it doesn't work, we have to trouble Ay-Tee-N-Tee to run a rural line. I have a hunch the line still works. Vita's phone was never turned off, but the phone bill hasn't been paid in oh, forty-odd years. Way past due, even by your Uncle Fritz's standards."

"Ooo, that bad?" Casey strolled to the trunk and examined a colorful, embroidered doily in a late afternoon sunbeam.

"Two dollars and forty cents a month." Whit bragged.

"How do they pay the help? Do they use robots?"

"No, they use Ernestine and Louise."

"Same thing." Casey put the doily on the counter. "Surely they don't number-please all day for free?"

"No. We're special-cased because our ghostselves fronted capital." Whit moved to another aisle. "The operators work for the hardware store doing the ordering and bookkeeping, and they number-please at the same time. We graciously agreed to keep it that way. Unless you want to change it, Mister Co-CEO."

"My interest in phones is talking, texting and the occasional voice-mail." Casey put down a doily. "Are we getting a phone at Vita? Do we have to pawn all your clocks to pay the back bills?"

"Vita's former owners' stock came with the house. The phone bills ticked up to less than two grand. It was a complicated deal in the first place, and some of the records were lost in the fires." Whit turned into another aisle. "We get interest–"

"I'm not interested."

"–On the original owners', investment. One point two percent." Whit paused for effect. "For well over forty years, it's a lot," Whit said.

"Queen Lizzie will never sell Big Ben."

"Easily covers the arrears on our phone bill."

"I was afraid we'd have to skip lunch," Casey said.

"The phone company's hamstrung. Boxed in."

"I'd never have guessed–unless I picked up a phone and rapped with Ernestine for two seconds." Casey moved to a tall chest on chest covered with spot resist glass pieces, all blue.

"So, I made Laurel an offer."

"Too bad he didn't refuse." Casey affected his best Italian movie mobster.

"He did."

"Great!"

"But then he made a counter offer."

"Do we need a counter? Think Aunt Myrtis would like this twisted-handle spots basket." Casey held the piece aloft. "It's Thirties, like her. Not a nick or a chip on it. Unlike her."

"If she doesn't already have three of them, she'd love it."

"Okay, I'll get it for myself." Casey went toward the counter, stopped. "Or maybe not." He set the glass basket back on the chest. "So bottom line, cut to chase, final analysis, all said-slash-done, cards on table?"

"I invested an additional sum and sourced Laurel to operate the company for us at present perks. There's no payroll. He'll handle staffing as a contractor."

"In that case, I'll get the basket to keep my boyfriend in," Casey said, "Because he is a definite basket case."

"Awww. Here's the deal. Laurel keeps the income from the phone bills to operate the system, and nothing changes except who owns it."

Casey set the basket on the showcase. "But now we're responsible for the whole bit and katoodle. Better get your Uncle Shyster to throw up a corporate smokescreen. LLC in the Dry Tortugas. Umpty-dozen holding companies. He knows the routine."

"Already in progress. And that's Schleider, not Shyster?" Whit puttered in the contents of a sideboard, holding up a pair of glass vases for Casey to admire. "I'll get Randy to set up the books. We have to pick up the accounting cost. Aren't these just like yours?"

"Those are taller. Dings and nicks?"

Whit brought the vases over and set them down.

Casey rubbed the rims of a vase and flipped it over to look for a Pontil mark. "Hand blown. Like you, Whit."

"Imp. Anyway, Ernestine retires soon. She has so many years in the saddle the horse is worn through. Louise, the other operator, is leaving soon to take care of her mother in North Carolina. So, we hit an opportunity window. Laurel's using our capital to propagate the nighttime system so every phone set will receive and forward calls anywhere on the network."

"Like any phone in Atlanta since Rhett took off for Charleston. I'm getting the vases." Casey headed for the front counter, nodded to Cecil and brought the vases back. "Or not. Cecil says these aren't the only ones here, and the others have richer color."

"Here, I'll take them." Whit replaced the vases. He rubbed a finger over the shelf, which bore no dust ring, and looked around at the open door, the ceiling fan, and back at the shelf. "Perfect like Vita. Too perfect. You don't think?"

"I prefer not to. Maybe tomorrow I'll think about that." Casey struck a histrionic pose and sat in a squeaky chair at a roll-top desk. "Whit," he said after a moment, "I'm familiar with what we do with clocks: Haul them back to Atlanta and bore friends and unsuspecting strangers with intricacies of their features, construction, and collectibility. What—I hesitate to ask—shall we do with our new phone company collection?"

"Nothing."

"Great plan. I'm for it."

"For now."

"Uh-oh."

CHAPTER THIRTY-THREE

The Building Boom

Isabel flounced into the shop and took off her stylish straw hat. "Aren't you two the talk of the town?"

Cecil looked up, yawned.

"Hey, Isabel." Casey waved. "Gossip mill at it again?"

Whit hnmphed. "Grapevine break. How was your lunch?"

"Fine as always. Now, where should I start?" Isabel took up her accustomed position behind the glass showcase and glanced over the items Whit and Casey had placed there. "Buying the phone system? You boys starting a building boom with the construction at Vita?" She looked up. "Or best news yet, your motorcycling friend bullying the town's biggest bully. Twice!"

"All that in one lunch? *Sixty Minutes* eats their heart out. If they had one." Casey puzzled at the doily Isabel handed him. "No like?"

"There are better, handmade ones around here without the yellowing this one has at the corners."

Casey looked around. "In that roll-top trunk?"

"Could be." Isabel hefted the clocks. "Excellent choices, Whit, both of these. I've got books you can check, but you probably already know this one's a superb example of the style."

"I figured." Whit leaned against a dresser. "Erica's in the news? And the phone deal. Not the hearse sisters?"

"I almost forgot the hearse," Isabel said. "Those gals are in the news, and you, too. New citizens after all the years."

Whit whistled. "The gossip fence knows things we don't."

"Quick, order a reprint of the Social Register." Casey passed an antimacassar to Isabel, who laid it on the counter.

"Great workmanship, retains its bright colors. Used very little, if at all. There are others like it, different shapes."

Whit smiled. "The gossip mill is ahead of ourselves," he said. "Our moving here–when and whether–depends on things yet undecided. Why would anybody care?"

Casey opened a black lacquered trunk, looked for a nod from Isabel, and dug in.

"You guys are something else," Isabel said. "The Mendels haven't had as many diners and sleepovers since the town clock chimed for no reason. The hardware's sold more plumbing supplies and building materials than Old Man Laurel's even seen since the Volunteer Fire Department project. Your order for all that plastic pipe really got him going."

"Contractors buy local," Whit said. "Saves time."

"And the Four Broads." Isabel laughed. "In one afternoon they nearly wiped Laurel out of lawn tools."

Casey mimicked Cilla's accent. "'Da Broads know a bargain when we see one.'"

Isabel laughed. "To hear Gertie tell it–and I'm sure she's embroidered the story as much as this dresser scarf–the hearse crew is about to change their name to 'Four Broads and a Big Ol' Redneck.' Phil took Cilla to a baseball game and sprung for matching Braves caps."

"Atlanta is great," Whit said. "Thirty-eighth floor, everything within a block–shopping, banking, restaurants. Art galleries and antique stores. Clocks. The problem is: my father's building twin condo complexes next to ours–Phase II and III–so our phase sounds like a nightmare and will for a while."

"Riveting, cement trucks beeping, yelling." Casey added in mock sadness, wrist to forehead, "it even drowns out Whit's clocks." He sighed dramatically. "Two huge towers, a snail's marathon at a time. One is in the way of our view and another right next to it. Seven in the morning, 'thanks a hell of a lot,' in the immortal words of Miss M. Last night till dark-thirty."

Cecil blinked and swished his tail.

Casey moved a box of trinkets to the floor and curled up beside it on an oval rug. "Where do you find all this stuff?"

"I have two sisters–Fort Worth, Texas, and Rhode Island–somewhere near Providence, but don't hold that against her. That's Nadia. She and I are twins. Yes, identical. Nadia has a book shop–collectibles, mostly. She buys estates to get the books. I get everything else, but I have to fight for the jewelry sometimes. Is your Vita construction finished?"

Whit came over to the showcase. "Almost. Stan finished the electrical yesterday. Did you meet him? Gertie teased him unmercifully about–well, you know Gertie. There was nothing wrong with the wiring, amazingly, but I wanted everything in conduit for safety, and a larger service. Four hundred amps."

Casey put trinkets away. "Whatever an amp is."

Whit thought. "Amps are like sex, the more you get the merrier you light up when someone flips your switch. Vita's roof was perfect, but I had a coating put on. The old drains were lead, so Stan's plumbing sub replaced them. We changed the supply to copper–bigger for the irrigation system, which should be hooked up today."

"You should see the access road," Casey said. "The Broads are doing a fabulous job. Whit got one of his father's firms to create the design, all the way to the main road."

"So that's why the heavy equipment hauled through town like an orange parade." Isabel said.

Whit continued. "We put in mature plants so it won't look scrawny while the plants take hold. The paving bricks are in concentric swirls to echo the iron gate. Lots of motion."

"A picture postcard on the hoof," Casey said.

Whit touched the Deco clock. "I have problems that a construction crew can't fix."

"You mean doubts?" Isabel asked.

Whit coughed. "Doubts, with a capital 'G.'"

CHAPTER THIRTY-FOUR

Electric Bumps

"I have a serious doubts-with-a-G problem. If it weren't for Casey I'd totally wig out. Bonkers."

"Bonkers-*er*." Casey corrected. "Whit wouldn't admit that Vita's grass doesn't grow. His high-tech sprinkler system waters lawns that haven't needed a sprinkler or a mower in decades."

"It's not possible," Whit said, emphatic.

"Anything we don't understand, we think is impossible," Isabel said. "Anything else?"

"Stan's crews rebuilt the well," Whit said. "New pump, pipes, pump house, tool shed. They had the aquifer tested for everything known to man. The curse, you know?"

"And?"

"Nothing. The labs—we had three redundant tests—they all said there's no way water can come out of the ground that perfect. And no way three tests could match exactly, which they did, tit and jottle." Whit moved to Casey's side.

"We talked about it, fought about it, and agreed to disagree," Casey said. "We know there's something afoot out there that doesn't yield to science or physics, Ohm's law, or even gravity. But so what?"

"Whit," said Isabel, "you two–"

Casey interrupted. "There's more."

"Lots more," Whit said. "My roofers put a high-density sealer on—get this!—the barn." Isabel gasped.

"It stayed materialized," Whit said, "while four men climbed all over it. When they finished, they came back from lunch to collect their tools and ladders, the barn was gone."

"Scared them *witless,*" Casey said. "Their tools were on the ground where the barn wasn't. They couldn't even smell it."

Isabel nodded. "That was Friday? Okay, that explains the high speed pickup chase that blasted through town. I sensed something spirit-driven, but I suspected liquid spirits."

"The liquid came later," Casey said. "They're probably still hung over." He apologized, "Whit bought the phone company. I wasn't consulted."

"I was consulting you when Isabel came in," Whit said.

Isabel filed another card. "I didn't mean to intrude on a private meeting."

Casey smirked. "Not private. Cecil overheard every word."

"Then your secrets aren't safe," Isabel admonished. "Cecil's a big tattle. What are you going to do with the phone company?"

"Nothing." Casey said, proud.

"For now," Whit added. "When Laurel struck his deals there was no such thing as a digital network."

"How much did you have to pay for the company?"

Whit smiled. "I promised not to tell."

"A few kilobucks and his second-best bed," Casey said, smirked. "I didn't promise. Besides, Cecil would blab if I didn't."

"So that's what Richardson's up to," Isabel said. "More of today's gossip."

"Richardson?" Whit asked Isabel.

"Richardson?" Casey asked Whit.

"He left his card." Isabel looked through a small walnut box on her desk. "'Richard C. Richardson, Stellar Cellular.' I signed on. Couldn't turn down a deal."

Whit waved the card away. "Stellar's the winning bidder so far, but you might get another company coming around. Even a better offer. *They're* putting up the capital."

"Shrewd, Whit," Casey said.

Isabel dabbed hand lotion onto her palms.

"We have to lease them some space for equipment." Whit wound the Deco clock carefully. Its gentle ticking elicited a whisk of the tail from His Greyness. "Bryson's going from number-please to state-of-the-art. Erica has it planned out. Did you meet Erica? You'd know if you did. She rides a Harley."

Isabel perched on the desk. "Heard about, but didn't see. Reb ran over here in a stew, saying Erica knocked old Bob Roberts out, right in front of the Shell."

"Embroidery," Whit said with a laugh. "Erica's a little, okay, she's a lot aggressive. She likes her men big, burly, and cowering at her feet. She didn't actually slap Roberts. She made him kiss her boots. Or so she told us."

Isabel laughed. "Ol' Bob Roberts does not cower."

"He does now." Casey smiled, wicked. "Erica is way experienced in such things."

"Impossible."

"Anything we don't understand, we assume is impossible," Whit quoted. "Erica said she hit the Shell to get gas. Casey told her to avoid it so of course that's where she went. Roberts made a tacky remark and she made him regret it. Next day, she gassed her hog, made him apologize and invited him to kiss toe. 'Commanded' probably, with a ladylike slap of encouragement."

CHAPTER THIRTY-FIVE

Hog Heaven

"Erica has been a friend of ours since 'Erica' was 'Eric,'" Casey said.

Isabel looked at Casey. "I've rarely seen a more attractive woman, and I *know* women. She's a man?"

"Not any more," Casey said. "I'm not telling tales out of school, she'll tell you herself. Before she became a beautiful woman, she was an attractive man. You'd recognize her family name from the *Journal*'s political columns."

Isabel stood up. "That explains the vibe I got from her."

"Erica's a great person," Whit said, "with odd taste in men. Maybe from being one herself. Reformed, so to speak."

"She has quite a following of breeder men," Casey said. "Some real lookers."

"Tell her to be careful," Isabel warned.

"She can definitely handle Roberts," Whit said. "We'll see if Roberts can handle what Erica dishes out."

Isabel jingled-fluffed her hair. "Ever since she bulldozed through town, I've sensed different energy from over there."

"Except in stuff-kicking mode, Erica's a pussycat." Whit licked the back of his hand and rubbed his cheek, catlike.

Isabel laughed. "Careful, Whit. You still have to negotiate with Cecil for these clocks."

"Ha!" Casey closed the trunk. "*This* is the one."

Whit accepted a lacy linen from Casey. Holding a pretend jeweler's loupe to his eye, he inspected it professorily. "*Ja?*"

"Herr Büllenscheissenindernogginkopf, this is the find of the day."

Whit stored the imaginary loupe in an imaginary vest pocket and turned the pillowcase over. "Where do you wind it up? Where are its chimes? Hands? Moon cycle?"

"If you hadn't looked so close, you might have seen." Casey smoothed the linen. "No Mozart, no ticktock, no mouse."

"Then why is it the find of the day?"

"It was salvaged from the C.S.S. Bowsplit in Savannah Hahhhbuh aftuh the Wawwuh of Nawthun Aggression. While still filled with actual horse feathers, it was the decisive weapon in a historic bedroom brawl between General Beauregahhd T. Bumfuddle and his second-favorite mistress, over custody of the last duck-down comforter in the Old South." Casey looked around at Whit and Isabel, both smirking. "Why, this amazing pillowcase nearly singlehandedly caused General Booftuddle to give up sleeping with extracurricular women. If it hadn't been for this l'il ol' pillowcase, the general would have been deprived of his comforter and would have snoozed through reveille, instead of moving to Bayou La Cash, Mississippi, out of the cold. I'll spare you details of his illustrious career." Casey took a breath. "Fast-forward to now. Bweuioooowip! The occasion demands that we honor General Doomfuttie's memory with a milkshake."

"Oh, you're hungry." Whit hnmphed.

"Famished. Cash us out please, Isabel. We've got people to go, places to eat, snacks to see. Charge my stuff to Cubic Zirconia Jim here."

Whit took out his checkbook.

Isabel smiled, held up the Deco clock for Cecil's appraisal. "Cecil thinks this is a bargain at the price marked."

Whit saluted the cat. "It sure is. I'd pay twice that."

"Okay, twice that." Isabel grinned at Casey, jotted on a pad and held up the doilies. "Cecil?"

His Greyness ignored her.

"Lagniappes. Cecil's not keen on them. The pocket watch? A really beautiful one. "Cecil?" Isabel put the watch down. "He's not impressed. Not too rare, but perfect condition and working order. I'm not getting 'original' vibes from it. There were lots of knock-offs. Lagniappe, too."

Whit nodded. "Knock off or not, no way I could pass it up."

"It is, after all, a clock," Casey said.

"The general's pillowcase and the rest—gifts for a future house warming." Isabel caught Casey's blue-eyed gaze. "Soon?"

"If the clatter *chez nous* gets any worse, we're moving *somewhere,* and soon." Casey smoothed a tatted doily.

"What's left before you move in?"

"Ghosts," Casey mouthed.

"Just the ghosts." Whit nudged Casey. "Beat you to it."

Isabel laughed. "I'm amazed the spirits have allowed all that work, but since they did I promise they're delighted. Yet, perhaps you'd like Cecil and me to check for lingering troubles."

Whit eyed His Greyness, who blinked lazily. "Sure."

Casey grinned. "Please do. I'm flabbergasted that Whit agrees, but I'm glad, too."

"The library is almost finished," Whit said. "That's Ben–handsome guy with the purple van? 'Cabinets Fit for a Queen.' He's rooming in town because he lives all the way over in Covington. Excellent woodworker. He built a computer hutch into the library's front wall. Duplicated the old mill-work, matched the materials, even reproduced the marquetry."

Isabel hand wrote a receipt. "You guys are definitely on the spirits' good guy list. I'll get you a box." She winked at Casey. "I've got the original peach crate that General Boeuf himself used."

Whit pocketed the pocket watch and gathered the Deco clock to his heart. "Care to join us at the café, if Cecil doesn't mind tending the store?"

"Great idea. I could use another belt of Gertie's insanely sweet tea."

CHAPTER THIRTY-SIX

Shakes and Pie

"Them two eats free," Mrs. Mendels shouted.

Gertie tap-tapped Whit's shoulder with her order pad and surreptitiously puckered a kiss to Isabel. "What y'all want? Git plenty, Mama's treatin'."

"Milkshakes," Whit said. "Except Isabel wants sweet tea, right?"

Isabel nodded.

"Chocolate." Whit said.

"I know what that'n wants." Gertie tap-tapped Casey on the shoulder. "He gits chawklit ever' time. There's lemon meringue pie yonder from dinnertime. It's a miracle there's s'much's a crumb left. Most ever'body's had t' git a piece, 'specially m'new fee-ahn-says."

"Okay." Whit nudged Casey.

"Me too."

Isabel shook her head. "When is the wedding?"

"Cain't rightly say," Gertie said. "Them men's a-hedgin'. I'm startin' t'think the best one of 'em's done already married. Ain't that a kick 'n th' head?"

"That would be Stan?" Whit smiled. "Stan's as married as men can get in Georgia."

"I shoulda knowed. They ain't all married up, are they?"

Casey shrugged. "Who knows. And Who isn't telling."

"Gertie," Isabel said, "have you seen your other fiancé Phil today?"

"No, I ain't." Gertie yelled toward the kitchen. "Shakes 'n pie, Mama! No need to het up th'grill." She turned to Isabel. "Phil went gallivantin' to ol' Miz Plunk's with 'is new squeeze, Cilla. In that ol' hearse."

Whit nodded. "She hired Stan to redo her house, and I hooked her up with the Broads to restore her gardens."

"Cilla might be prospectin' fer landscapin' work, but I reckon that ain't what Phil's a-doin'. He took 'is tools."

"Curious," Isabel said. "He always brings their cars in with his wrecker. Something about getting parts."

"He ain't in the wrecker," Gertie said. "He's in that ol' hearse. Awww, lemme go he'p Mama with them shakes."

"Git the phone, can ya?"

"Shore nuff, Mama." Gertie jogged to the front counter. "Café hol' on a sec." She set the handset down, set the four-position shake maker going and hurried back to the phone. "Now what c'n I do fer ya?" She spoke loud enough for everyone to hear. "Say, aren't you that good lookin' feller I waited on at dinnertime?" She put down the phone and yelled. "Casey! Fer you."

Casey scampered to the phone, returned in a minute. "Pool questions. Kidney shaped after all. You don't mind?"

"As long as it's okay with our ghos–I mean, Forces We Do Not Understand," Whit said.

Isabel chuckled.

"They like us staying true to their original," Casey said.

"That was Bo calling from Vita?" Whit made finger victory signs. "Vita's phone works."

Gertie pranced to the window table, swooped a huge tray down and doled out treats. She set a helping of bread pudding for herself at the space beside Whit. "Scoot over a little, Hon. I got time t' keep y'all company while y'eat yer pie."

"Great," Casey said. "Mmmm, this shake is *soooo* good."

"Shore nuff," Gertie bragged. "Hon, don't suck it down s'fast er y'll git a headache." She gaped out the window. "Land sakes! Look who's a-comin' yonder."

Casey put his milkshake down and gaped.

Whit's jaw dropped. "Unbelievable."

Isabel gawked. "You're talking about the car, Whit. I'm more amazed by who's in it."

A vintage Chrysler Maybach rolled to a gentle stop in front of the café. Its four occupants headed toward the door.

CHAPTER THIRTY-SEVEN

Out by the Pool

"**W**ho called this prayer meetin'?" Gertie pat-patted the four new customers in turn as they filed past. "We jus' need a preacher t' have a weddin' party." She pointed with the pad to Whit and Casey. "That round-de-round booth in the corner'll hold ever'body. Mama! Look who the cat's drug in!" The guests settled into the glossy red vinyl as Gertie hurried off.

Mrs. Mendels peered in, tsk'd and shouted. "Y'all're shore a sight to beee-hold."

Gertie returned with sweet tea and ice water.

"I'll get y'a spoon, Hon," Gertie whispered to Casey, not interrupting the conversation. She brought a folding chair, wordlessly handed Casey a long-reach spoon, rushed off to bring a tray and a foot-high stack of paper napkins. "I'll set here so's I c'n git up without scrounging past y'all. I got a feelin' that phone'll ring. It always does the minute I set down."

Isabel stood up. "I'll go close the shop. I wouldn't miss this 'prayer meetin',' as Gertie calls it, for a new bracelet."

"You gittin' phone's-gone-ring vibes too, Izz?" As Isabel nodded, Gertie sat down. The phone rang.

Mrs. Mendels dried her hands with her apron. "I'll git it."

Isabel turned, grimaced. "I'm sensing more than the phone, Gertie," she warned. "Something much bigger."

"Casey," Mrs. Mendels said. "It's your pool man."

Isabel blew a secret kiss to Gertie and left.

At the table, Gertie deftly rolled knife, fork, and coffee spoon into a napkin. She swiped a yellow, pre-glued strip of paper around each pack and stacked the kits in the plastic tray. She pointed with a knife out the window. "T'day's plumb full of surprises."

Erica paraded her Harley, part walking, part riding its throaty idle. Her hair whipped against the face of her passenger–her "bitch" in traditional parlance.

"That's y'all's friend," Gertie reported to Whit. "And Ol Bob Roberts with her."

Gasps all around.

Whit took in the exotic car parked in front. "Never mind Erica," he said. "And definitely never mind Roberts. I haven't found out about the car. Isn't that a Maybach? I didn't think there were any around outside of museums."

Casey came back to the table, exchanged nods all around. "Nothing serious," he said.

Whit pointed out the window.

Gertie folded a napkin. "Erica had somebody with her."

"Riding bitch? Who?" Casey looked around the table.

"Ol' Bob Roberts." Gertie winced.

Whit hnmphed. "Casey, don't just stand there embarrassed. Say 'pardon *mon Français*' and sit down."

Yvette and Yvonne said simultaneous hellos.

"Good to see you, Casey," said Mrs. Plunk. "Don't apologize. I know about riding bitch, and not from reading comic books. We're having too good a time to be offended. I'm teasing Whit about my old Maybach."

Miss Trudy patted the seat next to her. "Sit here by me. Gertie, I'd love a slice of lemon meringue when you get a minute. Do you want one, Kath?"

"I'd love one."

Mrs. Mendels peered toward the dining room and tsk'd. "I'm mighty glad to see you out and about, Kath."

"Tru and the twins keep hounding me to visit more," Mrs. Plunk said with a sigh. "I hope you're well, Ellen," she said.

"Real good," Mrs. Mendels said. "I reckon I've still got what it takes."

"Great to see you, Ellen," Miss Trudy said. "Casey, we've been pumping Whit for information, but he keeps changing the subject to dreary old cars. How are your renovations going?"

"Whit's happy, *ergo* I am, too." Casey grinned. "He's the resident Virgo. Now that everything is perfect, it looks like we can start moving in after the weekend. If Whit can unglue his gaze from that car long enough."

Whit hnmphed. "It's not every day you see a fine rare automobile like that."

"Don't get too excited, Whit," Yvonne said, "we can probably be talked into letting you drive it."

"While we plan a proper welcome," Yvette said. "This town parties once a year, on the Fourth of July. That's too soon to plan anything, and we don't want to wait until next July."

"Indeed not," Mrs. Plunk added. "I want a celebration in the Plunk manner. Tru, can you see to it? Something memorable." She patted Whit's forearm. "Like we had in the Maybach days. Arrange something that will take a year to live down and a hundred sections of gossip fence to tell about."

Miss Trudy spoke gently. "We old birds need to leave party plans to the young." She looked at Yvette, who acknowledged with a nod of gratitude and a co-conspirator's grin.

"We'll take care of it, Mama," Yvonne said. "Something cozy on the terrace." She waited for an answer, didn't get one. "One of Miss Tru's great dinners if she's willing."

Miss Trudy nodded. "With time to special order the ingredients, *bien sûr*? Old cognac, ancient port, *des fruits*. Everything but cigars and absinthe. I'll see if I can remember how to do a *Saint Honoré*." She accepted a slice of pie from Gertie. "This looks delightful."

"Nothin' fancy." Gertie apologized. "It ain't Fronnn-sayyy, but Mama makes it right here, and it shore is good."

Miss Trudy tested the pie's texture. "*Parfait*." She saluted Gertie and Mrs. Mendels with the fork. "As always."

Yvonne eyed Mrs. Plunk. "Fess up, Mama. Cozy on the terrace isn't what you had in mind."

The woman shook her head, emphatic.

"She'd hire an army of caterers," Yvonne said.

"Plus a wait staff of thirty and the philharmonic," Yvette continued.

Mrs. Plunk laughed. "Just the symphony will be fine."

Yvonne gave Miss Trudy a pleading look.

"Kath, *ma cherie*," Miss Trudy said.

"All right," Mrs. Plunk said. "I'll settle for chamber players if you promise Satie and Monpou." She turned to Miss Trudy. "And nothing beats Tru's Bananas Jazz Foster."

"Try the pie, Kath," Miss Trudy said. "It isn't flambé, but it is so delightful."

"Mmm, exquisite. Now, about that *Saint Honoré*."

"Thanks, Mama." Yvette said. "The Volunteer Fire Department building is booked for the Fourth, but we can get it later."

"Monpou in a tin can?" Yvonne tsk'd.

"Quite," Mrs. Plunk said. "That building would swallow the double basses whole. Do use the terrace, then. Schedule with the Four Broads so they can make it presentable."

Mrs. Plunk folded her napkin. "Oh, this is going to be fabulous. I hope I can still get into my pearl-studded gown. Dinner jackets under the stars *une autre fois*!"

Whit implored with his eyes. "Surely you're not thinking formal in the heat."

"Whit doesn't like doing drag as a penguin," Casey said. "But can we please hold the major festivities till later." Casey looked around the table. "Whit and I will host a do at Vita once all the work is completed. Save the major action for that. Informal, but in keeping with Vita's grandness."

"Excellent," Mrs. Plunk said. "So much like Tonio and Paul. Do let me hire an orchestra. You're putting Vita's old canopy back? That always was the perfect setting for the musicians."

"I'm having the new canvases made from the sketches Yvonne found in the basement," Casey said, "just like the ones that burned, shading part of the pool–as re-planned last night."

Mrs. Plunk twinkled. "They expressed their wishes?"

Casey made eye contact. "The 'force we do not understand' moved Bo's layout stakes. Now it's more of a small lake than a large pool. Ten laps and you're Guinnessed."

"That's Tonio," Mrs. Plunk said.

Whit laughed. "Build it like the 'force we do not understand' wants it. Now, as to this party?"

"Par-teezzzzzz," Yvette corrected.

"Oh, we had *so* many parties–I and Tonio, Paul, Dmitri, Tru." Mrs. Plunk sighed. "We'd go from Vita to my house and back. Sometimes we spilled over into town. That got us in trouble with Roberts. He and Dmitri never got along. Dmitri had that hot temper." She took a long breath. "Roberts' little brother caused a lot of it. He and Dmitri–I think Roberts was jealous, really. The worst part for Roberts was losing the affections–using the euphemism–of his little brother.

"I and my husband did the free love thing before the tie-dyes. I had other love interests. Dmitri too." Mrs. Plunk gazed out the window. "That poor little dog of his." She broke off.

CHAPTER THIRTY-EIGHT

Dmitri's Dog

Mrs. Plunk took a breath. "I've never told anyone. Dmitri and I left one of our parties at Vita. In the wee hours. We had the Maybach's top closed because of a cold downpour. We'd never use the tunnel with guests around–*le grand secret*.

"I drove, because Dmitri was more drunk than it's possible for one human to get. And liquor always made him amorous." Mrs. Plunk smiled. "Bret and Dmitri climbed in the back seat. The rain was so hard I couldn't see. Brett was very handsome, and I was more than a little jealous. Dmitri could be *so* inconsiderate about his other lovers *quelquefois*." She put a hand on Miss Trudy's wrist. "That poor little dog Sasha. Dmitri's first love, I always teased. A gift from his blue-eyed ballet boy. What was that boy's name? Something Russian. *Danseur incroyable*. Dmitri couldn't be without the little dog, although he adjusted easily to being without the bitchy dancer. We smuggled Sasha into the country in one of my hat boxes–quite an adventure that was.

"The poor thing chased cars. Had a limp to show for it, but that didn't stop him. Dmitri kept him inside on account of it. I don't know how the dog got out, or how he got over to Vita in the rain. Sasha ran after the car, yelping, running back and forth. I couldn't see the dog or the driveway. And I hit him without knowing it. Bret found him the next morning in a puddle of blood and rain."

Yvette nodded. "So that's–?"

"Dmitri was unconsolable." Mrs. Plunk continued. "He never forgave me. Moved into the carriage house at Vita–with Bret. They buried Sasha, I don't know where. It took the Robertses weeks to notice Bret was gone, then they couldn't stand him leaving. It wasn't the homosexual thing. Bret told me his brother and his old man had both been taking advantage–another euphemism–for years. Old Man Roberts threatened to send the sheriff for Dmitri, as a pervert, and for Tonio and Paul, for kidnapping. Bret told Tonio about the abuse, and the war began."

Mrs. Plunk looked up. "Today's the first time since–Sasha–that I've ridden in that car. Well, don't let me bore you with my sad tales." She paused. "Whit, did Stan get in touch with you? He had some structural question. About my house?"

"We talked. I'm sorry, your floor plan would require substantial structural modification–steel beams for support."

"Then beams it is," Mrs. Plunk said with finality. "I'll have it the way I want it."

"You couldn't stay there during construction," Whit said.

"I wasn't planning to live in all that noise."

"I can relate." Casey grumped.

"You and Miss Trudy could move into the cottage with us for a while," Yvette said.

"Last resort, girls," Mrs. Plunk said. "I and Tru will travel for a while, and then Ellen can put us up here in town, like the old days. Besides, we're–"

Conversation stopped dead. Mrs. Mendels yelled into the dining room. "Go look, Gertie! This'n ain't no drill!"

"Fire!" Gertie ran to the window. "I see smoke yonder!"

As the fire alarm saturated the air with its mournful wail, Mrs. Mendels hurried to where Gertie stood.

"This is too much," Mrs. Plunk said. "Where is it, Gertie?"

The twins joined Gertie at the window.

"West," Yvette said, agitated. "West, Mama."

"West." Whit said. "That's Vita."

Casey stored his spoon in the empty milkshake container. "Should we go try to save some things?"

"Stay here," Yvette said. "There's nothing anyone can do but wait for the fire crew. The buildings are so old and dry, by the time any of us get there it'll be too dangerous."

"We'll run out there," Yvonne said.

"Yes do," Mrs. Plunk said. "Pedal the metal. The car can handle it."

Mrs. Plunk scowled. "Just like years ago. First you see Roberts, then you see smoke. If that's my house or Vita, and I don't personally kill that man, somebody please do it for me and I'll gladly take the rap."

The twins zoomed away in the Maybach. Gary Mendels emerged from the bed and breakfast. Hitching up his suspenders, he put his head in the café and shouted, "Ever'body all right?"

"I reckon," said Mrs. Mendels. "You be careful."

"Don't you climb no ladders, Papa." Gertie said.

Mendels hurried across the street to the fire department, where several dusty pickups convened.

"Whatever is on fire, if it's no more than a litter barrel," Mrs. Plunk shook her fist. "*C'est décidé*! I am *going* through with what I came to town for. Tru, let me out. I've got some damn banking to do!"

Miss Trudy scooted out of the booth. "I'll come with you, Kath."

"Brush fire." Gertie said, more hopeful than confident.

The Volunteer Fire Department building's wide steel door rolled open. A burgeoning crew of volunteers ducked under it, donning gear as they approached the lone, ancient American La France firetruck.

Mrs. Mendels snatched up the phone. "Hello... Thanks." She handed Casey the phone. "Ernestine said your carpenter man at Vidah called in the fire. Talk to 'im."

"Have mercy!" Gertie clapped her hands. "Yonder comes Roberts ag'in, on the back of that motorcycle. The nerve! Ain't even waitin' f'th'smoke t'clear." She tsk'd, leaned toward the window. "Y'all's friend Erica's puttin' 'im off." Gertie propped her hands on her hips. "Now she's a-smoochin' 'im. On the lips. Ha! An' then slaps 'im one."

"That's Erica." Casey took the phone from Mrs. Mendels.

Isabel flounced in, joined Gertie at the window. "What do you make of it?"

"Mixed up." Gertie grumped. "That motorcycle's done messed up m'concentration."

"I'm getting confused energy, too," Isabel said.

Whit waved to Isabel. "Can you tell what's burning?"

"Woods," Isabel said, "near a building, a farm, maybe. A barn–not yours." She locked her fingers with Gertie's and held them wide. "Let's close our eyes and pool our energy."

Casey pointed to the phone. "This is Stan at Vita. The smoke's in the woods close by. Vita's wall might contain it, but Stan's worried the trees could be lost."

"What a shame," Whit said. "Camellias as old as the ones outside that serpentine wall would be difficult to replace."

Casey sighed. "A mansion in a moonscape." He put the phone back to his ear and listened, nervous.

"Yonder comes Phil in that ol' hearse," Gertie said.

"Stan says our barn reappeared." Casey smirked.

Whit hnmphed. "Just in time to burn down again?"

The Four Broads' hearse screeched to a panic stop in front of the Volunteer Fire Department. After giving Cilla a lightning-fast peck on the cheek, Phil swapped his

Braves hat for his fire fighter's helmet and ran to the firetruck. Cilla stood for a moment and crossed to the café.

"Ready to roll," Gertie said to no one in particular.

The elderly fire truck groaned, roared, and bounded out of the fire station in a glint of polished red. The urgent wail of its siren modulated the continuing din of the fire alarm. With Phil wheeling to make the turn, it swerved into the street and streaked past the café as helmeted volunteers clung to its sides like comic characters in a silent movie.

"Stan's sending his crews with all the extinguishers," Casey said.

"Good thinking," Whit said. "Hey, Cilla, good to see you."

Cilla hugged Whit and Casey in turn. "Your friend spotted the smoke and called in the fire," she reported breathlessly. "The phone operator called Mrs. Plunk's where Phil was working on her cars. I had to rush him back."

"Casey," Whit said, "tell Stan not to take chances."

"I told the Broads to turn on all the sprinklers," Cilla said. "There's not much wind, so there's a good chance the fire won't jump the wet sod."

"Thanks for the hope," Whit said. "Um, Isabel, are you getting anything?"

Isabel nodded. "The danger's not over, but I'm feeling it will be shortly."

"That's what I'm getting' too, Gertie said.

Mrs. Mendels plucked the phone's handset off Casey's shoulder. "The bank, please, Ernestine, but keep Vidah on the line. Ed? Let me speak to–Kath? This here's Ellen. It ain't your house or Vidah, but 'tain't over yet. Y'all're welcome. Y'all come on back when ya get done. Ernestine, how 'bout pluggin' this feller back into Vidah."

CHAPTER THIRTY-NINE

Setting the Woods on Fire

"Stan? Was that an explosion?" Casey turned to Whit. "Stan says it isn't getting any bigger or any closer."

Isabel held her palms high. "Explo–I sense... not the woods, a building. Gertie?"

Gertie shut her eyes. "I'm a-seein' machinery or something. And some men."

"Suits and ties. Not firemen?"

Gertie agreed, her eyes closed. "Maybe investigators."

Whit laughed. "Amazing, the accuracy with which you've both predicted the *present*. Open your eyes." He pointed to the street. A black van rolled up in front of the café.

"They can't be investigating the fire, 'cause it ain't over," Gertie objected.

"It's over," Casey said with relief. He cradled the phone on his shoulder. "The smoke is dissipating, and Stan says the Broads just saw the firetruck heading back. They're leaving the sprinklers on as a precaution." Casey thanked Stan, thanked Ernestine, thanked Mrs. Mendels, and hung up the phone.

"What a relief." Whit patted the seat beside him. "Okay, Mister Commentator, are we cutting to a commercial break or is Headline News up next?"

"Very funny, Mister Communications Mogul."

Two suits smoothed blue ties, tugged coat sleeves crisp and headed into the café.

"Friends of yours?" Mrs. Mendels checked her Timex. "Land sakes! With all th'excitement I ain't put m' ham on to bake. I hope ever'body's in th'mood fer meatloaf agin t'night. Gertie, git them new fellers set up, willya. Ain't no more fried chicken gizzards, if that's what they want, and y' daddy gobbled up the last of the oysters."

As the Maybach rolled to a stop in front of the café, Cilla scooted out of her seat. "I'll go get Phil."

"Y'might's well set a spell," Gertie said. "Them boys've always got a bunch of cleanin' an' organizin' t'do after they git back from a fire. Best part'f'a'hour at least. Let me getcha some pie and a sweet tea."

"Stick around Cilla," Whit said. "Casey wants a report on our landscaping project. Don't you, Casey?"

"Um, sure." Casey rubbed his middle. "I love meatloaf almost as much as I like Texican fried cheesecake with mango sauce. And dried papaya slices. And milkshakes, yum. And–"

The suits sat at the far end of the counter. Nervous.

"Make that hot tea with honey and lemon, and I'll pass on the pie." Cilla winked at Casey. "I've got a hot date."

"Me too," Casey said.

"We were testing the last of the irrigation lines when the smoke started," Cilla said. "Have you seen it?"

"Not lately," Whit said.

"I'll get my camera out of the hearse." Cilla said. "I got some shots this morning."

Gertie leaned close to Casey's ear. "I was tryin' t'get across to her that I ain't got claims on her man. We tease an' all, but Phil an' me's just good friends. I got t'let her know without lettin' on about me an' Isabel."

"Leave it to Phil." Casey advised.

"I reckon." Gertie put her smile back on, freed her order pad from her apron, and sauntered to where the suits sat. "Howdy, y'all. What c'n I getcha?"

Mrs. Plunk bustled in from the bank, pulling Miss Trudy by the arm. "Maybe that will rid this town of its sordid past." She made her way through the restaurant. "Is that Gertie or Ellen? My old eyes can just make out someone behind the counter."

"It's Gertie," Gertie said. "Glad y'all're back."

"Bring us some coffee, please. Extra, extra cream. Too bad you don't serve cognac."

"Miz Plunk, these two gentlemen's a-waitin' t'see ya," Gertie said. "This'n's a looker, too, an' he's dressed to preach." She fluffed her hair. "I was just a- plannin' m'weddin' when this'n here up an' sez they flew in special t'meet you. But I got plenty other fee-ahn-sayz. You c'n have 'em."

"Extra, extra cream." Mrs. Plunk adjusted the position of her purple satin pillbox hat. "Looking for me? How nice to be sought after again."

The suits turned around. "We're here about your paintings," impeccable blue worsted said, took her hand. "I'm Will Radling, Executive Director, and this is Ray Carell, our curator for acquisitions." Armani silk, bluish gray with a subtle pinstripe. Classy. Saks.

"Pleased to meet you at last," Carell said.

"Acquisitions, eh?" Mrs. Plunk laughed. "Don't get your hopes up." She shook Radling's hand as though firing him from a menial job. "I waited for you gentlemen half an hour at my home," she said, handing their business cards to Miss Trudy, whom she introduced as "my life partner."

"We apologize," Carell said. "We got lost." He and Radling sat down.

"Our cellphones quit several miles out, so we couldn't call you to reschedule." Radling glanced at Isabel, who smiled sympathy. "There was nothing but woods for over an hour, some of it on fire–I hope there's no danger. Finally, some woman on a motorcycle offered to lead us into town." He shrugged. "We came in here looking for a phone, and– Gertie, is it?–told us you'd be back shortly, so we waited."

Carell smiled, sheepish. "I'm glad we caught up with you."

Mrs. Plunk glowered. "Forgiven. Let's get on with it."

Radling perked up. "Just some papers to sign. We'll send a courier to transport the artworks. At your convenience, of course." He arranged papers in stacks on the table.

"I figured you got lost." Mrs. Plunk touched the array of papers and beckoned to Yvette. "This is going to take a while. You and Yvonne take Whit for a spin in Dmitri's Maybach."

"We don't mind waiting, Mama. We're talking over our plans with Cilla about renewing your gardens," Yvonne said.

"And Gertie's bringing us lemon pie." Yvette handed Whit a dainty key ring. "You and Casey go check on Vita. Okay, Mama?"

Mrs. Plunk waved approval.

"Wow!" Whit grinned. "Cilla, may we borrow your camera? I'd love a picture of us in the Maybach."

Cilla pushed the camera across the table. "Hold on a sec." She retrieved a memory chip from her pocket. "Use this geeky film thing. The other one's full from this morning."

Mrs. Plunk jabbed an index finger on the paper that Miss Trudy read to her. "When I brought these *bagatelles,*" she said, "your museum would have considered them vulgar, bordering on the obscene. Now my trashy trifles are quite the art find."

"Beardsleys? Quite." The dashing Carell gushed. "We were hoping to convince you to *donate* or perhaps bequeath–" Glimpsing a stern look, he left off.

"I'm happy to lend them for your exhibition–"

"We app–"

"I'm major renovating, so they need to be out of my house for a while, but I want them back. On schedule. You can try to wheedle them out of my heirs after I'm gone." She turned to Miss Trudy, who picked up the next paper. "This one covers what?"

"I want a look at the cool car," Cilla said. She followed Yvette and Yvonne to the sporty vehicle. "Wheeeooo," Cilla whistled. "Twice as long as my hearse, and curves like Mae West's corset. What did you say this is?"

"Maybach," said Yvette. "'My,' as in 'wish I had *my* shawl ya'll,' and 'back' as in 'oh my aching.' I suppose it's correctly 'bock.' Rhymes with Johann Sebastian? Back in Mama's day–rhymes with paleolithic–it was a high-end dream machine that Chrysler admiringly named after a German designer. They couldn't name anything after that *other* car pioneer, Hank Ford, see? Careful when you start it, Whit."

"It floods," Yvonne said. "Don't pat the gas."

Yvette continued. "They stopped making these when homage to German designers became politically incorrect."

Whit stood in front of the stretch-limo-sized sports car. He rubbed the gleaming grille affectionately, felt the fluid lines of its decoration and bug-eye headlights, and trailed his fingers over the sculpted swoop of a fender.

"Uh-oh," Casey said. "My boyfriend's in love with a dune buggy. Where will I survive? How will I go?"

"Jealous." Whit sighted down the long hood.

"Get in." Yvette nodded to Casey, who hopped in on the passenger side.

Whit took his time getting into the car, got out, got back in. "It looks like it's still in the showroom."

"Until today the poor thing hadn't been out of our carriage house in decades," Yvonne said. "When we were girls we'd sneak and play in it"

"Rare times when we were home from Europe," Yvonne said.

"We'd pretend we were at a polo match, spread a tablecloth on the lawn near the car and lay out *brioches* and jam for our dolls and imaginary friends."

Cilla got in the back seat. "I love the red interior. Phil put the new tires on this morning. Even the spare had rotted from sitting for so long. He spent all morning working on the brakes and such. Amazing that he had all the parts."

Whit puzzled. "Thirty-nine?"

"Nineteen thirty eight." Yvonne boasted. "Glaser Cabriolet. Mama says Dmitri always called it his last white stallion. They stopped keeping horses after he bought this nag." She petted the car's side panel as though stroking a racehorse. "Tonio and Paul kept horses till their barn burned."

"A couple months after the fire, Roberts was in the county jail, drunk, bragging about setting it, but the thugs he was talking to had such bad reputations no jury would have believed them on so much as the time of day, so he was never prosecuted."

Yvette pointed to the sky. "If that cloud comes this way you'll have run for cover. Closing the top might be tricky."

"It probably works like my Dad's Cord," Whit said.

Yvonne shook her head. "The old material is brittle, and the mechanism hasn't moved in decades."

"If it rains, just put it back in the Plunks' garage and we'll pick you up in the hearse," Cilla said.

Yvette agreed. "Good plan. Start it up, Whit."

"Jahhh," Casey said. "Geputten ze footen on ze gasss."

Whit handed the camera to Cilla and hugged Casey, who tilted his head toward Whit's and mugged.

Click.

"Let me see, let me see."

"Don't worry, Casey," Whit assured. "You'll look great. The camera never lies." He started the Maybach. "I can't believe I'm driving this car. It's unreal to even see one."

"Come on, Cilla," Yvonne said. "Let's go talk garden."

CHAPTER FORTY

The Persistent Poodle

Click. Casey framed Vita Sempre's iron gate with Cilla's camera. He inspected the picture, in which a long-haired white cat sat like an Egyptian goddess. The real world, if you can call it that, had no cat. "Brace myself." The blue gaze he laid into Whit's eyes spoke volumes. "The welcoming committee is non-existent Pywacket." He patted Whit's shoulder, soothed.

Preoccupied, Whit ran appreciative fingertips over the dash of the vintage Maybach. "Pffft! I spotted ghostpuss disappearing." Whit admired the car's controls with his hands.

"As I was saying, uselessly I perceive, I understand how our Deco ghosts spook you. You've even had to admit they exist, Mister Denial." Casey tapped the camera. "See, they pose for portraits. So, if you're not okay with this?" Casey indicated the escape route with his eyebrows.

"Thanks, O Considerate One, but I can deal with it." Whit hnmphed. "I'm over it all. Whoever's ghost is next in line, please take a number."

"Whit, I want you to know it's fine with me if we don't move here," Casey soothed. "We can take your Dad up on one of his rental properties, or buy something else, or hang out in St. Tropez for a year." Casey glared at the cat, who jumped into space and disappeared.

Whit dallied with the Maybach's controls. "After raising a Houston stink, for which I blush with embarrassment, I'm so can't-be-bothered now. If you can share turf with our ghostselves and their paranormal pets, then so can I. It'll be a non-stop adventure. Now, apply your baby blues to Cilla's camera and record this for posterity. Don't crop off the fruit trees."

Click. "It's beyond beautiful. A lane paved with cobblebricks, wide enough for actual cars." Casey panned the camera. "Here kitty."

Click.

"No, that's a rabbit. Works well with the Forties Chic original." *Click.* "Excellent motion." *Click.* "Enough puppywoods for a festival when they bloom."

"Puppywoods?" Whit laughed.

"Baby dogwoods. Ohhhh, Whiiit." Casey fluttered his eyelashes, cooed. "Thank y'all sooo much for putting Tara back like it was before the wawwuhh. Y'aw a fine gen'l'man to do such a favor faw a lady."

Whit nodded. "Suht'nly. Ah've got a surprise, but hold on while I hop out of this fancy carriage we borrowed." Whit turned his back and pretended to fiddle with the gate's lock.

Click.

"What was that noise?"

"Me takin' a pick-chuh." Casey brandished the camera.

"See anything different?"

Casey checked the camera's display. "Looks fine."

Whit showed off a keychain-bound controller that he fished from his pocket. He pointed the device at the entrance and pushed its button. With a gentle hum, the gates swung in and stopped just short of their iron catches. "The gates are hooked to electronic locks and detectors all around the serpentine wall. If anybody even gets close, it lets us know. If we don't reset it from inside the house within two minutes, it turns on the sprinklers." Whit hopped into the Maybach.

"Careful it doesn't douse the spirits," Casey said.

"After dark it also flashes. See those uplights under the–puppywoods, as you call them?" Whit acknowledged Casey's approving nod. "Floodlights, too."

Another nod. "Fiberglass posts, smart. With your fetish for landscape lights, we'll brown out the town when you throw the switch."

"*Automatic* switch," Whit corrected, boasted. "Other stuff too, when Erica irons out an odd interface. Cameras are mounted above the columns. Don't bother straining your eyes, you'd never find them. The video feeds go wirelessly to the new computer niche in the library. We can remotely operate the gates if anyone rings–" he pointed. "–our new video gatebell."

"Luvvvly."

"I decided to add more smoke and heat sensors, plus another back up power source and a fire suppression system."

"Wonderful," Casey said, disinterested. "Look. Cilla's camera got a grand picture of your excellent ass."

"Shall we join our ghost contingent inside?" Whit drove in, stopped just past the house and shut off the engine. "Pears, more puppywoods." He pointed. "Chinaberries, mimosas, and speaking of ghosts, our barn is back from the umpteenth dimension."

Casey snapped with a dismissive flip of his wrist. "I'm not in the mood for fright. Let's ignore it."

"Great idea. You're taking off your clothes?"

Casey batted his eyelashes. "Are grapes in season?"

Not yet. But sex in grape arbors is perennial."

"Hurry up!" Whit ran toward the Maybach from the grapevine covered gazebo.

Casey cartwheeled great nude circles across the yard, past the barn. "Right after I read some beads!"

Flash! Lightning, due east.

"One Mississippi." Whit hopped on one foot as he slipped into his pants. "I'll turn the car around while you dress. Two and a half Mississippis." He tucked in his white shirt, unbuttoned. "Casey! Quick, before the rain starts. We can just make it to Plunk's. Four and a half Mississippis. Where are–? No way the disappearing barn. I am NOT waiting out a storm in there. Six Mississippis. Come on! Seven Mississ–"

Rumble-umble-ble! A brisk wind further tousled Casey's hair.

Flash!

"One Mississippi. Hurry up!"

Casey kicked the barn's siding with his bare foot, winced. "Earth to spirits: You will NOT interrupt my concentration on–on none of your business what on. Either leave this smelly barn on Planet Vita or keep it out of my sight." He kicked the barn again. "Get it?" *Kick.* "Got it?" *Kick.* "Good."

Whit babied the vintage car, allowing it to sputter to life and fizzle before starting it again with the gentlest pat on its accelerator. "Come on, don't flood out," he coaxed. "Five– Mississippi's. Casey, let's go!"

Boooooom-rumble-umble!

Casey limped, stormed, skipped, bounded to the Maybach, tossed his clothes in the seat, and dived in after. "Giddyup! I'll ride bareback so I can moon that barn."

"Hold on!" Whit floored the accelerator.

Flash!

Yap-yap-yap-yap-yap!

"One–What is that?–Mississippi. Two–"

"A dog? Chasing the car."

Yap-Yap!

"It's *the* dog. Four Mississippis. The ghost dog." Whit swerved to the opposite edge of the driveway. The poodle kept up, chasing the front wheel.

Booommm-umble-umble-umble!

Flash! Yap-yap, yap-yap.

"One Mississippi. I'm trying to get away, but it stays right with us." Whit leaned out the car and shouted. "Pooch! Ooze back into whatever dimension you came from." He blew the horn, frantic. "Vaporize! Go chase the barn! Turn yourself into protoplasm and seep into the paving bricks! Anything, but get out of our lives! Three or is that four Mississippis." Whit threw his hands up. "Great, now he's running in front of the car." He let off the accelerator, swerved into the planter, spewing gravel from the tires as he braked. "That has to be the poodle that dripped into the kitchen when we first came to look at this haunted palace." He steered wildly, swerved onto the lawn, braked, accelerated. The poodle kept pace.

Booom! Flash! Yap-yap.

Casey clambered into the back seat. "I'll try to figure out how to close the top."

"Careful." Whit stomped the brakes. "If we can lose this kamikaze poodle we can still get to Plunk's. Dog, get away! Go dog! Bye, puppy! He's wet, but it's not raining yet. Three and a half Mississippis."

"This top feels like it would disintegrate if moved," Casey reported. "Oh, Whit, please try not to kill the dog–even though he's already dead."

Whit crept forward, slow. "Dmitri and his trick of the evening in a rainstorm. It's another time warp––"

Flash!

Casey jumped to the left.

"Playing out again like a B movie fifty years later."

The yapping dog kept up. Whit speeded up to outrun it.

Boooooom-umble-umble-um! Yap-yap. Yawpyawpyawp–

"That was close. More like an Alablamma than a Mississippi." Whit stomped the brake with both feet, fishtailing the car to a jolting stop, stalling its engine. The dog's yapping turned to yelping, muffled, and stopped.

Flash!

"Where did the poor thing go?" Casey hopped out and looked around. "Under the car?"

Boooooommm!

"He's not behind us," Whit said.

"Did you miss the pooch somehow?"

Whit restarted the engine. "I didn't run over the dog. I stopped just before we turned poodle into puddle."

Flash!

"You're sure, Mister Graphic Description?"

"Yes, Mister Sheepish Look."

Casey blew upward, bounced a lock of hair from his forehead. "Then what happened to the hound?"

Booooooooommm!

"He beamed himself to wherever dead ghost dogs that chase cars go when they miss getting killed for the umptieth time. Some shopping mall needed a dog zombie. Where does our barn fly off to when it disappears? Like just a few minutes ago when we–uh-oh. I felt a raindrop."

Flashcrack-rumbleumbleumbleumble!

"Ooo, that last disco light show and bass boogie were micro Mississippi's apart," Whit said. "It's Plunk's garage or drown. I hope we can make it before Noah rows by in his wire canoe."

Casey punched the button on the electronic gate controller, twisted around, commanded it to close behind them.

"Thanks," Whit said. "'Pedal the metal!'" He did exactly that.

Flash!

"Here's the turn to Plunk's. Hold on!"

FlashBoooooommmmmmmmmmmmmmmmmmmmm!

CHAPTER FORTY-ONE

Stormy, Wetter

"Negative ten Mississippi's that time." In the end stall of Mrs. Plunk's white clapboard garage-né-stable, Whit inspected the Maybach for rain. He groomed the thoroughbred, stroking a few beads of moisture with affectionate swirls of his shirttail. Just outside, occasional huge raindrops pelted the clay. A strong wind whipped Casey's hair.

Ethel, Phil's dualie, brightened the paddock.

"Heyyyy! Perfect timing!" Casey tucked in his shirt, not buttoned, and smoothed imaginary wrinkles from his jeans. "Whit rolled the fancy jalopy into the garage just in time," he said.

Flash! Crack-booommmmmm!

Isabel opened the truck's window and leaned out.

Flash!

"Vibes off the scale," Isabel said. "Not even counting the storm. I was worried about you two, thought I'd come and check."

Flash! Boooommmm!

"We're fine," Casey said. "Boy have we got stories."

Isabel's bracelets flung atonal treble against the deep bass thunder. She beckoned. "I've got news, too. Hop in or be drenched."

"Run for it, Casey. I'll close the doors."

Flashboooooooom! No Mississippi.

Casey dashed for the pickup, slid to the middle of the seat. "'Move yer bloomin' arse,'" he quoted-shouted at Whit.

Flashcrackbooooommmm! Rain. *Major* rain.

"Uh-oh." Whit uselessly umbrella'd a hand over his head as he swung the heavy wooden doors closed and ran. He arrived soggy, poured himself into the seat and yanked Ethel's door closed behind him. "Thanks for the rescue."

Flash!

"You're wet!" Casey said.

"It's raining," Whit said.

Booommm!

Isabel laughed. "I loved that movie."

Casey smoothed the water off Whit's face and trailed a fingertip down his wet chest. "'I like men with this many... muscles,'" he misquoted.

"Gertie and I used to sneak out to the midnight movies anytime *Rocky Horror* was playing. It was a long drive in the middle of the night, but we could neck in the dark balcony while toast and rice sailed over our heads. You have stories?"

Flash!

"Nooo," Casey said. "You first, then me."

Isabel turned Ethel's windshield wipers to maximum bail and took the truck out of gear. "I can't see a thing. We'll sit this out for a few minutes. Okay, shortly after you left in the Maybach, we found out what was burning."

Booommmm!

"That wasn't the woods," Isabel said. "It was Bob Roberts' liquor stills."

Flash-crack-booommm!

"Old Dirk Woodward came over to the café. He's a fire department volunteer, a retired sheriff's deputy. Phil sent him to get coffee. He's had trouble with his heart so they won't let him do much. Anyway, Dirk–"

Flash-booommm!

"–Dirk said the fire was on Roberts' granddaddy's old farm. It hasn't been Bob's property for decades, but he never worries about trespassing. The house burned down long ago, but a ramshackle old shed survived, and that's where Roberts has been making his liquor. Him and his daddy before him."

"Cozy," Casey said. "White lightning as a family value. Springer for days."

As the truck's wipers flap-flapped against the torrent, Isabel dabbed her dainty handkerchief at condensation on the windshield. "Roberts had an electrified fence around his still. Good thing Phil spotted it before somebody got injured. Dirk said Roberts had plowed a ring that contained the fire. Only one building burned–the stills, the mash, Roberts' stock. And his propane tank. That's what the explosion was. It was almost gone when the volunteers got there and too dangerous with the propane, so once they were sure there was no one in the building they sprayed water on the field around it and stayed clear."

Flash!

"We've been warned about Roberts' icky-face squeezings," Whit said. "Let me guess, the fire was no accident."

Isabel blotted-jingled at the opaque windshield. "Intentional, undoubtedly. But it makes no sense for him to torch his own stuff."

"Revenoors." Whit slicked his rain-soaked hair.

"If the feds destroyed it, they'd cart Roberts off for moonshining and he'd make license plates, like last time." Isabel stowed the handkerchief in her bosom. "Besides, they wouldn't leave the fire unattended."

Boooom!

"Okay, Casey, now you."

"Sooo, at Vita it rained, not frogs, but dead ghost wet dog," Casey said with relish. "Accent on 'ghost?'"

Isabel dabbed the windshield. "You saw Sasha?"

"He ran after the car as we were hauling 'A' to beat the rain. Exactly like Mrs. Plunk said, he ran in front of her car."

Flash!

"Wow." Isabel dabbed-jingled. "We'll get going soon."

"No hurry," Whit said. "Unless Phil needs Ethel."

"He and Cilla went to Atlanta in the hearse with the Plunk twins." Isabel dabbed. "They're going to a Braves game and get rained out."

Boommmm!

"Sasha chased the Maybach," Casey said, "and the Maybach chased the dog, shortly after we were not very chaste while the barn disappeared with a boom. Sasha ran in front of the car, but Whit didn't flatten him. And the dog disappeared. Poof."

"Ohhh," Isabel said. "That explains the energy I've been feeling. It's wonderful you didn't hit Sasha. Maybe he can rest."

"That's a concept," Whit said. "Ghosts resting. Do they take coffee breaks? A nice holiday after a season of haunting? Disappearing takes a lot out of those protoplasmic nonentities."

Flash.

Isabel put the truck in reverse. "I was about to wish Ethel had oars. Do you mind if we drive into Vita on the way back? I'd like a closer feel for this energy bump."

"Okay with me, if Whit's willing."

"Just don't flatten any dogs." Whit handed a controller to Casey.

Booom!

"The barn was there when we rolled up in Plunk's dune buggy," Casey said. "We walked by it on the way to the arbor, wink-wink. There we were, making with the grapes, and the barn blinked itself into its other dimension like somebody flipped its switch. Wham! Like the sky was about to fracture. And the smell! Not a good thing for... *grapes*."

Whit cast his eyes skyward.

"Whit laughed it off. He's awesome." Casey petted Whit's cheek. "We get back to... *grapes*, and there we were on the brink of *wine*, and wham! The barn reappeared! Again with the thunderclap and the skunk-o-matic. Totally blew the mood, and there were clouds moving in and fireworks in the sky in the distance." Casey took a breath. "We had the Maybach sitting there topless. Whit was mad and so was I. *Interruptus* doesn't feel good. Twice!"

"Gertie and I know about interrupt-us. We deal with it every time Gertie's mama gets up in the night. She's got a bad case of religion and Gertie won't come out to her."

Thunder. Distant.

Isabel wheeled Ethel into Vita's re-sculpted, re-landscaped, re-paved access road. "This is gorgeous."

"Thanks. Whit's the best."

"Shucks," Whit said. "T'weren't nothin'."

Isabel applied Ethel's brake. "Hmmm, seems like the barn was trying to alert you to the approaching storm."

Casey held up the controller. "Open, sez me." The gates obeyed.

"Cool." Isabel stopped in front of the barn. "Open your window please, Whit." Isabel pushed up her sleeve and herded her jingling bracelets away from her wrist. She opened her window and extended her arm. "Take my other hand."

"A séance in a pickup," Whit said.

"Let your mind float," Isabel said, "you especially, Casey. Together we make a powerful receptor."

CHAPTER FORTY-TWO

Les Mecs

"Hey, Izz, Whit, Casey, 'bout time y'all got back here. Ain't been no men t'flirt with in two hours." Gertie stacked clean dishes, inspecting each one. "We was startin' t'think y'all'd drownded."

"Whit did." Casey smirked. "His whole life flashed before my eyes."

"I'll go park Ethel." Isabel hurried off.

Miss Trudy patted the window seat beside her. "Come and sit, *mes beau mecs*. Yvette and Yvonne went off with Phil and Cilla to get Phil a new Braves cap–or so he thinks."

Casey slid into the seat beside Whit. "Another rainy night in Georgia," he quoted-sang-parodied.

Whit hnmphed. "I didn't know the Braves could swim. But speaking of rain, Casey's got quite a story."

"As do I." Mrs. Plunk sipped from her cup. "And you boys need to know. This afternoon when I and Tru went to the bank, I bought the delinquent mortgages on Bob Roberts' gas station, his house, and the lot behind it where the blacksmith shop was before it burned. Old Ed Beasley's too wimpy to foreclose."

"It's causing trouble with the auditors. He's beside himself with anxiety." Miss Trudy acknowledged Casey's smirk. "Even more than usual."

Mrs. Plunk continued. "He sent registered letters saying the bank was selling the loans." She sipped her *café au lait*, extra-extra *lait*, a decaffeinated brew that Mrs. Mendels concocted under Miss Trudy's tutelage. "I'll own those liens outright Monday after the Fourth of July."

"From what I've heard of Roberts," Whit said, "you'd get a better ROI from a trip to Vegas."

"Quite probably," Mrs. Plunk said, sipped.

"Ooo," Casey said. "You want to evict him."

Whit hnmphed. "Vegas would be more fun."

Mrs. Plunk tapped the air with a forefinger. "Quite right, Casey. Roberts has disturbed the peace around here for too long. He's a crook, an arsonist, a bootlegger, a moonshiner, a bigot, a blackmailer, and an ass, the 'son and heir of a mongrel bitch,' quoting the Bard." She raised her cup. "Roberts brought down the curse–him and his family now mercifully deceased. I'll take great pleasure in putting him in the street with the rest of the garbage." She sipped summarily, as if sipping settled the matter.

Miss Trudy nodded, confirmed. "His moonshine is what burned this afternoon."

Mrs. Plunk set her cup down with a clink. "Unless he can raise substantial cash–and I sincerely hope he can't–he'll be out of his house, out of his station, and out of this town." She put a hand on Whit's arm. "Getting rid of Roberts is my return on investment."

Miss Trudy pressed on. "We hired the meanest lawyer in Atlanta."

"To put the courthouse dogs on Bob Roberts," Mrs. Plunk said with relish.

"Remind me to make an appointment for a brush-up with our Tai-kwan-do-karate-jiujitsu-knife-fight instructors," Casey said.

Miss Trudy spoke up. "We created a convoluted hierarchy of holding companies. Roberts will deal with a bureaucracy of lawyers, magistrates, and bailiffs."

"Tru worked out that angle," Mrs. Plunk said with pride.

Casey whistled. "We won't breathe a word. Wouldn't dare."

"Not a syllable," Whit said. "For our own sake, as well as yours. Thanks for forewarning."

"Tru is taking me to an eye specialist in Rochester, New York, whom everybody says is the best in the world. I'm hoping he can restore my sight or improve it considerably."

Casey waved at Gertie, crooked his elbow in a drinking motion, described a large glass with his hands, plunked imaginary ice cubes into it, and operated an imaginary drink dispenser over it. "Do you think Roberts will leave town?"

Gertie answered the pantomime with a grin and a nod.

"I intend to make sure of it," Mrs. Plunk said. "When they padlock his house, I fully expect Roberts to break the lock. The magistrates will handle that, to his great dismay." She gulped the warm elixir. "I'll have the place razed as soon as possible so he can't burn it–like the blacksmith shop."

Gertie set a glass and two straws in front of Casey. "Double shot of vanilla like y'always want. Anybody else need anythin'?"

Mrs. Plunk held up her cup. "Please."

"No one in town would rent so much as an outhouse to him," Mrs. Plunk continued. "He'll stay with his cronies for a while, but he's no longer a source of what they put up with him for."

Miss Trudy added, "Vita's ghosts have dogged him with bad luck for so long there's no place he's welcome. Besides, nobody has enough fire insurance."

"I expect the Shell will be torn down by late August. He put up the station as security to re-roof his house after a windstorm. Roberts couldn't qualify for the loan, but Ed felt sorry for him." Mrs. Plunk tsk'd.

"Beasley was probably under great pressure from Roberts to do his wimp act," Miss Trudy said.

Whit broke in. "We got the Maybach into your garage before the rain hit. It stayed dry, only a few drops of water and I wiped those off. It was fabulous. Thank you."

"Thank the twins," Mrs. Plunk said. "I presented it to them this morning."

Casey elbowed Whit. "Whom do we thank for Dmitri's poodle?"

Mrs. Plunk grabbed her cup with both hands. "Sasha?"

"He chased the car, just like you said earlier."

Mrs. Plunk grabbed Miss Trudy's hands. "After all these years. You didn't...?"

"No," Whit said proudly. "We missed the non-existent dog somehow."

"Isabel drove Ethel out to pick us up, and we rode over to Vita, and the barn stayed put since this afternoon when it blinked on and off like a carnival ride. And Isabel said it was trying to get our attention because we were, well, distracted, but now it's resting and doesn't smell any more, and there was no sign of Sasha that second time after we missed it the first time, and she said he's resting, too, meaning Sasha, and probably won't be back because his spirit is satisfied." Casey came up for air.

CHAPTER FORTY-THREE

Urbanites' Lament

Whit meandered around the hilly Bryson area, rarely out of third gear. "Nice of Amos to roll our Fiat into Phil's service bay when he saw the rain coming," he said. "I'm just driving," he explained to Casey's third puzzled look. "I was so worried about the Maybach I completely forgot–" He patted the dash. "–about our little red speeding ticket maker." Whit turned onto a narrow, blacktopped road. "Just as well it was out of Roberts' fanbelt slicing range, too."

"Looks like a grand sunset after that rain." Casey thought a minute. "Heavy on the fire-engine red considering the afternoon's events."

"And the coming cosmic battle."

"Plunk versus Roberts," Casey said. "Fifteen rounds and a game of ice hockey. Loser has to tip the ambulance drivers."

"Remind me to never tick Plunk off. She's the hoary hellgrammite from the south portal of hell," Whit said.

"Fifty years of being a recluse chilled her out like vintage vinegar. Only not as mellow."

Whit drove aimlessley. "So, move to Vita? Take a chance on being in the Plunk vs. Roberts crossfire? Suffer more months of unsleepable construction at our condo? Move into Dad's rental unit? Or take a suite at the Hyatt-Regency?"

"I'm thinking," Casey said.

"'Stewing' is more like it, but let's hear it."

"Okay, clock backward. Untick, untick. Bing! The thrill filled Thirties. An ever so convenient Fire at the sugar factory takes out Plunk's parents, with whom she was having a tiff. Was it notorious firebug Roberts? At her request, perhaps? Or were those lucifers struck by the dubious debutante herself, PMS'ing about her Parisian lesbian fling thing?"

"Good questions," Whit said. "From all accounts she hardly needed more fortune. Besides, if she paid Roberts to do his torch act, or if he knew she did it, she would never dare take Roberts on–even after fifty years. There's no statute of limitations on murder, even in Georgia."

"She was acquitted, so she's immune," Casey said. "She didn't need loot, but to satisfy her old man's will she married Dmitri and hatched up actual twins–*got* to hurt. I bet she was drummed out of Savannah's elite Lesbian Baking Society. Probably lost points off her U-Haul Discount Card for it."

"Stereotypes. For shame!"

"Sorreee."

Whit squinted into an imaginary magnifying glass. "I conclude Roberts didn't set that fire. As for the baby thing, maybe she plied both banks of the sexual identity Seine. The rich-and-famous-women's sexual revolution was a hot ticket. Plath? Chanel? Sand? Collette?"

"Not in that order, but yes, that whole third sex thing."

"Maybe she fell in love with a gay man." Whit touched Casey's thigh. "It happens."

Casey blew a kiss.

"Dmitri the player, too. Making out with Bret in the back seat when she flattened Sasha. Did you detect a foot-wide vein of jealousy in that story?"

"Poor Sasha," Casey said.

Whit turned onto a winding valley road. "What happened to Bret? Nobody's seen him since the fire." Whit hnmphed. "We know Dmitri and Bret survived. Phil saved them from the burning gate house. The others, we don't know. As for piano virtuoso me and spritely ballerino you, poster boys for the McCarthy blacklist?"

"No wonder they disappeared." Casey smoothed his hair. "If anyone toasted Plunk's *vielles* for her, the underworld-connected alter-us would qualify as usual suspects."

"I'm sure we didn't do it." Whit pointed to a rainbow near the pinkening horizon. "The vibes would be off the scale. Why are you laughing?"

"You. Discussing vibes."

"I'm in tune with the metaphysical compost, now."

"I'm proud of you, but that's 'cosmos,' not 'compost'?"

"I'm proud of me, too," Whit said, "and if I had a shrink I'd expect him to say the same. And I chose 'compost' advisedly. Euphemistically, even."

"Because?"

"It stinks for not being understandable on the obsessive compulsive anal retentive plane."

"Okay, Mister Pocket-Protector-Wearing, Slide-Rule-Cherishing, Notebook-Hoarding, Algorithm-Loving Engineer. I understand, and that makes me proud of you."

"Thanks, I think." Whit headed the car into the sunset. "So, our ghostselves? Dmitri's ghost? The Bretghost? Have we all gone on to that big jazz club in the sky? Did Sashaghost whip out his transit beam and return us to Transylvania? Or are we still 'crawling, on the planet's face?'"

Casey contemplated a long minute. "We didn't croak in the fire. I got that from Isabel, but I sense it, too. Our alterselves couldn't deal with the loss of our beloved horses in the fire. Couldn't live under the threat of violence and misdeeds from the likes of Roberts. And Congress. So we hauled cute cans and never looked back."

"Through the tunnel?"

"Maybe we hid in our catacombs till the smoke cleared, so to speak. How long has it been since we met or passed a car?"

Whit mused. "Half an hour or so."

"See? Even today, we wouldn't even need night to escape."

"We'd need transportation."

"So, we do the secret subterranean thing to our pal Plunk's where she's sleeping off her Chartreuse and doesn't see us. We bribe her help to take us to the train station. Zoom to Club Med. Montmorenci, whatever. Our alterselves had plenty of money. Dmitri was probably on thin ice, with HUAC poisoning the melting pot. Bret couldn't return to his thug fam, so there wasn't any coming back."

"We're seventy-five? Eighty?" Whit hnmphed. "Somewhere in all that happy-ever-aftering, we might have died."

Casey gasped. "Dmitri was from beyond mere France, from a long line of gypsies, tramps and thieves. Siberian, via Romania and France? He had kin who could summon all manner of magic."

"So why didn't we phone home? Or at least write to our lifelong friend, pal, spouse, and maybe partner in crime?"

"The letters got misdirected." Casey gasped. "Ooo, that just popped out from the paranormal plane."

Whit eyed a cloud with a purple halo. "The sky is going to be gorgeous over the lake when we cross the wooden bridge. I'll head that way in a minute."

"You actually know where we are?"

"Enough to get us home. One more question. When do we move, or do we?"

Casey tipped an imaginary hat. "Pull over to the side of the road. Quick."

"Why?" Whit braked to a gentle stop.

"Shut off the engine... Now, what do you hear?"

Whit listened. "Crickets. Frogs in some pond–that creek with the old wooden bridge. And a mockingbird just behind us singing his heart out. A tractor, far in the distance–maybe the hayfield a couple miles back."

Casey curled an arm around Whit's shoulders and kissed his cheek. "We can go now."

"Go? I like it here."

"So do I. Does that answer your question?"

CHAPTER FORTY-FOUR

For Sale

At noon, a sign went up in front of Roberts' Shell. "For Sale / Or Lease / Bundrick Rlty & Prpty Mgmnt & Ins." Abe Bundrick himself installed the red, white and blue placard with a star-and-stripe background. He studied it, saluted it, repositioned it, reinstalled it, moved it, straightened it, and pasted strips of silver duct tape over "Or Lease." After viewing the sign from the opposite street corner, from the left and right sides of the property, and from the center of the street, Bundrick adjusted his clip-on tie and ambled across to Phil's Gro & Ser Sta.

With nods and howdy's to Phil's regulars in their accustomed chairs leaned against the front wall, he sidled inside. The porch crowd squinted and guffawed at Bundrick's sign, sipped Yoo-Hoo, remarked about cold spells in hell, sat, spat, fanned gnats, and contemplated distant cumulonimbus portending rain.

"Howdy, Abe," Phil said, not looking up. "Mess o' Sundays since you come callin'." He extricated himself from the engine of a well worn pickup and waved a socket wrench by way of a handshake. "Good t'see ya, but b'fore y'say a word, I seen that f'sale sign when you first stuck it up. Y'a-wastin' y'time a-trottin' over here. I don't reckon you could pay me to take that station, considerin' the evil eye that's always come down on it. Jes f'arguments, how much is Ol' Roberts a-wantin'?"

Phil went outside, followed by Bundrick, who nodded quick hello-goodbyes as he hurried past. "Where's he goin' in such a rush?" Phil asked.

"T'th'Tourist," Reb said. "Him'n' Ol' Gary Mendel been on the wagon together f'a month. They tak'n off several times a day t'go't'meetin's, some of 'em way out past Beulahlan' Church."

"Well I'll be." Phil raised his new Braves cap, smoothed his hair, settled the cap. "Y'all won't b'leve what Roberts is askin'. I'm half a mind t'go look."

Amos twisted, elicited precipitous creaks from his chair. "The devil hisse'f wouldn't have that prop'ty to add a new wing onto hell."

Reb didn't turn around. "Ya jes' got shed of one place that's hainted. Reckon y'want t' try agin?"

"If Roberts is sellin' out, maybe the bad luck'll leave with 'im," Phil said. "Hand me one of them peaches, Amos. Y'all right. I ought t'jus' fergit it."

"Trane! Hey!" Roberts yelled from his gasoline island.

Amos spat.

Reb spat.

"What?" Phil spat, even though he didn't chew.

Roberts beckoned. "Want a look?"

Phil bellowed a gruff "nahhh" and muttered to Reb, "I don't want t'git struck by lightnin'."

Reb and Amos snickered, spat.

Roberts swaggered across the street. As he neared the deep shadow of the station's overhang he pulled his Cat cap's visor forward over his eyes. "Don't let bad times get in the way of a good deal." He ducked into the shade. "Let's you and me talk."

"I'm a-listenin'." Phil scowled, followed Roberts inside. In two minutes flat the two men emerged.

"Reb, Amos," Roberts greeted. "Y'all awright?"

"Fine." Reb spat.

Amos grunted, spat. He opened his pearl-handled pocket knife to peel a fist-sized peach that he selected from a weathered wooden crate propped next to his chair.

Roberts growled loud enough for all to hear, "I'm a-leavin' Bryson."

Bud inhaled his hand-rolled cigarette deeply, coughed, studied it, exhaled. "Umnhhh."

"Rides a Harley?" Amos spat.

"That's her." Roberts looked from one man to the other. "Seems like nobody's had as much damn bad luck as me. Lightnin' an' windstorms. Always my station, leave ever'body else alone."

Amos spat.

Roberts continued. "An' them damn yellow jackets ain't missed a summer in I don't know when. I still got a welt on my neck from that'n that nailed me last week. It's a plague. Like I been a-sayin' all these years." He pointed to the station. "I can't keep glass or even plywood in them back windows. Somethin' busts 'em out just in time fer winter.

Damn kerosene heater won't stay lit, and the woodpile stays wet when it ain't rained in a month."

"Them's the haints a-gittin' even," Amos said.

"It's the f'k'n bad luck and the plague on this f'k'n town," Roberts boomed. "My porch roof's a-leakin' agin. Sposed t'last fifteen years and didn't even make five. I'm mighty tempted t'stick fire to it all. But I don't reckon Erica'd have anything t'do with me if I did, so I ain't gonna." He fanned gnats with his hand.

"I reckon you won't," Phil warned. Loud. "You burn anything, and I mean so much as a leaf, and your ass is *mine*—Erica won't git none. You got that, Bob Roberts? You hear what I'm a-sayin'? Set one more fire and you won't live long enough f'th'smoke t'clear. Ain't a jury around here wouldn't *thank* somebody fer killin' you, and you know that fer shore and certain."

"Trane, I ain't settin' no more fires."

"How 'bout yore still?" Reb spat. "You set that'n."

"I done that fer Erica. Them feds was swarmin' around askin' questions, but I done that'n to convince Erica I'm serious about hangin' up liquor. And I am. That woman's set me afire, and I'm done with all of it."

Phil folded his arms and glowered.

"You seen I plowed that field to keep the fire from gettin' t'th'woods."

"I seen that electric fence, too. Coulda killed somebody."

"It was switched off. Anyway, I'm clearin' out, an' I shore would like t'git a little money out of my property."

"The way we heard it," Reb reported, "every time your girlfriend comes to town she whups your ass."

"I git licks in, too, but Erica's the only woman I ever met that could hold 'er own with me."

Amos spat.

Reb spat.

Roberts cleared his throat. "She owns a big farm t'other side 'f Atlanta. Needs me t'take care of her farm equipment. And her. I ain't turnin' this'n down."

Phil hnmphed.

"I'm letting the station go fer ever what I c'n git out'f't. The house, too." Roberts shooed gnats from his face. "If y'interested, the house is gittin' foreclosed, an' I reck'n the station too, soon enough. I got might near enough to pay 'em off, but I ain't gonna." He scanned the men's faces. "Any o'y'all got a little cash, y'oughta buy it."

"I got two dollars saved up," Reb offered.

"I know better'n that." Roberts looked from frown to frown, to Phil's fierce scowl. "Bundrick's got the papers, and I give Ol' Ed Beasley power of attorney. Go do business with them. I reckon y'got till right after the Fourth of July barbecue t'make up your mind b'fore the f'k'n lawyers surround it like dogs on a pork chop. After that they c'n take it to hell with 'em s'far as I care. I ain't plannin' on comin' back."

"I'll see ol' Ed Beasley when 'e gits back t'th'bank after he eats," Phil said. "I ain't saying yay or nay, just thinkin'."

Roberts lifted his cap, grinned and left.

"Y'reckon Erica give 'im that shiner?" Reb said when Roberts was out of earshot.

"Reckon she didn't?" Phil laughed.

"Y'all think Roberts knows what kinda woman he's a-gittin'?" Amos snickered. "Or what he ain't?"

"I hope he don't," said Phil. "But I b'leve he does."

"Why's that?" Amos passed Phil a peach.

"A little birdie," Phil said.

"A birdie named Cilla." Reb snickered.

Phil bit into the peach.

"What else that little birdie tell you, Phil?" Reb selected a peach for himself.

"Plenty," Phil muffled, his mouth stuffed. "I got t'git Old Man Frye's pickup finished so's I can go see what ol' Ed Beasley knows about this."

CHAPTER FORTY-FIVE

Clock Shopping

In the window at Isabel's antique shop, His Regal Greyness settled into an afternoon sunbeam as though preparing for a Knickerbocker nap. He pawed, rattled the metal cup against the old picture frame and re-re-re-readjusted his angularities. With scrupulous attention to detail, Cecil assessed the Snoozability Quotient of several positions before settling on paws-glassward, his woolly tail draped over the window ledge. In mid-testdoze, the door opened with a brassy clang.

"Hey, Cecil," Casey greeted an imperious yawn. "Where's Isabel?"

"She's here." Isabel shouted from the shop's far reaches, "checking in some new items. I got tons of new goodies since you guys were here a couple days ago."

"Izz!" Casey exulted, extracted a stack of snapshots from Whit's back pocket. "What do you make of these?" He spread the photos on the glass showcase.

"Oh my!" Whit approached a great-great-grandfather clock of European descent and New England upbringing.

"What do I make of what?" Isabel didn't move. "I'm up to my ears in stuff right now. Tell me which piece and I'll yell out what I know about it. Has Whit spotted the new clock?"

"Spotted it? He's already calculating how to get it home. No way it'll fit in my Saab." Casey stroked Cecil's chin. "I brought some things that you *have* to see. I can't describe them, because they're *unnn*describable. I'm not sure I even believe them, and I *know* Whit doesn't! Come look. Incredible, I promise!"

"Things you brought? Antiques?"

"Not just from another time, but another dimension. *Twilight Zone* stuff. But I know you're busy so we can come back later." Hiding a wicked smirk from Whit's knowing glance, Casey turned his attention to Cecil's soft belly.

Isabel put down her pen and clipboard and jingled through the aisles. A windchime factory in a hurricane. "Wow!" She picked up one of Casey's photos. "Definitely worth the interruption." She picked up another, squinted at it, splashed it with strong sunlight from Cecil's window. "Like you said, these are–" Another print. "Completely." And another. "Unnn–" Another. "Beee–" One more. "–leeevable!"

"My sentiments exactly," Whit said. "Speaking of unbelievabile, what do you know about this clock?"

"It's not half as incredible as these photos." Isabel held eye contact with Casey. "Hey, Cecil!" She held up two photos for His Greyness to inspect.

"Ffffft!" The cat's eyes glared. He leapt to his feet, hissed, arched his back, fluffed his fur, twitched his tail.

"That cinches it," Isabel said.

"It's okay, Cecil." Casey soothed, petted, rubbed. "It's only a sequel to a bad dream." He pushed a print to Isabel. "Isn't this is a sexy picture of Whit driving the Plunkmobile? Even though the poodle to his left–beside those orbs of light–got killed decades earlier, and the ghostperson in the back seat is only half there."

"Enough with the backseat Banquo and dead dog mugshots," Whit said. "Let's move on to important matters: this clock. German, or around there? Maybe early-Nineteenth?"

"Squeeze behind it and look at the back, about even with the pendulum bob." Isabel studied the prints in turn.

"Hmmm, double hinges. A secret door? Let's see if–"

"Wow," Isabel said. "Great picture of Whit, but that transparent figure just peeking in. Getting caught on purpose, I think." She touched a print. "Bret trying to materialize."

"'Got to be good looking 'cause he's so hard to see?'" Casey quoted-sang-parodied.

"Spirits rarely sit for portraits," Isabel said. "Orbs appear in photos often, and there's a bunch of them here. What, Whit?"

"Any idea what this half-eroded sticker says?"

"'Vvvormzzz,'" Isabel said. "A city on the Rhine, very fashionable, wealthy industrial center around the mid Twentieth. Rubble after each of the wars. That's where it was made, I think." She turned back to Casey. "By now, Sasha would be–I couldn't even count the dog years. And Bret would be pushing sixty. Here he's maybe early twenties. And *blue* eyes. The whole Roberts clan has brown."

Casey agreed. "A hottie."

Isabel flipped through the prints. "I'm into women, but I know a hunk when I see one. The flirt's shirt is open."

"Look closer, Izz." Whit said. "He's a stripper after Casey's own heart. His shirt opens as you go through the stack. If Cilla hadn't stowed the camera, we'd have ghost porno. Now, this Worms-eaten clock? Please?"

"Have Mrs. Plunk and the twins seen these?" Isabel asked.

"They invited us for dinner, so we'll startle them then." Whit said. "We showed Gertie just now. Casey dragged her away from arranging an elopement with my friend Jan. You'll meet him in a minute."

"Jan pronounced with a 'Y' but spelled with 'J' is Whit's way-hunk-o-matic part-Swiss blond audiophile friend," Casey explained. "He followed us over to help Whit wedge a home theater system into Vita—the big room with the blank wall."

Whit hnmphed. "Gertie pronounced the photos 'devil works.'"

Isabel splayed her fingers over the array of snapshots. "That means she didn't get any signals. No clairvoyance. I'm getting nothing, too."

Whit cleared his throat. "*Und Klatschen die Uhr?*"

Casey laughed. "Jan-with-a-'J' has Whit in *Deutschespeak* mode. Jan-with-a-'J' speaks French and English fluently, but his German is almost as bad as Whit's—with a 'T' for 'terrible'. It's a wonder either of them made it through Herr Doctor Brindl's fancy Swiss university."

"*Summa cum laude, danke schön*," Whit reminded.

Casey smirked. "I offloaded these from Cilla's camera while Whit and Jan-with-a-'J' watched, so no way anyone could have tinkered with them. I took the camera chip to Tenth Street for prints, and theirs are the same as my inkjets: dead dog, diaphanous stripper in the twins' battle wagon."

Whit hugged the clock like a beloved relative. "Clock? Pretty please?"

"It's a good thing Jan-with-a-'J' brought his Jeep-with-a-'J.'" Casey chuckled. "I have a feeling we're about to adopt a new clock-with-a-'c.'"

His Royal Greyness sat up and looked around.

"Sorry, Whit," Isabel said. "I was distracted by unreality-with-a-'U.' Superb condition for a clock that old." She winked at Casey. "And really old for being in such good condition."

"Very," Whit said. "With a 'V.' Now give!"

"It's not in any of the books I checked, but my sister dug up something on it. I'll get you the note she sent." Isabel rummaged among the papers on her desk.

"Whit wants it, with or without pedigree," Casey said. "Hey, Cecil! How much for the Kaiser's crazy clock?"

"I'm afraid the clock's going to be quite dear," Isabel said. "My sister said it came over from Germany in the late Thirties with a family that managed to get out before the war. It headed west and then spent some quality time on Cape Cod. She happened to be in Provincetown. Here's what she wrote." Isabel jotted the clock's price on the perfumed, rice paper envelope, flashed it to Casey, who whistled, and handed the note to Whit, who scanned it, refolded it, and stashed it in his back pocket.

"Sold!"

"Sorry about the high ticket," Isabel said. "Cecil? Aren't you going to give our best customer a discount?"

Casey squinted into the window and quoted-parodied, "Never give a Whit an even break."

CHAPTER FORTY-SIX

The Tall Clock

Jan (with a "J") Jansen flashed a grin.

"And speaking of suckers." Casey introduced Jan before Whit could whisk him off to admire the tall clock.

"Isabel the All Seeing, we finally meet," Jan said. "I've heard so many nice things about you it's like we've already met." Whit pulled him away.

"Approve?" Casey asked Isabel.

"Yummy," she said. "And so charming. But I'll stick to women. I'm more familiar with the territory."

"He and Whit—" Casey winked. "Before I came into the picture. They outed each other in college, explored the 'territory' and then found other interests. In Whit's case, *moi*."

"And Jan?" Isabel prompted. "A man that cute can't be single more than ten minutes at a time."

"Jan met a nice *artiste* crawling home from the Marais—Pierrôt, of the French persuasion, roof-over-'O'." Casey described a circumflex accent with his hands. "They're still together, like Whit and me. Roof-Over-'O' has a commissioned piece to finish and couldn't join us this afternoon."

"They live in Atlanta?"

"Across the hall from our condo." Pierrôt naturalized."

"Casey," Jan said. "Pick out some quilts for my Aunt Inez. We'll use them temporarily to cushion Whit's new clock."

"Get plenty," Whit said. "Grandpa clock is no Lilliputian."

Wrapped up tighter than Nefertiti's bosom, the Worms-crafted clock defied being shoehorned into Jan's Jeep. Exasperated, Jan, Whit, and Casey wrestled it into the store.

"It refuses to go." Whit complained to Cecil, who suspended his nap to observe the struggle. "Too bulky."

"And heavy." Jan grumped. "Is this thing granite?"

"It's old." Isabel handed out paper towels for cleanup. "People get heavier with age, why shouldn't clocks?"

"Hnmph!" Jan said.

Isabel smiled. "Phil might let you borrow Ethel. He's going out with Cilla, but they'll take the hearse. Just call and I'll come let you in. Louise can always find me."

"Louise?" Jan puzzled.

Casey pointed out the dialless phone. "Ernestine and Louise are the town's phone system. More gossipy than Fox, more immediate than CNN, less credible than the bar floosies on Cheshire Bridge."

Whit thanked-but-no-thanked. "I'll just send professionals with a forklift."

"Wise decision," Isabel said.

Byes and hugs said and re-said, hugged and re-hugged to Isabel and His Purring Grayness, Whit and Casey dragged Jan away.

Casey started his car and gazed at the side mirror, past Jan's Jeep (two J's) into the sky. "Just as well your clock's staying here. Those clouds might not hold their water for an hour's drive."

Jan pulled up behind.

"Drive slow, please," Whit said, "so Jan can follow. He has zero sense of direction."

"'You take the only road out of town,'" Casey parroted, crept away from the curb.

"Jan could get lost in a one-car garage." Whit readied Vita's gate gizmo.

"Gorgeous, just gorgeous, the whole place," Jan said for the eightieth time. "But there has to be a reason this whole wall is blank."

Casey sat at the piano. "Look, no hands!"

Rachmaninoff's "Vocalise."

"Nice," Jan said. "A player?"

"Of sorts." Whit hedged. "I've been wondering if the blank plaster was put there to hide something."

"Hmmm." Jan felt the area with his palms.

On the piano a long-haired, white cat preened, curled into a melon-sized ball, licked his paw, and settled down to nap.

Whit scribbled in his notebook while Jan framed the blank wall with his digital camera. *Beep.* The flash startled Casey, but the purring fluffball took no notice.

"Ben can build new millwork in front and finish it with matching coves and crowns," Whit said.

"Acoustics?" Jan snapped his fingers, clapped. "Test. Test. Mmm, nice."

"Excellent in fact," Whit said, "although I can't imagine why. What did you say?"

"Nothing, Casey said," said Casey. "Nothing at all." The cat rubbed, squirmed, and responded in proper feline manner to Casey's attention.

Whit suggested a perspective view. "From here?"

Click.

Jan looked around at the piano. "Whose kitty?"

"Cats rule!" Casey quoted-parodied. "Let's just say he came with the house."

The cat swished his flocculent tail. "Know any Gershwin?" Casey asked. The piano obliged with "The Man I Love."

Casey petted the cat through the chorus. "Swing it." The piano cut to swing time, restated the theme and brought the song to a dramatic end with an arpeggiated major seventh.

Casey and Jan applauded.

Whit caught Casey's glance. "Bat out some Beethoven." The piano played Mussorgsky's "Pictures at an Exhibition."

"Is that thing voice activated?" Jan turned to observe.

"Not very well," Casey said. "Beethoven this is not."

The piano pounded out the first four notes of the Fifth Symphony, *forte fortissimo*, and started the Moonlight Sonata."

"How in the world?" Jan puzzled.

"You really don't want to know what's going on behind the curtain," Whit capped his pen. "We have what we need."

Jan walked over to the piano and petted the cat. He held out the camera. *Click.* "Thanks for the concert." He patted the piano and rubbed the cat. When he took his hand away, the cat changed to ceramic.

Jan idly reached out to pet the cat again, but recoiled. "What happened to your cat? He was here a second ago."

"You really don't want to know that either." Whit pulled Jan toward the front of the house.

"Trust Whit on this," Casey said. "Let me tell you about our phone system, a mud-filled pothole on the communications superhighway. Did you know we own it?"

Whit interrupted. "Let's offload your camera's pictures to my computer before you head back to the city."

"I'll email them. I know you have a dinner." Jan looked at the cat figurine, whose position had changed.

"Broadband hasn't been invented in Bryson." Casey grumped.

"And you guys are going to live here?"

"Soon," Casey said. "Maybe. Good riddance steel riveting at dawn-thirty every day. You and Pierrôt don't get as much of it 'cause you're across the hall. For us it's unbearable."

"But the barn you told me about? The dog? The ghosts?"

Whit hnmphed. "There's no such thing as ghosts." He clicked the mouse. "The camera's transferring now."

Jan's eyes widened as a picture scrolled onto the screen.

"Not again," Whit said. "What is it with these ghosts and cameras?" He grabbed Jan's arm to keep him from fleeing. "They're hams, but otherwise tame."

CHAPTER FORTY-SEVEN

Under Construction

Arriving at precisely seven o'clock, Whit and Casey found the gated entrance to Mrs. Plunk's property resurfaced, edged with new brick planters, and redolent of summer flowers and fresh mowed lawn. They found her mansion latticed with painters' scaffolding, the trees around her front porch in stable condition, recovering from drastic pruning. Scattered implements indicated progress on a sprinkler project worthy of Augusta National. Or *Les Tuileries*.

"Everything's a mess." Yvette apologized, greeted, hugged.

"It's been neglected for so long," Yvonne said, hugged. "We'll have to use the side entrance. The plasterers have the front rooms walled off with ladders."

Yvette led the way to a semicircular side porch. Its two-story columns gleamed white at their tops, but near the ground remained a begrimed gray, splotched with painters' putty.

"Mama's being amazingly patient. She bribed the Broads to take this evening off," Yvonne said. "Everything will be pretty much done when she and Tru get back."

"We talked her out of removing walls," Yvette said.

Yvonne added, "The steel beams didn't scare her, but logic somehow prevailed."

"Good," Whit said. "What she wanted was way out of character with the house."

"That was the logic that prevailed." Yvonne grinned.

"We left the big sitting room for last," Yvonne added. "It's still presentable enough for dinner."

Whit consoled. "We understand construction mess."

"Do we ever." Casey waved the snapshots. "I can't wait to show you! You won't believe it even after you see it, and we got some more at Vita just now that we didn't bring because we didn't have time to print them out and our friend Jan with a 'J' was in a big gay tizzy to get his cute buns out of there, but those are even more unbelievable and I can't wait to show them to you, too, because you will not believe them, and I wish we'd had time to make prints before we left."

Whit smiled. "Casey can't wait for Show And Tell."

Miss Trudy gathered plates, took away confitures, and presented a tray teetering with *petits chocolats.*

Casey protested *patisseries* weakly. "Oh I couldn't!" He plopped a fist-sized strawberry thickly coated with dark chocolate onto his plate. "No, really." He selected a *petit four* swirled with white chocolate, dollopped with raspberry jam.

Miss Trudy pointed to a *pain au chocolat.* "If sin were edible, *this* is the definitive recipe."

"Ahhh," Casey said as if discovering America. "*Chocolatine.* I love those." He heaped two of the them onto his dessert plate.

"*Pain au chocolat,*" Miss Trudy corrected. "*Chocolatine* is the South of France."

Casey took a bite, swooned with pleasure, palmed his fork and gave two thumbs up. He worried his *petit four* in half and popped both halves into his mouth. "MMM!"

"*Coq au vin* and now this," Yvonne said. "Miss Tru, you have truly outdone yourself."

"*Absolument,*" Mrs. Plunk said. "Casey, Whit, I have *un petit supris* for you. It's not as exciting as your photos of Sasha–thank you for understanding my tears. Yvonne, would you?"

"I'll go get it," Yvette said.

"Tru and I are off to pursue the wild *foie gras, quoi-quoi,* in hopes of restoring my sight. We'll be back for the Fourth of July celebration, and I hope you'll join us."

"I haven't talked Casey into it yet."

Mrs. Plunk raised a hand. "It's a tradition that I and my friends started after the war, a benefit for local charities. This time it's for a new firetruck. For the first time in a lot of years I've felt like participating."

"Mama's friend Amos oversees the food," Yvette broke in. "He ran a great barbecue house in town until he retired."

"There's a fiddling contest, too," Yvonne said.

Mrs. Plunk tsk'd. "It's more fiddling than contest. My friend Ellen always wins. Nobody can touch her gospels. But maybe you boys don't like barbecue. Or bluegrass?"

Casey rubbed his middle. "It's hard to think roast pig in the presence of *pain au chocolat.* If food were sex, *here* is the orgasm!" He returned Miss Trudy's grin. "I'm more Zydeco than bluegrass, but I'm convinced. Should we bring a nice Merlot?"

Yvette apologized. "No, it's a G-rated event."

"Churchy types," Yvonne explained. "Besides, keeping alcohol unwelcome has always excluded certain undesirables."

"No problem," Whit said. "Wagons ho!"

"Goody," said Mrs. Plunk.

Yvette handed her a decorated, leather-bound quarto.

"Thank you." Mrs. Plunk cradled the volume. "I've been so reclusive, so unsocial, inhospitable." She touched Casey's prints. "Oh, how I wish I could see these. But it's easy for me to imagine Sasha, Brett. And you boys in these photos and at Vita, which they loved. Tonio's *fermata*. Their respite from fame, politics and fighting families."

Mrs. Plunk placed her palms on the volume in her lap. "This was Paul's. During the barn fire Tonio and Paul were seen trying to save their horses, and running after Roberts, who was chasing Bret with a buggy whip. Phil pulled Brett and Dmitri out of the burning gate house. What happened to any of them after that, no one knows.

"I waited for Dmitri to come home. At daybreak I telephoned, and when no one answered I checked the cars, the smoldering ruins, the café. Phil wasn't back from the emergency room yet. I even got up the courage to call Roberts' house. He hung up on me. When still no word by the middle of the day, I went over to Vita, fearing what I hoped I would not find.

"I stole through the tunnel, so as not to tangle with the deputies that were investigating the fire. I thought I'd find Dmitri, maybe the others, in the tunnel or in the house. Hiding, sleeping. Or dead. I checked crannies that only I and they knew." She touched her cheek with her napkin. "Next day came a depressing downpour that washed out the roads. I sent my gardener out in the Dusie to search. He didn't get two miles before getting stuck in the mud. Phil pulled the car in, and went out searching in his wrecker. In a few days, when the sheriff couldn't leave a deputy any longer, I locked the gate."

Mrs. Plunk swayed back and forth slightly, cradling the volume in her arms. "I reported them missing and kept checking Vita. The last time I went I found this book on the dining room table, and I knew they were not coming back. This is Paul's journal. He kept it as long as I knew him, many volumes over the years, and often showed it off as he added to it. This one has photos from his ballets, programs from Tonio's piano recitals. Sketches, cartoons. There are photos of the two of them with Dmitri at the Opera House, and some of Bret brushing the horses. Skiing, sailing, Paris, Lucerne, Amsterdam. Athens. Clowning around at Vita."

She turned pages. "I can't see these now, but I remember this one from its fold. Paul teased me unmercifully because I creased it accidentally. It's Dmitri at the piano with

Bret, Tonio and Paul. And here--" she turned the book around. "Tonio with Paul at their crazy dining room table."

"Mmm," Casey said. "Two chairs."

"There's a dozen more chairs somewhere in the basement. The day of the fire, Paul added this picture."

"It's exactly like Casey's photos," Miss Trudy said.

"I figured so," Mrs. Plunk said. "I've got the caption memorized: 'Dmitri's toy. Alas, someday Bret will grow up, but Dmitri insists not.' I got this out to give it to you, and to let go of it. This book was all I had of good-bye, and all I could stand for memory." She passed it to Casey.

"We'll take care of it," he assured.

"Don't," Mrs. Plunk said, urgent. "I want you to put it in the fireplace at Vita and burn it."

CHAPTER FORTY-EIGHT

Out and About

"It's been an exciting week in Lake Woenotgone,'" Whit quoted-parodied. He queued the Fiat at a battered traffic light for I-75 northbound. "Vintage Volvo, three trucks, and Oldsmograannywagon. Then us."

"To think I almost opted out of that Fourth of July Fiddlin' Contest Pig Pickin' Hoedown Parade and Coming Out Party."

"Three trucks, then Granny. Old Amos gets the Big Pink Bloomers trophy for nerve. "

"'Fellers.'" Casey wheezed in passable Amosspeak, "'I been a-thinkin' f'a while, an' fer what time I got left, y'all call me Amanda.' In front of everybody. Then off he sails like he's on a cloud before anybody can say a word and reappears picking banjo in high drag for the gospel sing-a-long."

"One pickup, then grannymobile. Amanda's outfit was worthy of the Peonies' Garden Geriatric Girls Charity Review." Casey described the party gown with his hands. "A lovely lilac figure-enhancing off-the-shoulder strapless affair of elegant chiffon." He fluffed imaginary sleeves. "Accenting a bounteous bogus bust replete with razor burn. I'll speak with her on the down-low about depilatories."

The unrelenting traffic nearly squashed a slow-moving truck.

"Yikes!" Casey covered his eyes. "That took courage."

"That took insanity."

"I meant Amos-Amanda," Casey said. "Luckily, I was spared a coming out drama. *Mom* told *me!*"

"Hnmph! I tried, remember? We sat Dad down after dinner, but every time I edged toward the subject he left his glasses in the study, had to go pee, went to get the *Journal* from the den, wanted more sherry, needed something for digestion."

"Deniable plausibility–didn't want to know what he couldn't admit to already knowing," Casey said. "Glad you let him off."

"Denial indeed. He knows. Or he can ask my mom or one of my stepmoms and they'll be glad to enlighten him." Whit glowered. "Oldsmogranny's a big chicken."

"In this traffic, she'll be barbecue chicken if she's not careful. What's that sound? Is this dune buggy whining for another bifurcated trifurballator already?"

Whit zoomed onto the highway, listened, smirked, shifted, merged, accelerated, shifted. "That's your surprise. Glove box."

"You bought me a music box? This thing is locked."

Whit patted his pants pocket. "Nope. Something else. Key's in here."

"Keepers finders." Casey attacked. The key bounced under Whit's seat. "Oops." He entwined an arm through Whit's legs to feel under the seat. "Does this not-a-music-box relate to your grampa clock with a mind of its own and an iron will to match?"

Whit hnmphed. "Quiet Weeksville can neither forget nor ever live down those ghosty photos of *Papaclock* letting us know where he wants to be, and next to what piano."

After refusing to go with Jan to Atlanta, the clock made itself visible in a photo Jan took at Vita.

"Poor Jan with a 'J' was beside himself to get out of there."

Whit pointed to the glove compartment. "Look while you hear the music. If it stops, wait till it starts or you'll ruin the surprise."

"Surprise! Phil's big announcement at the barbecue?"

"Running off to get hitched? The biggest surprise was that the grapevine never knew," Whit said.

Casey mimicked. "'Weren't no time fer lollygaggin' aroun' a-stuffin' cake in our pieholes. I had tractors to overhaul.'"

"Oil to change, baseball games to attend, caps to buy," Whit said. "They make a happy couple. Still, I always thought she was a faithful follower of Lady Lesbos."

"Surprise! She's a practicing hetero. Getting plenty of practice, from all accounts." Casey sat up, dangled the key. "No thanks to your lane-changing, Mister Lane Changer."

"The music stopped, so hang on."

"You want me to sit here holding the key to Pandora's glove box and not look at what's making with the diatonics?"

"Worth it, I promise." Whit said quickly, "Surprise, Erica's new toy: guest of dishonor at the Fourth of July festival, Bob Roberts."

"Think anyone knew the leash Erica dragged him in with was tied to his jewels?" Casey jangled the keys.

"Not yet," Whit said. "They know if they frequent the right bars or surf the Internet for five seconds."

"Ed-the-human-worm Beasley knew. The look on his face!"

"So, while Plunk's in Yankeedom planning to foreclose Roberts' property, he strolls in where he isn't welcome with wads of cash for the donation jar. Amends?"

"You know Erica and her steps." Casey put a hand toward the glove box.

"Wait for the music."

Casey smoothed his clothes. "Who bought Roberts' property for cash in the nick of time before Plunk's lawyers descended?"

"Us," Whit said.

"Say whahhht?"

"Our LLc bought it–Erica's suggestion. The impending foreclosure made it bargain basement. Stellar needs space for their equipment. We'll lease it to them for a profit. Plunk approves. I phoned her at the hospital. Her eye operation was mildly successful."

Casey threatened the glove box with the key.

"Wait, wait. Music first, then look."

"She collected Dmitri's insurance. Like she needed an extra million?" Casey put on his best Plunk impression. "'Principle, dears. And I do not believe the pure tee gossip that uppity detective dug up. Soviet spy, indeed. Not my Dmitri!'"

"Guilty or not, the Romanians executed him. And deported Brett. There's the ditty. Open the sesame."

"Goody. Whit, there's nothing here but my cell pho–-"

"And?"

"Wowww, my celll phooone."

"And?"

"Rachmaninoff. Does this meannn?"

"This means it's ringgg-inggg. Answer it."

Casey put the phone lovingly to his ear. "Hello, I think. I can hear you fine. Three bars out here. I'll tell him. *Ciao*. Erica says the system has been functional since breakfast."

"Surprise!" Whit took the exit ramp toward Bryson.

"Sad. Impersonal beeps, intrusive technology from which it's not possible to hide. It's like being propelled into the future without asking to go."

"So turn the phone off."

"Ummm, someone might text me." Casey pocketed the device.

At the Bryson Café, Whit sat with Casey by the window. Gertie high-fived from the kitchen. Perched on swivel stools at the counter, several customers waited for their food while they chatted on their cellphones. With each other.

Attired in a ruffled teal creation from Barbara Dwyer/Sky City Designs for every day wear, the office, or that special party occasion, and accessorized by an extra-wide patent leather belt in basic black with a gold-filled buckle, Amanda née Amos clutched a mint green smartphone to her ear, careful not to disturb her earrings. Fresh pierced. "You git any calls from outside of Bryson yet?"

"Not yet, Amanda. Have you?" Two seats away, Reb spoke into his chrome phone.

"Nope. I dialed all over Atlanta tryin' t'find more shoes big enough–" Amanda wore the sequin pumps she debuted at the Fourth of July barbecue. "None of 'em called me back yet." She sipped her tea like a junior leaguer. "Call waitin's goin' off. This's Jimmy," she said. "I'll ask 'im if he's talked to his family in Warner Robbins. Bye."

Jimmy's call came from across the aisle, five feet away.

Gertie waved a smartphone as red as her hair. "What's't y'want, Mama?"

From the kitchen, Mrs. Mendels spoke into her basic black cellphone. "Gertie, y'got t'git this food on the table."

"Shore 'nuff, Mama. I got 'nother call, but I'll catch the counter while I–Hello? Hey, Reb. Jes' text Mama's number with whatcha want on y'to-go order."

"Shore," Reb said. "Phil an' Cilla's a-plantin' flower beds around 'is house, an' he wants me t'bring 'em two oyster dinners."

"July ain't got no 'R'," Gertie chided. She delivered plates of food, squeezing the phone to her ear with her shoulder. "Text Mama 'bout th'oysters. I'll fix y'tea 'fore y'leave so th'ice won't melt." She dropped off Amanda's fried chicken. "Hon," she whispered, "y'need t'learn 'bout cheek rouge. Come by t'night an' me an' Izz'll show you how t'do it."

Amanda nodded thanks and resumed her cell conversations. Plural.

Gertie looked up, brightened. "Here's m'two favorite fee-ahn-says come t'cheer me up." She tap-tapped Casey on the shoulder with her phone. "I'll be right back'n'git y'all set up. How 'bout writin' y'cell number on the back of m'order pad with ever'body else's, so's I can punch it into m'phone."

"Gertie!" Mrs. Mendels yelled, ominous. "We got t'talk."

"I'll dial y'up in a minit. I'm a-talkin' t'Izz right now."

"That's just what I mean. We got t'talk, an' I mean *talk*!"

"Gimme a sec and dial m'number."

"We got girl talk t'talk, girl," Mrs. Mendels warned, loud, "an' I don't mean on no cellphone. You hear?"

"What on earth? Mama?"

CHAPTER FORTY-NINE

Can You Hear Me Meow?

His Regal Greyness graciously permitted Casey to bestow a thorough ear rub. "Everyone has phones glued to their heads," Casey said.

Isabel smirked, held up her powder blue model. "Whit's moving crew called a minute ago. 'Two Hunks and a Big Pink Truck?' They got lost, but should be here about now."

"They're coming for Whit's humongous clock after they unload a phone gizmo at the hardware."

"And meanwhile?" Isabel primped, jingled, stashed her phone on her desk. "I sense you need to talk."

Casey curled catlike on a Victorian cushion of red tasseled velvet. "The truck hunks are bringing our bags and baggage."

"And you have questions? Concerns? Issues?"

"Yep, yep, and yep."

"Casey, if I thought there was the slightest danger–"

Casey shrugged. "The scary stuff has calmed down. The barn quit disappearing." Shrug. "Whit even trusts it enough to store the world's largest supply of garden hose in case of fire." Shrug again. "The piano still plays, and the glass cat squirms and purrs when touched. It's entertaining, now, instead of scary."

"Those special effects are probably permanent."

"Whit finds it charming. He pets the cat figurine constantly. Gets him purring– meaning the cat. Whit, too, really. He's become chummy with the spirits, even conducting a tour of Jan's plans for the home theater system."

"Cool."

Casey fidgeted. "We've been coming over in the afternoons bringing stuff, getting things arranged." Casey held eye contact. "Yesterday, I caught them red handed. The ghosts? They were, well Paul was. Are you going to make me blurt this out or can you just read my mind?"

Isabel stared into Casey's blue gaze, gasped. "Ghost Paul had sex with Whit?"

"You're amazing. That's exactly it. But not actually 'had' sex, fortunately–otherwise I would already be on *Court TV* for pre-meditated ghosticide. What happened was, I caught Ghost-of-Paul *trying* to make out with partner-of-Casey."

"Ghosticide?" Isabel laughed. "But go on."

"There are open relationships, and there are Whit and Casey. We're long term. If I caught those ghosts, why, I'd, I'd–"

"Ghosticide."

"Do you suppose the pre-ghostified Tonio and Paul slept around? Surely they know what each other is up to–now, in the spirit world–and who they're up to it with."

Isabel pondered, nodded. "Maybe."

"I was outside sunning. Nude. Face down. Almost napping. And I felt a hand on my, my–"

"Thigh?"

"Farther north, but that will do for discussion. I thought it was Whit, because who else would have their palm on my... thigh? So I went 'Mmm' like I always do."

Cecil sat up.

"I thought he was trying to lie down on top of me. I felt the weight, but no touch. I twisted around and glimpsed–someone, a fleeting reflection in my sunglasses on the table." Casey shuddered. "A proverbially dark and handsome man. Nude! He looked like the photos of Tonio. Just a glance and he was gone. Fortunately."

"Wow." Isabel leaned forward.

"Tonio appears in mirrors, so he isn't a vampire?"

"Works in the movies."

"That's a relief. Anyway, the weight I was feeling disappeared instantly. I jumped up, and no one was there. A minute later I felt a hand on my... *thigh* again." Casey took a deep breath. "Well, I let him have it. For *real*."

Isabel stifled a laugh.

"That impudent ghost got a first-class piece of my mind. I told him my–thigh–is totally off limits, along with everything connected to it and everything even close to it, north or south of it, and *never not ever* even think about touching my anything or my anything else, anywhere, any time, any way. I threatened to scratch their ghost eyes out if either one of them so much as breathed hard in my direction."

"Good for you. I think."

"But then I thought: Where was Whit?"

Cecil swished his tail, blinked.

"In the library with the computer, that's where Whit was. And I thought, while naked Tonioghost is getting fresh with me outside, *where* is Paulghost? Sooo! I ran and peeked in. And what did my wondering eyes behold? Whit! He had his clothes off and his eyes closed like he was being *smooched*." Casey made with the eyebrows, scrunched his mouth. "Which he was. I couldn't see anyone with him, but he obviously thought he was not alone. And he *wasn't*!"

"I get the picture," Isabel said.

"Not the whole *porno* picture, fortunately. Or, you know." Casey sharpened his index finger and drew it across his throat. "G*hosticide*."

Isabel nodded.

"So I stormed in, *ghostus interruptus,* in the nick of time before anything I would not want to mention could happen."

"Whew?"

"Whew! Ghost of Paul transparentized himself on his way out. I stepped in and, um, finished what *ghostus* had been trying to *startus* before *interruptus*. Cuddle-cuddle. Whit stuck his cute nose back into his computer. As I passed the new bathroom in the hallway, there stood Paulghost." Casey paused. "Naked!"

Isabel set her bracelets aflutter.

"Quite the specimen, very much up to all accounts."

"What happened?"

"I gave it to him, too. Both barrels. I told him the same thing I told Tonio: Whit's off limits, I'm off limits, limits are off limits. No hanky, no panky, no touchy no feelie, no fooling. And *no* fooling around. Ever! My rules, my way, or I'll tear their ghost heads off by the roots and bowl them down the road to oblivion." Casey mimed the threat.

"Good for you."

"Ghost vaporized, and I got in the shower, but the wetter I got, the more I thought about Whit being almost seduced, the madder I got. I stormed to the piano, dripping, and kicked it."

"Barefoot?"

Casey nodded, winced. "It didn't do any good. So I beat it. And cussed it proper. I noticed the ghost-of-Paul cat was in a different position from when I kicked the piano, so I threw him at the window. The window didn't break, and porcelain pianopuss morphed himself back into a furry feline, scampered across the rug, hopped onto the piano, and turned himself back into glass."

"So now you're having second thoughts about moving in?"

"Definitely."

Isabel's desk phone rang. "Someone's using the old system?" She passed it to Casey without answering it.

"Hello? Thanks, Ernestine." Casey parked the handset on his shoulder. "The movers are taking the phone contraption up the stairs now. Ernestine's bringing Whit to the phone."

"I think you've already done what needed to be done, but Cecil and I could try and contact the spirits for you."

"I contacted them pretty good." Casey socked his palm. "But we would appreciate anything you can do. And thanks for the sounding board." Casey listened at the phone. "Heyyy... Okay, tinker with your new toy, Whit. I'll go handle the movers and your clock. The truck is pulling up outside, now."

Whit nodded to His Royal Greyness, who replied with a yawn. "Isabel, did the guys get the clock on the truck okay?"

"You mean the Bench Press Duo? They hardly worked up a sweat." Isabel smirked, jingled. "Oh, and Casey said to please bring him a shake from the café. The dust cloud outside is from him leaving to lead the truck hunks to Vita." Isabel put her paperwork down. "Something on your mind, Whit?"

"Yes. Do you want to read it, or should I spill?"

"Talking helps sometimes."

"It's the spirits." Whit sighed. "I caught one of them trying to, to, to neck with me."

"Wow."

"I finished planning the new theater system and had the drawings ready to go to the courier, when I noticed one of the dimensions was different. So I checked my notes, and found I had copied it wrong. No way it would have fit. I looked at the screen, and some other things changed–while I watched."

"Geek ghosts?"

"Exactly. I'm glad they caught that error. That part's fine. What's not fine is that in the middle of all this, one of the spirits tried to, to, to make out."

"No!"

"I felt hands massaging the back of my neck. I thought it was Casey, but I should have known, because he never interrupts when I'm working, and he was outside napping and tanning." Whit cleared his throat. "Well, not-Casey-but-I-thought-it-was soothed me out of my clothes and into–"

"Necking?"

"For purposes of discussion, yes. The–necking–wasn't quite the way Casey always does. So I opened my eyes, and in the reflection from my computer screen I caught a glimpse of Paul."

"You saw the ghost?"

"Plainly, and nude. Only a brief moment, but it was definitely Paul. Fortunately, Casey came in just then and took over, where–" Whit shivered. "Where Paulghost left off."

"Hmmm," Isabel smiled.

"I was so happy Casey cut in. I see you already know where I'm going with this. Mindreader. Anyway, we cuddled awhile and then Casey went out and I heard him yelling in the hall, laying a totally regal cussing on Paulghost. He chased Paul out to the piano and threw a major temper tantrum." Whit took a long breath. "Casey told me that Tonio had just tried the same thing with him, which is why he came to look in on me and caught–you know." Whit sighed. "Casey and I are permanent, and I'm not willing to share me or him with anybody, much less ghosts from the sordid past, or the present, or future, or any other dimension, any planet, or any clock shop."

"And you have second thoughts about moving in?"

"Definitely!"

CHAPTER FIFTY

The Recalcitrant Clock

Isabel leaned forward in her squeaky wooden desk chair and popped her cellphone open, as though confident it would soon ring. "Oops." She snapped it shut, smiled up at Whit, and reached for her ancient deskbound phone just as it rang. Without answering she handed the receiver to Whit.

His Feline Highness enthroned himself in the store's cluttered front window, an admirably napworthy spot on sunny summer afternoons.

"That was Casey," Whit said. "The German clock acted like it was bolted down just now. The mover hunks couldn't unload it from their truck. Mere gravity isn't to blame. Any ideas?"

Isabel primped, her bracelets a-jingle. "The spirits know they can make their wishes known through me." She held eye contact. "Your clock has an inhabitant, Whit, though I don't know if it was inhabited when I got it."

"'Occupied'? Like airplane loos when you need one?"

"Something like that." Isabel laughed.

"You read the future like Yoda reads the Force, Izz, so I believe you, illogical as that sounds."

"Sometimes the future isn't decided until *after* you try and read it." Isabel smiled, her eyes alight. "And sometimes I'd rather not know the future until it has mercifully passed."

"*Touché.* So, challenge your Tarot *cartes des visites*, rub some Kirlian Kryptonite onto your obsidian crystals, and please help me divine what's up with my fugitive from Sotheby's auction block. It's sooo fine. Taller than any of my grandfathers with their hats on, and a decorated pendulum bob the crowned heads of Europe would dump the Holy Grail for. I'm happy to have it, but it refuses to go home with me. Twice!"

Isabel put her fingers to her temples and closed her eyes. "Hmmm. It sure didn't want to go to your Atlanta condo."

"Its 'inhabitant,' did he-she-it think it was headed to a boring museum? My clock collection isn't in a museum, although it's way worthy. I've been diligent, and lucky, and thorough."

"Hmmm. Museum wasn't the issue," Isabel said, her eyes tightly closed, hands aloft.

Cecil looked up, blinked, winked, and adjusted his position.

"Hmmm." Isabel tilted her head ceilingward, touching her fingertips to her temples, her bracelets jingling. "The inhabitant is connected with your ghostly counterparts." Isabel opened her eyes. "I should have suspected before. I'm seeing a pattern. It showed itself in those ghostly pictures your friend Jan shot. And today, it let the hunks load it into their van–"

Two Hunks and a Big Pink Truck Moving Company, read the side of the huge–yes, pink–moving van. *We Put Motion in Your Ocean.*

Whit snapped his fingers. "It went willingly."

"Hmmmm, it *loved* being manhandled into the pink truck." Isabel grinned. "Spirits communicate best when happy. Hmmm. The clock wanted to be moved, but not to Vita."

"Then where?" Whit glanced at Cecil, who twitched a whisker.

"Hmmm. We know that already." Isabel put her palms on the desk. "The hunks brought the rest of your stuff from Atlanta, right? Moving day."

"If we don't chicken out." Whit stroked His Feline Highness.

"Vita was the right direction. Do you have the photos Jan took?" Isabel applied hand cream, setting her bracelets jingling like an angry windchime.

"The ones with *wunderclock* next to the piano are on my computer."

"Hmmm. Mrs. Plunk has pianos, and she lives just past Vita. Whit, your clock wants to go to Mrs. Plunk's."

"I'll tell Casey." Whit seized the phone. "Ernestine, hook me up to Casey's cell number, please." Whit parked the receiver on his shoulder. "Bryson's number-please phones can now call the new cellular system." He whispered, "and the operators don't get to eavesdrop." And sang, "'All things just keep getting better.'"

"Hey, Sweetie," Whit said to Casey, on the phone. "I'm calling on Isabel's land line left over from the Paleolithic, and you're answering on your Twenty-First Century Freeway Driving Hindrance and Tourist Infuriator."

Isabel answered her cell. "What's wrong, Gertie?" Her voice wavered. "Quit crying a sec and tell me what happened, Honey."

"It's working great." Whit bragged. "Hold on a sec. Izz? Is everything all right?" He spoke into the phone. "Izz is talking to Gertie on their cells."

"She didn't!" Isabel slumped in her chair.

"Is my clock still glued to the pink truck's tailgate?"

"She said what?" Isabel sat back with a thump and gripped the edge of the desk.

Cecil sat upright and blinked.

"Izz? Are you okay? You look like you just saw a ghost. Casey? Not even Wally could budge it? Atlas' understudy?"

"Gertie, it'll be all right," Isabel said into the phone. "I sensed something major brewing, but didn't want to face knowing what it was. Don't worry, Honey. Hold on a sec." Isabel caught Whit's concerned glances. "Gertie's mama found out about Gertie and me." She spoke into her cell. "Don't think about that right now, Honey." Looked up at Whit. "Her mama caught us sneaking a kiss on the firetruck during the Fourth of July festival," Isabel said. "One little smooch. Gertie? How did she even see?"

"Ewww. She has that industrial strength religion."

Isabel sighed. "They both do. Me and Gertie worked through it years ago between us, but her mama, well–"

Whit pointed to the phone in his hand. "Pale news by comparison, but Casey figured out my clock was trying to hitch a ride to Plunk's. Not even–" Whit struck a bodybuilder pose. "–Wally of the continent-sized biceps could budge it from the truck, so Casey remembered Vita's piano is a concert grand–Izz? Is everything all right? With Gertie?"

Isabel shrugged, worried. "I'm not sure." She spoke into the phone. "Cry, Honey," she consoled. "Cry if you think it'll help, even if you know it won't." She spoke to Whit. "All these years we were so careful keeping our big secret. From Gertie's Mom, and particularly from the town gossips. This cellphone's the first time we've been able to have a private phone conversation."

"Stellar Cellular aims to please."

Isabel slumped on her elbows on her desk. Her bracelets fell silent. "Now that we can coo in each other's ear privately, we're busted." She listened at her phone. "Cry, Honey. Let it all out." She gave a long sigh. "I had no idea Ellen Mendels was anywhere around. The dormers on Bryson Tourist. She climbed up there to snap photos with her old Argus like she always does, and–and she took our picture. Kissing." Isabel sighed. "Really, it's a relief, to finally come out of the Bryson Bed and Breakfast walk-in closet."

"I'll go see what I can do," Whit said. "I'm good with family outings. With six stepmothers and counting, I've had lots of practice–every time one of their sons or daughters breaks the news. I think I have a couple of Lesbigayfam Atlanta support group brochures in the Fiat. Besides, I need to pick up milkshakes for Casey and the truck hunks."

"Thanks, Whit," Isabel said. "Gertie, you're not going to bear this by yourself. I'm coming over, and Whit too. We'll face this together, and we'll get through it. I promise."

CHAPTER FIFTY-ONE

Pride in Prejudice

Whit leaned against Vita's barn and flirted like a street hustler. "Heyyy, Cutie, what up?"

"Dish!" Casey slupped chocolate delectable through twin straws and brandished his metallic blue smartphone. "Don't make me call Dial-A-Gossip."

"Okay." Whit snapped to attention, mimed a drum major's pose and marked time. He whipped his engineer's pen from his pocket protector and used it as a baton to strike up an imaginary band, making kazoo-like sounds for a Sousa-esque intro. "Isabel and I marched on the Bryson Café. Bxxt-bx-bx-bxxx-bxxx. Like Pride, but just us. We rainbowed our way straight-I-mean-gaily-forward up the middle of Main-as-in-only Street. If there had been any traffic we would have stopped it. If the burg had a traffic light we would have run it. If it had a city council we would have awed them into turning Town Hall, if it had one, into a shrine for the Village People."

Casey stage-sighed. "Our very own Pride at our soon-to-be country home-sweet-ghost-infested-home. Was there no press? Did *Out* send a photographer? Was he cute?"

"Just me and Izz, marching through Georgia one city block on our way to the café. Bxx-bx-bx-bxxt bx-bxxx. Considering Mrs. Mendels' religious fixation, I expected to have to go into Pastor Fuzz mode and argue theology for an hour," Whit said. "The other chocolate shake is yours, too—no way the whole thing would fit in one go-cup. Gertie met us, crying, at the door, but before I even got started, her mama one-upped me."

"She what?"

Whit shrugged. "*She* lectured *Gertie*. I was proud of her, even though I couldn't get a syllogism in edgewise."

"What about her notorious churchiness?"

"Just as Isabel and I got there, Mrs. Mendels was telling Gertie–her words: 'Girl, God don't mind, and I don't either.'" Whit thumped an imaginary pulpit. "She was well read on her Merrick. In between her exegetical studies."

"Unbelievable," Casey said.

"I should have taken notes. Mrs. Mendels handed in her theology homework on time, I'll say. Get her an organist and a circus tent and she could–well, you'd have to elide whole sentences into a string of syllables and apostrophes to get the full effect. It was awesome."

"Ayyy-MEN!" Casey said. "Are they looking to practice up on their exorcisms?"

"Exorcism is for demons," Whit corrected. "Our beautiful new country home has paranormal spirits."

"Rossini the cat?"

"Spirit," Whit said. "Sweet little pussycat wouldn't harm a ghost mouse." Rossini materialized behind them, unseen, and seated himself to eavesdrop.

"Then how about the non-existent barn we're leaning on?"

Whit dismissed it with a wave of his arm. "Spirits. According to Isabel, they are the racehorses that incinerated in it when our pre-incarnations disappeared. Its antics stopped weeks ago after you read its beads."

"The little wet dog?"

"Spirit," Whit said. "You did notice he's stopped getting run over every afternoon?"

"The rug still lops over in the living room. The piano still plays with itself, and we won't even mention that episode where our ghostselves tried to have peoplesex with us."

Whit grimaced. "They're sorry for that. You said so yourself, Mister In-Tune-With-The-Cosmos Cuss-Out-The-Spirits Throw-Ghostcat-Into-Window."

Rossini hopped through a hole in the space-time discontinuum.

"Anyway, Mrs. Mendels and Gertie propped on the front counter–" Whit demonstrated "–while Isabel slumped over the table in the window. Izz and Gertie cried and Mrs. Mendels tried to comfort her daughter and daughter-in-closet-in-law. Gertie's mom showed off the pictures from the Tourist's dormer window."

"You and me kissing and hugging?"

"Yep, plus Phil smooching his heterosqueeze Cilla, plus Isabel and Gertie making with the liplock on the firetruck when they thought no one could see."

Casey vacuumed the last of his shake. "I'm sorry I was hassling with your stubborn clock and couldn't help hug them through their outing crisis."

"I thank you, and my clock thanks you."

"All is well in Gertieland. Should have known from the way Gertie's mama sailed through the Amos-Amanda episode."

"Amanda walked in on the story right at the end. She found ladies' shoes large enough from that place in Charlotte you sent her to, and Gertie has taught her how to apply makeup better. The town is being admirably supportive. I wouldn't say Amos–I mean, Amanda–looks *good* as a seventy-year-old-woman now, but at least she doesn't look like a clown in prune drag. Gertie said that since she and Isabel are now outed, Amanda could be her bridesmaid if Isabel wants a girl-girl wedding."

"Awwwwww."

"Anyway, Amanda's fine, Gertie's fine, Mrs. Mendels is fine, Isabel's beside herself with fine, and we all hugged and ate pie and had a big gay cry."

CHAPTER FIFTY-TWO

Big Hand on the Twelve

Casey kicked off his Key West Sandals, landing them against the barn. "Ruby slippers, clap-clap, Mom with newly outed Lesbodaughter holds court with Extended Gender-misaligned Family. My excellent boyfriend takes notes. Everyone makes with the hankies. Fade to lavender, scroll titles. Color by Technicolor. Fabulous West Hollywood ending."

"We'll drop by so you can catch up."

"Meanwhile." Casey removed his shirt and hung it on a shutter hinge. "Your clocks are here, except for your most recent fugitive from the Smithsonian's clutches."

"Thank you."

"*And* your boyfriend."

"That hottie is here, too?" Whit shaded his eyes with his hand and pretended to look around. "Well, so you are. And nude. I feel complete. Big Gay Sigh. Except for my previously mentioned great-speckled great-great-grandfather clock? What's up with Herr Clock?"

"I had the pink truck hunks take him to Plunk's, where he permitted himself to be manhandled inside. Light like feathers, Wally claimed."

"To Wally, pianos are weightless trifles."

"True. Anyway, your clock is ensconced in Plunk's parlor. I smelled something baking. Maybe we can hit Miss Trudy up for a treat while you ogle your clockle."

"Meaning not drive home yet?"

"Uh, Whit? Your clocks-minus-one are here. Your clothes, your boyfriend. Your hat if you had one. Where, I hesitate to ask, would we 'drive home' to?"

"Oops, I forgot. We *are* home. Here, queer and all that."

Casey's eyes blazed vivid blue. "Got it! Do you want to see where I put the rest of your clocks?"

"Sure, but aren't you nude for a reason, Mister Bighand-on-the-Twelve?"

Casey grinned. "Grapes before clocks?"

"Way tempting, but we have our inaugural agenda."

"Okay, clocks, then agendas, then grapes."

Whit pointed. "Rear entrance!"

Casey cartwheeled across the lawn to the back door.

"Nice not to hear breaking glass anymore," Whit commented. "Wonder what calmed that down."

"Frankly my deahhh–"

"Point taken." Whit stopped at the porch. "Bighand on the ten-thirty."

In the kitchen, Casey pointed out a baker's dozen clocks, grouped according to type or era, on shelves and counters. Others leaned against the walls at the wide baseboards. "We can hang these wall clocks later."

"Good thinking. I'll have Stan pull outlets next week. Big sloppy kiss for your superlative interior design."

In the butler's pantry, more clocks mingled with the Lenox and Doulton. Casey collected a kiss. "Wait till you see the dining room. Your xillion mantel clocks–" He stopped at the door.

"Yes, Mister Bighand-on-the-nine?"

"Uhhh." Casey stared.

Whit followed his gaze to the piano. "Ohhh." He whipped out his cellphone. "Mrs. Plunk's land line, please, Ernestine." That took many seconds. "This is Whit. Is this Yvonne? Yvette, would you please take a look at the clock Casey brought over. ...Oh, just wondering if– ...You're serious. Is that Yvonne playing the piano? ...And it never did that before?"

"Look at all the clocks," Casey said. "Big clocks, little clocks, electric clocks." Casey waved his arm to take in the whole place. "Wind-up clocks. Mantel clocks, stand up clocks, cat clocks, puppy clocks, liquor bottle clocks and table clocks. French clocks, Swiss clocks, Brit and German clocks. And now, the stubborn clock that latched onto gravity's coattail and would not let go. The clock that insisted on bumming a ride next door. Weighs more than two hippos and a blue whale, has reappeared here. Poof!"

Whit stormed over to the clock, frowned, rapped it sharply. "Solid." He fitted the case key into its beveled glass door, opened it as if to reset its weights, and turned to Casey.

"Yvette said the clock is sitting right where you put it, and their piano is playing with itself–Rachmaninoff. When the music started they caught glances of Dmitri–Dmitri's ghost–tangoing with their mom who is still a thousand miles away."

"I so don't care."

"I figured. Our clone-of-clock has to be Brett. Hmmm, this one also has a panel on the back." He felt inside the compartment. "Empty."

"Are there two clocks or one?"

"Two, formerly one. And this clock is Brett." Whit cleared his throat. "Tonio, Paul, Brett: May I present my Very Significant Other, the sweet and beautiful Mister Nudist himself, Casey Bighand-At-Eight DePaul, the love of my life. Casey, meet Tonio and Paul Ghost and their friend Brett Ghost." Whit gestured broadly. "Dmitri went home to his fam."

"Plunk's husband's boytoy is a clock."

"Awesome clock, you have to admit," Whit pocketed the clock's key. "The good news is, this is the end of the news. Cue the theme song, scatter the purple pixie dust, scroll credits, and we all live gaily ever after."

"Pass the Jordan Almonds. Let's not stay for the double feature." Casey held out his hands. "You're in tune with the paranormal now? Rollerblading around the cosmic plane?"

"Let's go see Yvette and Yvonne. I've got a strong hunch about their clock's secret compartment."

"Then grapes?"

"Grapes, agenda, dinner, grapes, snacks, grapes-grapes-grapes."

"Wine!"

CHAPTER FIFTY-THREE

Happily After Ever

Comfortably low in the freshly planted trees that lined the grand new brick-paved boulevard, a mockingbird choir chirped in five-part harmony a euphonic welcome to their new hosts. Whit slow-coasted his red convertible as though oozing along a Pride parade. He braked to a ceremonious stop in front of the ironwork flourishes at Vita Sempre's wide entrance, and with a quick click of a blue keychain button commanded the gates to open. Whit nudged Casey and orated, accompanying his speech with theatrical swoops of his arms sidewise, rearward, and over the car's windshield toward the verdant grounds.

"Casey, my heart, fresh from the bower of celebratory grapes, welcome to our dream. Welcome, my mutual durable-power-of-attorney-executor, to our long-sought, much debated, fraught-over, fought-over, home in the country." He raised a finger toward the mockingbirds and opened his arms, gracious, appreciative, indicating the trees, the meandering drive, and the gate.

Casey followed Whit's gaze up the wide brick-paved path that climbed through a rainbow of summer flowers to the distant cottage–nay, mansion, trim and posh. He put on his best O'Hara, adjusted the chin strings of an imaginary sun bonnet, and opened his mouth to drawl, but sat silent.

Whit beamed. "Welcome to our rural refuge from the city that never lets you sleep. Fifty fabulous miles from terminal traffic jams, far out of antique car door denting distance of swarming SUV's and other predators." He inhaled deeply. "Far though maybe not far enough even yet from city smog. And most mercifully, magnificently and notably, beyond the construction noise that I hope our condo's newfound tenants will be able to survive without going further nuts."

Casey hnmphed, nodded.

Ev and Blake, construction company supervisors, moved in as Whit and Casey moved out. Before the morning's first crane operator climbs past their bedroom window, they'll be inhaling warm Krispy-Kremes in mid-commute to their own worksites. Grateful tenants, they sent their paint crew over to help Casey move his plants.

"So here we are," Whit said. "Xanadu at last, cozy on the edge of Tranquility Itself, two miles past the outskirts of nowhere." He modulated into mellifluous tones like a travelogue narrator. "And now as Bambi grazes at forest's edge–" Whit pointed.

Imaginary Bambi, but Casey nodded anyway.

"–While turtles sun themselves peacefully on the banks of a bubbling creek–"

"What's with all the poesy? Oops." Casey waved the soliloquy on. "Pray, continue, O thespian one."

Whit cleared his throat, opened his arms, addressed the overarching oaks. "Peacefully, ever quietly, and without the riveting and the shouting, the hammering, beeping, and the diesel roar." He smirked. "But soft quiet on yonder windows breaks, and grapes mature gracefully on gnarly vines in our sexy arbor," *wink*, "while thirty-foot camellias store up pink for next year's blossoms, we can ever carpe the diems of lazy afternoons, rap on our cellphones from library to poolside. And relish the wondrous joys of this sumptuous place. Erected in the past for the hedonistic pursuits of our pre-incarnations, it's renovated. Reborn. Reconstituted for our pleasure. Like Tang."

Pause.

"That's all."

Casey applauded.

Whit put the car in gear. "Wait, don't strip yet. You get to do the honors."

"The new-house ceremony. I almost forgot." Casey leaned over, squinted, and puckered up for a kiss.

Whit met Casey's lips with his own as he coasted the car into the grounds. "Ceremoh-neeezzz. Now the garland. Over your left shoulder. If it lands outside the gate you get to make a wish."

Casey retrieved a dinner-plate-sized wreath of blackberry vines and yellow roses from behind his seat. "Toss this thing?"

"Do I detect cynicism? Aren't you superstitious?"

"More than you." Casey solemnly sailed the wreath over his shoulder.

"Did you make a wish?"

"I did, and you've already come true."

"Awww." Whit revved the engine. "More superstitions. We don't want to leave anything to angry demigods or demi angrygods." He coasted the car forward. "I couldn't get any gargoyles shipped over, so I settled for local remedies."

"Sage, candles, hyacinths, aromatherapies. Garlic? Is there anything you missed? Are there any local gypsies still underemployed?"

"Doubt it. I've been quite thorough." Whit grinned.

"How about the hékahluahá-awannabealoha'awboloneyhoohah ceremony from the Hawaiian archipelago?"

Whit laughed. "Got that covered."

"Reggie the Scary doing his black polkadot mass thing?"

"Missed that, but it stays missed. Must not tempt Goddess."

"The Jamaican Blue Mountain Cursèd Chicken Effigy thing?"

"Skipped that, Mon. Don't have any blue chickens."

Casey beamed. "Okay, then keep an eye out for pre-op zombie capons, and let's hit it!"

Whit waited. "Should I have? "Reggie? Chicken?"

Casey's smirk spoke for him.

Whit held the controller aloft and commanded the gate to close behind them. He coasted past the house along a driveway strewn with rose petals and lined with baskets of fresh flowers. Whit pointed to the baskets. "Yours?"

"Nope."

"Nor mine. If there's a florist's card, I bet it's signed with a cat's paw."

Behind them, Rossini sniffed a flower basket.

"Or Brett the Clock, or Tonyghost Piano, or Paul the naked one well fixed for protoplasm." Whit parked near the barn, beside Casey's Saab.

Casey sniffed the air. "Roses for days. There can't be any flowers left this side of Mobile."

"Blue Chicken, eh? Now the threshold ceremony. Should we close the top?"

Casey checked the sky for clouds. "Fifty-fifty. Unless the Chicken Effigy Thing backfires."

With Japanese lanterns aglow around Vita's huge pool, lugubrious strains of Gershwin, Satie, and Debussy warmed the night amid the murmur of party conversation and the tink of cocktail glasses. The harpist and the lutenist made eyes at each other as they coaxed Vivaldi from their instruments.

"Cilla's due in April. Phil's hanging out on eBay bidding on Lionel train sets."

"After all these years Kath got a letter from Dmitri in one of Whit's clocks. Seems Brett spent his last days with an antique dealer in Provincetown. He put the letter inside Paul's last journal and sealed it up in the clock. It's like a message in a bottle. Took a decade, but the journal finally got to her."

"I heard Dmitri and Brett escaped to the South of France. They bribed the Romanians to say he was executed as a Russian spy, then lived the country life near Tonio and Paul's villa close to the old Toulouse canal—until Tonio fell ill."

"His heart? Paul mentioned their suicide pact and a cliff on a remote Greek island—but their bodies were never found. Brett and Dmitri went and helped with the search."

"Erica hasn't dumped Bob Roberts? That means he's a good lay and an abject servant. Ed Beasley saw the two of them at the Eagle last weekend."

"Must be serious."

"I'll get it." Casey closed the convertible's top, a simple process. He joined Whit in a puddle of ivy leaves and rose petals at the front door. "Me first?"

"Smells like your bathroom after one of your three-hour baths." Whit sniffed, smiled. "How come you get to go first?"

"Okay, Butch. Flip you for first."

"Heads or tails?"

Guests danced happily, some in step, as Vita Sempre's piano batted out a continuous medley of Gershwin songs, assorted polkas, show tunes, mazurkas, ditties, tangos, and the occasional Gymnopedie. Aglow in the corner near the gigantic fireplace with its gas logs alight, a young-looking, bejeweled Katherine Plunk twirled giddy with delight, dance after dance, arm in arm with graceful, elegant men in Forties silks.

"Heads it is." Whit extended his arms and winked an invitation.

"Thank you." Casey draped himself languidly over Whit's outstretched arms and held a big sloppy kiss while Whit carried him through the portal.

"Now me!" Whit hopped into Casey's arms.

THE END

www.ingramcontent.com/pod-product-compliance
Lightning Source LLC
Chambersburg PA
CBHW070815180626
46818CB00001B/282